American Ideals, and Other Essays, Social and Political

Theodore Roosevelt

Contents

PREFACE 7

I. AMERICAN IDEALS 9

II. TRUE AMERICANISM 17

III. THE MANLY VIRTUES AND PRACTICAL POLITICS 28

IV. THE COLLEGE GRADUATE AND PUBLIC LIFE 35

V. PHASES OF STATE LEGISLATION[5] THE ALBANY LEGISLATURE. 44

VI MACHINE POLITICS IN NEW YORK CITY 67

VII SIX YEARS OF CIVIL SERVICE REFORM 86

VIII ADMINISTERING THE NEW YORK POLICE FORCE 101

IX THE VICE-PRESIDENCY AND THE CAMPAIGN OF 1896 117

X HOW NOT TO HELP OUR POORER BROTHER 131

XI THE MONROE DOCTRINE 140

XII WASHINGTON'S FORGOTTEN MAXIM 150

XIII NATIONAL LIFE AND CHARACTER 164

XIV "SOCIAL EVOLUTION" 183

XV THE LAW OF CIVILIZATION AND DECAY 197

AMERICAN IDEALS, AND OTHER ESSAYS, SOCIAL AND POLITICAL

BY

Theodore Roosevelt

PREFACE

IT is not difficult to be virtuous in a cloistered and negative way. Neither is it difficult to succeed, after a fashion, in active life, if one is content to disregard the considerations which bind honorable and upright men. But it is by no means easy to combine honesty and efficiency ; and yet it is absolutely necessary, in order to do any work really worth doing. It is not hard, while sitting in one's study, to devise admirable plans for the betterment of politics and of social conditions ; but in practice it too often proves very hard to make any such plan work at all, no matter how imperfectly. Yet the effort must continually be made, under penalty of constant retrogression in our political life.

No one quality or one virtue is enough to insure success ; vigor, honesty, common sense,—all are needed. The practical man is merely rendered more noxious by his practical ability if he employs it wrongly, whether from ignorance or from lack of morality; while the doctrinaire, the man of theories, whether written or spoken, is useless if he cannot also act.

These essays are written on behalf of the many men who do take an actual part in trying practically to bring about the conditions for which we somewhat vaguely hope ; on behalf of the under-officers in that army which, with much stumbling, halting, and slipping, many mistakes and shortcomings, and many painful failures, does, nevertheless, through weary strife, accomplish something toward raising the standard of public life.

We feel that the doer is better than the critic and that the man who strives stands far above the man who stands aloof, whether he thus stands aloof because of pessimism or because of sheer weakness. To borrow a simile from the football field, we believe that men must play fair, but that there must be no shirking, and that success can only come to the player who "hits the line hard."

THEODORE ROOSEVELT.
SAGAMORE HILL,

October, 1897 .

I.
AMERICAN IDEALS[1]

IN his noteworthy book on *National Life and Character*, Mr. Pearson says: "The countrymen of Chatham and Wellington, of Washington and Lincoln, in short the citizens of every historic state, are richer by great deeds that have formed the national character, by winged words that have passed into current speech, by the examples of lives and labors consecrated to the service of the commonwealth." In other words, every great nation owes to the men whose lives have formed part of its greatness not merely the material effect of what they did, not merely the laws they placed upon the statute books or the victories they won over armed foes, but also the immense but indefinable moral influence produced by their deeds and words themselves upon the national character. It would be difficult to exaggerate the material effects of the careers of Washington and of Lincoln

[1] *The Forum*, February, 1895.

upon the United States. Without Washington we should probably never have won our independence of the British crown, and we should almost certainly have failed to become a great nation, remaining instead a cluster of jangling little communities, drifting toward the type of government prevalent in Spanish America. Without Lincoln we might perhaps have failed to keep the political unity we had won; and even if, as is possible, we had kept it, both the struggle by which it was kept and the results of this struggle would have been so different that the effect upon our national history could not have failed to be profound. Yet the nation's debt to these men is not confined to what it owes them for its material well-being, incalculable though this debt is. Beyond the fact that we are an independent and united people, with half a continent as our heritage, lies the fact that every American is richer by the heritage of the noble deeds and noble words of Washington and of Lincoln. Each of us who reads the Gettysburg speech or the second inaugural address of the greatest American of the nineteenth century, or who studies the long campaigns and lofty statesmanship of that other American who was even greater, cannot but feel within him that lift toward things higher and nobler which can never be bestowed by the enjoyment of mere material prosperity.

It is not only the country which these men helped to make and helped to save that is ours by inheritance; we inherit also all that is best and highest in their characters and in their lives. We inherit from Lincoln and from the might of Lincoln's generation not merely the freedom of those who once were slaves; for we inherit also the fact of the freeing of them, we inherit the glory and the honor and the wonder of the deed that was done, no less than the actual results of the deed when done. The bells that rang at the passage of the Emancipation Proclamation still ring in Whittier's ode; and as men think over the real nature of the triumph then scored for humankind their hearts shall ever throb as they cannot over the greatest industrial success or over any victory won at a less cost than ours.

The captains and the armies who, after long years of dreary campaigning and bloody, stubborn fighting, brought to a close the Civil War have likewise left us even more than a reunited realm. The material effect of what they did is shown in the fact that the same flag flies from the Great Lakes to the Rio Grande, and all the people of the United States are richer because they are one people and not many, because they belong to one great nation and not to a contemptible knot of struggling nationalities. But besides this, besides the material results of the Civil War, we are all, North and South, incalculably richer for its memories. We are the richer for each grim campaign, for each hard-fought battle. We are the richer for valor displayed alike by those who fought so valiantly for the right and by those who, no less valiantly, fought for what they deemed the right. We have in us nobler capacities for what is great and good because of the infinite woe and suffering, and because of the splendid ultimate triumph.

In the same way that we are the better for the deeds of our mighty men who have served the nation well, so we are the worse for the deeds and the words of those who have striven to bring evil on the land. Most fortunately we have been free from the peril of the most dangerous of all examples. We have not had to fight the influence exerted over the minds of eager and ambitious men by the career of the military adventurer who heads some successful revolutionary or separatist movement. No man works such incalculable woe to a free country as he who teaches young men that one of the paths to glory, renown, and temporal success lies along the line of armed resistance to the Government, of its attempted overthrow.

Yet if we are free from the peril of this example, there are other perils from which we are not free. All through our career we have had to war against a tendency to regard, in the individual and the nation alike, as most important, things that are of comparatively little importance. We rightfully value success, but sometimes we overvalue it, for we tend to forget that success may be obtained by means which should make it abhorred and despised by every honorable man. One section of the community deifies as "smartness" the kind of trickery which enables a man without conscience to succeed in the financial or political world. Another section of the community deifies violent homicidal lawlessness. If ever our people as a whole adopt these views, then we shall have proved that we are unworthy of the heritage our forefathers left us; and our country will go down in ruin.

The people that do harm in the end are not the wrong-doers whom all execrate; they are the men who do not do quite as much wrong, but who are applauded instead of being execrated. The career of Benedict Arnold has done us no harm as a nation because of the universal horror it inspired. The men who have done us harm are those who have advocated disunion, but have done it so that they have been enabled to keep their political position; who have advocated repudiation of debts, or other financial dishonesty, but have kept their standing in the community; who preach the doctrines of anarchy, but refrain from action that will bring them within the pale of the law; for these men lead thousands astray by the fact that they go unpunished or even rewarded for their misdeeds.

It is unhappily true that we inherit the evil as well as the good done by those who have gone before us, and in the one case as in the other the influence extends far beyond the mere material effects. The foes of order harm quite as much by example as by what they actually accomplish. So it is with the equally dangerous criminals of the wealthy classes. The conscienceless stock speculator who acquires wealth by swindling his fellows, by debauching judges and corrupting legislatures, and who ends his days with the reputation of being among the richest men in America, exerts over the minds of the rising generation an influence worse than that of the average murderer or bandit, because his career is even more dazzling in its success, and even more dangerous in its effects upon the community. Any one who reads the essays of Charles Francis Adams and Henry Adams, entitled "A Chapter of Erie," and "The Gold Conspiracy in New York," will read about the doings of men whose influence for evil upon the community is more potent than that of any band of anarchists or train robbers.

There are other members of our mercantile community who, being perfectly honest themselves, nevertheless do almost as much damage as the dishonest. The professional labor agitator, with all his reckless incendiarism of speech, can do no more harm than the narrow, hard, selfish merchant or manufacturer who deliberately sets himself to keep the laborers he employs in a condition of dependence which will render them helpless to combine against him; and every such merchant or manufacturer who rises to sufficient eminence leaves the record of his name and deeds as a legacy of evil to all who come after him.

But of course the worst foes of America are the foes to that orderly liberty without which our Republic must speedily perish. The reckless labor agitator who arouses the mob to riot and bloodshed is in the last analysis the most dangerous of the workingman's enemies. This man is a real peril; and so is his sympathizer, the legislator, who to catch votes denounces the judiciary and the military because they put down mobs. We Americans have, on the whole, a right to be optimists; but it is mere folly to blind ourselves to the fact that there are some black clouds on the horizon of our future.

During the summer of 1894, every American capable of thinking must at times have pondered very gravely over certain features of the national character which were brought into unpleasant prominence by the course of events. The demagogue, in all his forms, is as characteristic an evil of a free society as the courtier is of a despotism; and the attitude of many of our public men at the time of the great strike in July, 1894, was such as to call down on their heads the hearty condemnation of every American who wishes well to his country. It would be difficult to overestimate the damage done by the example and action of a man like Governor Altgeld of Illinois. Whether he is honest or not in his beliefs is not of the slightest consequence. He is as emphatically the foe of decent government as Tweed himself, and is capable of doing far more damage than Tweed. The Governor, who began his career by. pardoning anarchists, and whose most noteworthy feat since was his. bitter and undignified, but fortunately futile, campaign against the election of the upright judge who sentenced the anarchists, is the foe of every true American and is the foe particularly of every honest workingman. With such a man it was to be expected that he should in time of civic commotion act as the foe of the law-abiding and the friend of the lawless classes, and endeavor, in company with the lowest and most abandoned office-seeking politicians, to prevent proper measures being taken to prevent riot and to punish the rioters. Had it not been for the admirable action of the Federal Government, Chicago would have seen a repetition of what occurred during the Paris Commune, while Illinois would have been torn by a fierce social war; and for all the horrible waste of life that this would have entailed Governor Altgeld would have been primarily responsible. It was a most fortunate thing that the action at Washington was so quick and so emphatic. Senator Davis of Minnesota set the key of patriotism at the time when men were still puzzled and hesitated. The President and Attorney-General Olney acted with equal wisdom and courage, and the danger was averted. The completeness of the victory of the Federal authorities, representing the cause of law and order, has been perhaps one reason why it was so soon forgotten; and now not a few shortsighted people need to be reminded that when we were on the brink of an almost terrific explosion the governor of Illinois did his best to work to this country a measure of harm as great as any ever planned by Benedict Arnold, and that we were saved by the resolute action of the Federal judiciary and of the regular army. Moreover, Governor Altgeld, though preeminent, did not stand alone on his unenviable prominence. Governor Waite of Colorado stood with him. Most of the Populist governors of the Western States, and the Republican governor of California and the Democratic governor of North Dakota, shared the shame with him; and it makes no difference whether in catering to riotous mobs they paid heed to their own timidity and weakness, or to that spirit of blatant demagogism which, more than any other, jeopardizes the existence of free institutions. On the other hand, the action of the then Governor of Ohio, Mr. McKinley, entitled him to the gratitude of all good citizens.

Every true American, every man who thinks, and who if the occasion comes is ready to act, may do well to ponder upon the evil wrought by the lawlessness of the disorderly classes when once they are able to elect their own chiefs to power. If the Government generally got into the hands of men such as Altgeld, the Republic would go to pieces in a year; and it would be right that it should go to pieces, for the election of such men shows that the people electing them are unfit to be entrusted with self-government.

There are, however, plenty of wrong-doers besides those who commit the overt act. Too much cannot be said against the men of wealth who sacrifice everything to getting wealth. There is not in the world a more ignoble character than the mere money-getting American, insensible to every duty, regardless of every principle, bent only on amassing a fortune, and putting his fortune only to the basest uses— whether these uses be to speculate in stocks and wreck railroads himself, or to allow his son to lead a life of foolish and expensive idleness and gross debauchery, or to purchase some scoundrel of high social position, foreign or native, for his daughter. Such a man is only the more dangerous if he occasionally does some deed like founding a college or endowing a church, which makes those good people who are also foolish forget his real iniquity. These men are equally careless of the workingmen, whom they oppress, and of the state, whose existence they imperil. There are not very many of them, but there is a very great number of men who approach more or less closely to the type, and, just in so far as they do so approach, they are curses to the country. The man who is content to let politics go from bad to worse, jesting at the corruption of politicians, the man who is content to see the maladministration of justice without an immediate and resolute effort to reform it, is shirking his duty and is preparing the way for infinite woe in the future. Hard, brutal indifference to the right, and an equally brutal shortsightedness as to the inevitable results of corruption and injustice, are baleful beyond measure; and yet they are characteristic of a great many Americans who think themselves perfectly respectable, and who are considered thriving, prosperous men by their easy-going fellow-citizens.

Another class, merging into this, and only less dangerous, is that of the men whose ideals are purely material. These are the men who are willing to go for good government when they think it will pay, but who measure everything by the shop-till, the people who are unable to appreciate any quality that is not a mercantile commodity, who do not understand that a poet may do far more for a country than the owner of a nail factory, who do not realize that no amount of commercial prosperity can supply the lack of the heroic virtues, or can in itself solve the terrible social problems which all the civilized world is now facing. The mere materialist is, above all things, shortsighted. In a recent article Mr. Edward Atkinson casually mentioned that the regular army could now render the country no "effective or useful service." Two months before this sapient remark was printed the regular army had saved Chicago from the fate of Paris in 1870 and had prevented a terrible social war in the West. At the end of this article Mr. Atkinson indulged in a curious rhapsody against the navy, denouncing its existence and being especially wrought up, not because war-vessels take life, but because they "destroy commerce." To men of a certain kind, trade and property are far more sacred than life or honor, of far more consequence than the great thoughts and lofty emotions, which alone make a nation mighty. They believe, with a faith almost touching in its utter feebleness, that "the Angel of Peace, draped in a garment of untaxed calico," has given her final message to men when she has implored them to devote all their energies to producing oleomargarine at a quarter of a cent less a firkin, or to importing woollens for a fraction less than they can be made at home. These solemn prattlers strive after an ideal in which they shall happily unite the imagination of a green-grocer with the heart of a Bengalee baboo. They are utterly incapable of feeling one thrill of generous emotion, or the slightest throb of that pulse which gives to the world statesmen, patriots, warriors, and poets, and which makes a nation other than a cumberer of the world's surface. In the concluding page of his article Mr. Atkinson, complacently advancing his panacea, his quack cure-all, says that "all evil powers of the world will go down before" a policy of "reciprocity of trade without obstruction"! Fatuity can go no farther.

No Populist who wishes a currency based on corn and cotton stands in more urgent need of applied common sense than does the man who believes that the adoption of any policy, no matter what, in reference to our foreign commerce, will cut that tangled knot of social well-being and misery at which the fingers of the London free-trader clutch as helplessly as those of the Berlin protectionist. Such a man represents individually an almost imponderable element in the work and thought of the community; but in the aggregate he stands for a real danger, because he stands for a feeling evident of late years among many respectable people. The people who pride themselves upon having a purely commercial ideal are apparently unaware that such an ideal is as essentially mean and sordid as any in the world, and that no bandit community of the Middle Ages can have led a more unlovely life than would be the life of men to whom trade and manufactures were everything, and to whom such words as national honor and glory, as courage and daring, and loyalty and unselfishness, had become meaningless. The merely material, the merely commercial ideal, the ideal of the men "whose fatherland is the till," is in its very essence debasing and lowering. It is as true now as ever it was that no man and no nation shall live by bread alone. Thrift and industry are indispensable virtues; but they are not all-sufficient. We must base our appeals for civic and national betterment on nobler grounds than those of mere business expediency.

We have examples enough and to spare that tend to evil; nevertheless, for our good fortune, the men who have most impressed themselves upon the thought of the nation have left behind them careers the influence of which must tell for good. The unscrupulous speculator who rises to enormous wealth by swindling his neighbor; the capitalist who oppresses the workingman; the agitator who wrongs the workingman yet more deeply by trying to teach him to rely not upon himself, but partly upon the charity of individuals or of the state and partly upon mob violence; the man in public life who is a demagogue or corrupt, and the newspaper writer who fails to attack him because of his corruption, or who slanderously assails him when he is honest; the political leader who, cursed by some obliquity of moral or of mental vision, seeks to produce sectional or social strife—all these, though important in their day, have hitherto failed to leave any lasting impress upon the life of the nation. The men who have profoundly influenced the growth of our national character have been in most cases precisely those men whose influence was for the best and was strongly felt as antagonistic to the worst tendency of the age. The great writers, who have written in prose or verse, have done much for us. The great orators whose burning words on behalf of liberty, of union, of honest government, have rung through our legislative halls, have done even more. Most of all has been done by the men who have spoken to us through deeds and not words, or whose words have gathered their especial charm and significance because they came from men who did speak in deeds. A nation's greatness lies in its possibility of achievement in the present, and nothing helps it more than the consciousness of achievement in the past.

II.
TRUE AMERICANISM[2]

PATRIOTISM was once defined as "the last refuge of a scoundrel"; and somebody has recently remarked that when Dr. Johnson gave this definition he was ignorant of the infinite possibilites contained in the word "reform." Of course both gibes were quite justifiable, in so far as they were aimed at people who use noble names to cloak base purposes. Equally of course the man shows little wisdom and a low sense of duty who fails to see that love of country is one of the elemental virtues, even though scoundrels play upon it for their own selfish ends; and, inasmuch as abuses continually grow up in civic life as in all other kinds of life, the statesman is indeed a weakling who hesitates to reform these abuses because the word "reform" is often on the lips of men who are silly or dishonest.

What is true of patriotism and reform is true also

[2] *The Forum*, April, 1894.

of Americanism. There are plenty of scoundrels always ready to try to belittle reform movements or to bolster up existing iniquities in the name of Americanism; but this does not alter the fact that the man who can do most in this country is and must be the man whose Americanism is most sincere and intense. Outrageous though it is to use a noble idea as the cloak for evil, it is still worse to assail the noble idea itself because it can thus be used. The men who do iniquity in the name of patriotism, of reform, of Americanism, are merely one small division of the class that has always existed and will always exist,—the class of hypocrites and demagogues, the class that is always prompt to steal the watchwords of righteousness and use them in the interests of evil-doing.

The stoutest and truest Americans are the very men who have the least sympathy with the people who invoke the spirit of Americanism to aid what is vicious in our government or to throw obstacles in the way of those who strive to reform it. It is contemptible to oppose a movement for good because that movement has already succeeded somewhere else, or to champion an existing abuse because our people have always been wedded to it. To appeal to national prejudice against a given reform movement is in every way unworthy and silly. It is as childish to denounce free trade because England has adopted it as to advocate it for the same reason. It is eminently proper, in dealing with the tariff, to consider the effect of tariff legislation in time past upon other nations as well as the effect upon our own; but in drawing conclusions it is in the last degree foolish to try to excite prejudice against one system because it is in vogue in some given country, or to try to excite prejudice in its favor because the economists of that country have found that it was suited to their own peculiar needs. In attempting to solve our difficult problem of municipal government it is mere folly to refuse to profit by whatever is good in the examples of Manchester and Berlin because these cities are foreign, exactly as it is mere folly blindly to copy their examples without reference to our own totally different conditions. As for the absurdity of declaiming against civil-service reform, for instance, as "Chinese," because written examinations have been used in China, it would be quite as wise to declaim against gunpowder because it was first utilized by the same people. In short, the man who, whether from mere dull fatuity or from an active interest in misgovernment, tries to appeal to American prejudice against things foreign, so as to induce Americans to oppose any measure for good, should be looked on by his fellow-countrymen with the heartiest contempt. So much for the men who appeal to the spirit of Americanism to sustain us in wrong-doing. But we must never let our contempt for these men blind us to the nobility of the idea which they strive to degrade.

We Americans have many grave problems to solve, many threatening evils to fight, and many deeds to do, if, as we hope and believe, we have the wisdom, the strength, the courage, and the virtue to do them. But we must face facts as they are. We must neither surrender ourselves to a foolish optimism, nor succumb to a timid and ignoble pessimism. Our nation is that one among all the nations of the earth which holds in its hands the fate of the coming years. We enjoy exceptional advantages, and are menaced by exceptional dangers; and all signs indicate that we shall either fail greatly or succeed greatly. I firmly believe that we shall succeed; but we must not foolishly blink the dangers by which we are threatened, for that is the way to fail. On the contrary, we must soberly set to work to find out all we can about the existence and extent of every evil, must acknowledge it to be such, and must then attack it with unyielding resolution. There are many such evils, and each must be fought after a separate fashion; yet there is one quality which we must bring to the solution of every problem,—that is, an intense and fervid Americanism. We shall never be successful over the dangers that confront us; we shall never achieve true greatness, nor reach the lofty ideal which the founders and preservers of our mighty Federal Republic have set before us, unless we are Americans in heart and soul, in spirit and purpose, keenly alive to the responsibility implied in the very name of American, and proud beyond measure of the glorious privilege of bearing it.

There are two or three sides to the question of Americanism, and two or three senses in which the word "Americanism" can be used to express the antithesis of what is unwholesome and undesirable. In the first place we wish to be broadly American and national, as opposed to being local or sectional. We do not wish, in politics, in literature, or in art, to develop that unwholesome parochial spirit, that over-exaltation of the little community at the expense of the great nation, which produces what has been described as the patriotism of the village, the patriotism of the belfry. Politically, the indulgence of this spirit was the chief cause of the calamities which befell the ancient republics of Greece, the mediæval republics of Italy, and the petty States of Germany as it was in the last century. It is this spirit of provincial patriotism, this inability to take a view of broad adhesion to the whole nation that has been the chief among the causes that have produced such anarchy in the South American States, and which have resulted in presenting to us, not one great Spanish-American federal nation stretching from the Rio Grande to Cape Horn, but a squabbling multitude of revolution-ridden States, not one of which stands even in the second rank as a power. However, politically this question of American nationality has been settled once for all. We are no longer in danger of repeating in our history the shameful and contemptible disasters that have befallen the Spanish possessions on this continent since they threw off the yoke of Spain. Indeed there is, all through our life, very much less of this parochial spirit than there was formerly. Still there is an occasional outcropping here and there; and it is just as well that we should keep steadily in mind the futility of talking of a Northern literature or a Southern literature, an Eastern or a Western school of art or science. Joel Chandler Harris is emphatically a national writer; so is Mark Twain. They do not write merely for Georgia or Missouri or California any more than for Illinois or Connecticut; they write as Americans and for all people who can read English. St. Gaudens lives in New York; but his work is just as distinctive of Boston or Chicago. It is of very great consequence that we should have a full and ripe literary development in the United States, but it is not of the least consequence whether New York, or Boston, or Chicago, or San Francisco becomes the literary or artistic centre of the United States.

There is a second side to this question of a broad Americanism, however. The patriotism of the village or the belfrey is bad, but the lack of all patriotism is even worse. There are philosophers who assure us, that in the future, patriotism will be regarded not as a virtue at all, but merely as a mental stage in the journey toward a state of feeling when our patriotism will include the whole human race and all the world. This may be so; but the age of which these philosophers speak is still several aeons distant. In fact, philosophers of this type are so very advanced that they are of no practical service to the present generation. It may be, that in ages so remote that we cannot now understand any of the feelings of those who will dwell in them, patriotism will no longer be regarded as a virtue, exactly as it may be that in those remote ages people will look down upon and disregard monogamic marriage; but as things now are and have been for two or three thousand years past, and are likely to be for two or three thousand years to come, the words "home" and "country" mean a great deal. Nor do they show any tendency to lose their significance. At present, treason, like adultery, ranks as one of the worst of all possible crimes.

One may fall very far short of treason and yet be an undesirable citizen in the community. The man who becomes Europeanized, who loses his power of doing good work on this side of the water, and who loses his love for his native land, is not a traitor; but he is a silly and undesirable citizen. He is as emphatically a noxious element in our body politic as is the man who comes here from abroad and remains a foreigner. Nothing will more quickly or more surely disqualify a man from doing good work in the world than the acquirement of that flaccid habit of mind which its possessors style cosmopolitanism.

It is not only necessary to Americanize the immigrants of foreign birth who settle among us, but it is even more necessary for those among us who are by birth and descent already Americans not to throw away our birthright, and, with incredible and contemptible folly, wander back to bow down before the alien gods whom our forefathers forsook. It is hard to believe that there is any necessity to warn Americans that, when they seek to model themselves on the lines of other civilizations, they make themselves the butts of all right-thinking men; and yet the necessity certainly exists to give this warning to many of our citizens who pride themselves on their standing in the world of art and letters, or, perchance, on what they would style their social leadership in the community It is always better to be an original than an imitation, even when the imitation is of something better than the original; but what shall we say of the fool who is content to be an imitation of something worse? Even if the weaklings who seek to be other than Americans were right in deeming other nations to be better than their own, the fact yet remains that to be a first-class American is fifty-fold better than to be a second-class imitation of a Frenchman or Englishman. As a matter of fact, however, those of our country-men who do believe in American inferiority are always individuals who, however cultivated, have some organic weakness in their moral or mental make-up; and the great mass of our people, who are robustly patriotic, and who have sound, healthy minds, are justified in regarding these feeble renegades with a half-impatient and half-amused scorn.

We believe in waging relentless war on rank-growing evils of all kinds, and it makes no difference to us if they happen to be of purely native growth. We grasp at any good, no matter whence it comes. We do not accept the evil attendant upon another system of government as an adequate excuse for that attendant upon our own; the fact that the courtier is a scamp does not render the demagogue any the less a scoundrel. But it remains true that, in spite of all our faults and shortcomings, no other land offers such glorious possibilities to the man able to take advantage of them, as does ours; it remains true that no one of our people can do any work really worth doing unless he does it primarily as an American. It is because certain classes of our people still retain their spirit of colonial dependence on, and exaggerated deference to, European opinion, that they fail to accomplish what they ought to. It is precisely along the lines where we have worked most independently that we have accomplished the greatest results; and it is in those professions where there has been no servility to, but merely a wise profiting by, foreign experience, that we have produed our greatest men. Our soldiers and statesmen and orators; our explorers, our wilderness-winners, and commonwealth-builders; the men who have made our laws and seen that they were executed; and the other men whose energy and ingenuity have created our marvellous material prosperity,—all these have been men who have drawn wisdom from the experience of every age and nation, but who have nevertheless thought, and worked, and conquered, and lived, and died, purely as Americans; and on the whole they have done better work than has been done in any other country during the short period of our national life.

On the other hand, it is in those professions where our people have striven hardest to mould themselves in conventional European forms that they have succeeded least; and this holds true to the present day, the failure being of course most conspicuous where the man takes up his abode in Europe; where he becomes a second-rate European, because he is over-civilized, over-sensitive, over-refined, and has lost the hardihood and manly courage by which alone he can conquer in the keen struggle of our national life. Be it remembered, too, that this same being does not really become a European; he only ceases being an American, and becomes nothing. He throws away a great prize for the sake of a lesser one, and does not even get the lesser one. The painter who goes to Paris, not merely to get two or three years' thorough training in his art, but with the deliberate purpose of taking up his abode there, and with the intention of following in the ruts worn deep by ten thousand earlier travellers, instead of striking off to rise or fall on a new line, thereby forfeits all chance of doing the best work. He must content himself with aiming at that kind of mediocrity which consists in doing fairly well what has already been done better; and he usually never even sees the grandeur and picturesqueness lying open before the eyes of every man who can read the book of America's past and the book of America's present. Thus it is with the undersized man of letters, who flees his country because he, with his delicate, effeminate sensitiveness, finds the conditions of life on this side of the water crude and raw; in other words, because he finds that he cannot play a man's part among men, and so goes where he will be sheltered from the winds that harden stouter souls. This emigré may write graceful and pretty verses, essays, novels; but he will never do work to compare with that of his brother, who is strong enough to stand on his own feet, and do his work as an American. Thus it is with the scientist who spends his youth in a German university, and can thenceforth work only in the fields already fifty times furrowed by the

German ploughs. Thus it is with that most foolish of parents who sends his children to be educated abroad, not knowing— what every clear-sighted man from Washington and Jay down has known—that the American who is to make his way in America should be brought up among his fellow Americans. It is among the people who like to consider themselves, and, indeed, to a large extent are, the leaders of the so-called social world, especially in some of the northeastern cities, that this colonial habit of thought, this thoroughly provincial spirit of admiration for things foreign, and inability to stand on one's own feet, becomes most evident and most despicable. We believe in every kind of honest and lawful pleasure, so long as the getting it is not made man's chief business; and we believe heartily in the good that can be done by men of leisure who work hard in their leisure, whether at politics or philanthropy, literature or art. But a leisure class whose leisure simply means idleness is a curse to the community, and in so far as its members distinguish themselves chiefly by aping the worst—not the best—traits of similar people across the water, they become both comic and noxious elements of the body politic.

The third sense in which the word "Americanism" may be employed is with reference to the Americanizing of the newcomers to our shores. We must Americanize them in every way, in speech, in political ideas and principles, and in their way of looking at the relations between Church and State. We welcome the German or the Irishman who becomes an American. We have no use for the German or Irshman who remains such. We do not wish German-Americans and Irish-Americans who figure as such in our social and political life; we want only Americans, and, provided they are such, we do not care whether they are of native or of Irish or of German ancestry. We have no room in any healthy American community for a German-American vote or an Irish-American vote, and it is contemptible demagogy to put planks into any party platform with the purpose of catching such a vote. We have no room for any people who do not act and vote simply as Americans, and as nothing else. Moreover, we have as little use for people who carry religious prejudices into our politics as for those who carry prejudices of caste or nationality. We stand unalterably in favor of the public-school system in its entirety. We believe that English, and no other language, is that in which all the school exercises should be conducted. We are against any division of the school fund, and against any appropriation of public money for sectarian purposes. We are against any recognition whatever by the State in any shape or form of State-aided parochial schools. But we are equally opposed to any discrimination against or for a man because of his creed. We demand that all citizens, Protestant and Catholic, Jew and Gentile, shall have fair treatment in every way; that all alike shall have their rights guaranteed them. The very reasons that make us unqualified in our opposition to State-aided sectarian schools make us equally bent that, in the management of our public schools, the adherents of each creed shall be given exact and equal justice, wholly without regard to their religious affiliations; that trustees, superintendents, teachers, scholars, all alike, shall be treated without any reference whatsoever to the creed they profess. We maintain that it is an outrage, in voting for a man for any position, whether State or national, to take into account his religious faith, provided only he is a good American. When a secret society does what in some places the American Protective Association seems to have done, and tries to proscribe Catholics both politically and socially, the members of such society show that they themselves are as utterly un-American, as alien to our school of political thought, as the worst immigrants who land on our shores. Their conduct is equally base and contemptible; they are the worst foes of our public-school system, because they strengthen the hands of its ultramontane enemies; they should receive the hearty condemnation of all Americans who are truly patriotic.

The mighty tide of immigration to our shores has brought in its train much of good and much of evil; and whether the good or the evil shall predominate depends mainly on whether these newcomers do or do not throw themselves heartily into our national life, cease to be European, and become Americans like the rest of us. More than a third of the people of the Northern States are of foreign birth or parentage. An immense number of them have become completely Americanized, and these stand on exactly the same plane as the descendants of any Puritan, Cavalier, or Knickerbocker among us, and do their full and honorable share of the nation's work. But where immigrants, or the sons of immigrants, do not heartily and in good faith throw in their lot with us, but cling to the speech, the customs, the ways of life, and the habits of thought of the Old World which they have left, they thereby harm both themselves and us. If they remain alien elements, unassimilated, and with interests separate from ours, they are mere obstructions to the current of our national life, and, moreover, can get no good from it themselves. In fact, though we ourselves also suffer from their perversity, it is they who really suffer most. It is an immense benefit to the European immigrant to change him into an American citizen. To bear the name of American is to bear the most honorable of titles; and whoever does not so believe has no business to bear the name at all, and, if he comes from Europe, the sooner he goes back there the better. Besides, the man who does not become Americanized nevertheless fails to remain a European, and becomes nothing at all. The immigrant cannot possibly remain what he was, or continue to be a member of the Old-World society. If he tries to retain his old language, in a few generations it becomes a barbarous jargon; if he tries to retain his old customs and ways of life, in a few generations he becomes an uncouth boor. He has cut himself off from the Old-World, and cannot retain his connection with it; and if he wishes ever to amount to anything he must throw himself heart and soul, and without reservation, into the new life to which he has come. It is urgently necessary to check and regulate our immigration, by much more drastic laws than now exist; and this should be done both to keep out laborers who tend to depress the labor market, and to keep out races which do not assimilate readily with our own, and unworthy individuals of all races—not only criminals, idiots, and paupers, but anarchists of the Most and O'Donovan Rossa type. From his own standpoint, it is beyond all question the wise thing for the immigrant to become thoroughly Americanized. Moreover, from our standpoint, we have a right to demand it. We freely extend the hand of welcome and of good-fellowship to every man, no matter what his creed or birthplace, who comes here honestly intent on becoming a good United States citizen like the rest of us; but we have a right, and it is our duty, to demand that he shall indeed become so, and shall not confuse the issues with which we are struggling by introducing among us Old-World quarrels and prejudices. There are certain ideas which he must give up. For instance, he must learn that American life is incompatible with the existence of any form of anarchy, or of any secret society having murder for its aim, whether at home or abroad; and he must learn that we exact full religious toleration and the complete separation of Church and State. Moreover, he must not bring in his Old-World religious race and national antipathies, but must merge them into love for our common country, and must take pride in the things which we can all take pride in. He must revere only our flag; not only must it come first, but no other flag should even come second. He must learn to celebrate Washington's birthday rather than that of the Queen or Kaiser, and the Fourth of July instead of St. Patrick's Day. Our political and social questions must be settled on their own merits, and not complicated by quarrels between England and Ireland, or France and Germany, with which we have nothing to do: it is an outrage to fight an American political campaign with reference to questions of European politics. Above all, the immigrant must learn to talk and think and *be* United States.

The immigrant of to-day can learn much from the experience of the immigrants of the past, who came to America prior to the Revolutionary War. We were then already, what we are now, a people of mixed blood. Many of our most illustrious Revolutionary names were borne by men of Huguenot blood—Jay, Sevier, Marion, Laurens. But the Huguenots were, on the whole, the best immigrants we have ever received; sooner than any other, and more completely, they became American in speech, conviction, and thought. The Hollanders took longer than the Huguenots to become completely assimilated; nevertheless they in the end became so, immensely to their own advantage. One of the leading Revolutionary generals, Schuyler, and one of the Presidents of the United States, Van Buren, were of Dutch blood; but they rose to their positions, the highest in the land, because they had become Americans and had ceased being Hollanders. If they had remained members of an alien body, cut off by their speech and customs and belief from the rest of the American community, Schuyler would have lived his life as a boorish, provincial squire, and Van Buren would have ended his days a small tavern-keeper. So it is with the Germans of Pennsylvania. Those of them who became Americanized have furnished to our history a multitude of honorable names, from the days of the Mühlenbergs onward; but those who did not become Americanized form to the present day an unimportant body, of no significance in American existence. So it is with the Irish, who gave to Revolutionary annals such names as Carroll and Sullivan, and to the Civil War men like Sheridan —men who were Americans and nothing else: while the Irish who remain such, and busy them-selves solely with alien politics, can have only an unhealthy influence upon American life, and can never rise as do their compatriots who become straightout Americans. Thus it has ever been with all people who have come hither, of whatever stock or blood. The same thing is true of the churches. A church which remains foreign, in language or spirit, is doomed.

But I wish to be distinctly understood on one point. Americanism is a question of spirit, conviction, and purpose, not of creed or birthplace. The politician who bids for the Irish or German vote, or the Irishman or German who votes as an Irishman or German, is despicable, for all citizens of this commonwealth should vote solely as Americans; but he is not a whit less despicable than the voter who votes against a good American, merely because that American happens to have been born in Ireland or Germany. Knownothingism, in any form, is as utterly un-American as foreignism. It is a base outrage to oppose a man because of his religion or birthplace, and all good citizens will hold any such effort in abhorrence. A Scandinavian, a German, or an Irishman who has really become an American has the right to stand on exactly the same footing as any native-born citizen in the land, and is just as much entitled to the friendship and support, social and political, of his neighbors. Among the men with whom I have been thrown in close personal contact socially, and who have been among my staunchest friends and allies politically, are not a few Americans who happen to have been born on the other side of the water, in Germany, Ireland, Scandinavia; and there could be no better men in the ranks of our native-born citizens.

In closing, I cannot better express the ideal attitude that should be taken by our fellow-citizens of foreign birth than by quoting the words of a representative American, born in Germany, the Honorable Richard Guenther, of Wisconsin. In a speech spoken at the time of the Samoan trouble, he said:

"We know as well as any other class of American citizens where our duties belong. We will work for our country in time of peace and fight for it in time of war, if a time of war should ever come. When I say our country, I mean, of course, our adopted country. I mean the United States of America. After passing through the crucible of naturalization, we are no longer Germans; we are Americans. Our attachment to America cannot be measured by the length of our residence here. We are Americans from the moment we touch the American shore until we are laid in American graves. We will fight for America whenever necessary. America, first, last, and all the time. America against Germany, America against the world; America, right or wrong; always America. We are Americans."

All honor to the man who spoke such words as those; and I believe they express the feelings of the great majority of those among our fellow-American citizens who were born abroad. We Americans can only do our allotted task well if we face it steadily and bravely, seeing but not fearing the dangers. Above all we must stand shoulder to shoulder, not asking as to the ancestry or creed of our comrades, but only demanding that they be in very truth Americans, and that we all work together, heart, hand, and head, for the honor and the greatness of our common country.

III.
THE MANLY VIRTUES AND PRACTICAL POLITICS[3]

SOMETIMES, in addressing men who sincerely desire the betterment of our public affairs, but who have not taken active part in directing them, I feel tempted to tell them that there are two gospels which should be preached to every reformer. The first is the gospel of morality; the second is the gospel of efficiency.

To decent, upright citizens it is hardly necessary to preach the doctrine of morality as applied to the affairs of public life. It is an even graver offence to sin against the commonwealth than to sin against an individual. The man who debauches our public life, whether by malversation of funds in office, by the actual bribery of voters or of legislators, or by the corrupt use of the offices as spoils wherewith to reward the unworthy and the vicious for their noxious and interested activity in the baser walks of

[3] *The Forum*, July, 1894.

political life,—this man is a greater foe to our well-being as a nation than is even the defaulting cashier of a bank, or the betrayer of a private trust. No amount of intelligence and no amount of energy will save a nation which is not honest, and no government can ever be a permanent success if administered in accordance with base ideals. The first requisite in the citizen who wishes to share the work of our public life, whether he wishes himself to hold office or merely to do his plain duty as an American by taking part in the management of our political machinery, is that he shall act disinterestedly and with a sincere purpose to serve the whole commonwealth.

But disinterestedness and honesty and unselfish desire to do what is right are not enough in themselves: A man must not only be disinterested, but he must be efficient. If he goes into politics he must go into practical politics, in order to make his influence felt. Practical politics must not be construed to mean dirty politics. On the contrary, in the long run the politics of fraud and treachery and foulness are unpractical politics, and the most practical of all politicians is the politician who is clean and decent and upright. But a man who goes into the actual battles of the political world must prepare himself much as he would for the struggle in any other branch of our life. He must be prepared to meet men of far lower ideals than his own, and to face things, not as he would wish them, but as they are. He must not lose his own high ideal, and yet he must face the fact that the majority of the men with whom he must work have lower ideals. He must stand firmly for what he believes, and yet he must realize that political action, to be effective, must be the joint action of many men, and that he must sacrifice somewhat of his own opinions to those of his associates if he ever hopes to see his desires take practical shape.

The prime thing that every man who takes an interest in politics should remember is that he must-act, and not merely criticise the actions of others. It is not the man who sits by his fireside reading his evening paper, and saying how bad our politics and politicians are, who will ever do anything to save us; it is the man who goes out into the rough hurly-burly of the caucus, the primary, and the political meeting, and there faces his fellows on equal terms. The real service is rendered, not by the critic who stands aloof from the contest, but by the man who enters into it and bears his part as a man should, undeterred by the blood and the sweat. It is a pleasant but a dangerous thing to associate merely with cultivated, refined men of high ideals and sincere purpose to do right, and to think that one has done all one's duty by discussing politics with such associates. It is a good thing to meet men of this stamp; indeed it is a necessary thing, for we thereby brighten our ideals, and keep in touch with the people who are unselfish in their purposes; but if we associate with such men exclusively we can accomplish nothing. The actual battle must be fought out on other and less pleasant fields. The actual advance must be made in the field of practical politics among the men who represent or guide or control the mass of the voters, the men who are sometimes rough and coarse, who sometimes have lower ideals than they should, but who are capable, masterful, and efficient. It is only by mingling on equal terms with such men, by showing them that one is able to give and to receive heavy punishment without flinching, and that one can master the details of political management as well as they can, that it is possible for a man to establish a standing that will be useful to him in fighting for a great reform. Every man who wishes well to his country is in honor bound to take an active part in political life. If he does his duty and takes that active part he will be sure occasionally to commit mistakes and to be guilty of shortcomings. For these mistakes and shortcomings he will receive the unmeasured denunciation of the critics who commit neither because they never do anything but criticise. Nevertheless he will have the satisfaction of knowing that the salvation of the country ultimately lies, not in the hands of his critics, but in the hands of those who, however imperfectly, actually do the work of the nation. I would not for one moment be understood as objecting to criticism or failing to appreciate its importance. We need fearless criticism of our public men and public parties; we need unsparing condemnation of all persons and all principles that count for evil in our public life: but it behooves every man to remember that the work of the critic, important though it is, is of altogether secondary importance, and that, in the end, progress is accomplished by the man who does the things, and not by the man who talks about how they ought or ought not to be done.

Therefore the man who wishes to do good in his community must go into active political life. If he is a Republican, let him join his local Republican association; if a Democrat, the Democratic association; if an Independent, then let him put himself in touch with those who think as he does. In any event let him make himself an active force and make his influence felt. Whether he works within or without party lines he can surely find plenty of men who are desirous of good government, and who, if they act together, become at once a power on the side of righteousness. Of course, in a government like ours, a man can accomplish anything only by acting in combination with others, and equally, of course, a number of people can act together only by each sacrificing certain of his beliefs or prejudices. That man is indeed unfortunate who cannot in any given district find some people with whom he can conscientiously act. He may find that he can do best by acting within a party organization; he may find that he can do best by acting, at least for certain purposes, or at certain times, outside of party organizations, in an independent body of some kind; but with some association he must act if he wishes to exert any real influence.

One thing to be always remembered is that neither independence on the one hand nor party fealty on the other can ever be accepted as an excuse for failure to do active work in politics. The party man who offers his allegiance to party as an excuse for blindly following his party, right or wrong, and who fails to try to make that party in any way better, commits a crime against the country; and a crime quite as serious is committed by the independent who makes his independence an excuse for easy self-indulgence, and who thinks that when he says he belongs to neither party he is excused from the duty of taking part in the practical work of party organizations. The party man is bound to do his full share in party management. He is bound to attend the caucuses and the primaries, to see that only good men are put up, and to exert his influence as strenuously against the foes of good government within his party, as, through his party machinery, he does against those who are without the party. In the same way the independent, if he cannot take part in the regular organizations, is bound to do just as much active constructive work (not merely the work of criticism) outside; he is bound to try to get up an organization of his own and to try to make that organization felt in some effective manner. Whatever course the man who wishes to do his duty by his country takes in reference to parties or to independence of parties, he is bound to try to put himself in touch with men who think as he does, and to help make their joint influence felt in behalf of the powers that go for decency and good government. He must try to accomplish things; he must not vote in the air unless it is really necessary. Occasionally a man must cast a "conscience vote," when there is no possibility of carrying to victory his principles or his nominees; at times, indeed, this may be his highest duty; but ordinarily this is not the case. As a general rule a man ought to work and vote for something which there is at least a a fair chance of putting into effect.

Yet another thing to be remembered by the man who wishes to make his influence felt for good in our politics is that he must act purely as an American. If he is not deeply imbued with the American spirit he cannot succeed. Any organization which tries to work along the line of caste or creed, which fails to treat all American citizens on their merits as men, will fail, and will deserve to fail. Where our political life is healthy, there is and can be no room for any movement organized to help or to antagonize men because they do or do not profess a certain religion, or because they were or were not born here or abroad. We have a right to ask that those with whom we associate, and those for whom we vote, shall be themselves good Americans in heart and spirit, unhampered by adherence to foreign ideals, and acting without regard to the national and religious prejudices of European countries; but if they really are good Americans in spirit and thought and purpose, that is all that we have any right to consider in regard to them. In the same way there must be no discrimination for or against any man because of his social standing. On the one side, there is nothing to be made out of a political organization which draws an exclusive social line, and on the other it must be remembered that it is just as un-American to vote against a man because he is rich as to vote against him because he is poor. The one man has just as much right as the other to claim to be treated purely on his merits as a man. In short, to do good work in politics, the men who organize must organize wholly without regard to whether their associates were born here or abroad, whether they are Protestants or Catholics, Jews or Gentiles, whether they are bankers or butchers, professors or day-laborers. All that can rightly be asked of one's political associates is that they shall be honest men, good Americans, and substantially in accord as regards their political ideas.

Another thing that must not be forgotten by the man desirous of doing good political work is the need of the rougher, manlier virtues, and above all the virtue of personal courage, physical as well as moral. If we wish to do good work for our country we must be unselfish, disinterested, sincerely desirous of the well-being of the commonwealth, and capable of devoted adherence to a lofty ideal; but in addition we must be vigorous in mind and body, able to hold our own in rough conflict with our fellows, able to suffer punishment without flinching, and, at need, to repay it in kind with full interest. A peaceful and commercial civilization is always in danger of suffering the loss of the virile fighting qualities without which no nation, however cultured, however refined, however thrifty and prosperous, can ever amount to anything. Every citizen should be taught, both in public and in private life, that while he must avoid brawling and quarrelling, it is his duty to stand up for his rights. He must realize that the only man who is more contemptible than the blusterer and bully is the coward. No man is worth much to the commonwealth if he is not capable of feeling righteous wrath and just indignation, if he is not stirred to hot anger by misdoing, and is not impelled to see justice meted out to the wrongdoers. No man is worth much anywhere if he does not possess both moral and physical courage. A politician who really serves his country well, and deserves his country's gratitude, must usually possess some of the hardy virtues which we admire in the soldier who serves his country well in the field.

An ardent young reformer is very apt to try to begin by reforming too much. He needs always to keep in mind that he has got to serve as a sergeant before he assumes the duties of commander-in-chief. It is right for him from the beginning to take a great interest in National, State, and Municipal affairs, and to try to make himself felt in them if the occasion arises; but the best work must be done by the citizen working in his own ward or district. Let him associate himself with the men who think as he does, and who, like him, are sincerely devoted to the public good. Then let them try to make themselves felt in the choice of alderman, of councilman, of assemblyman. The politicians will be prompt to recognize their power, and the people will recognize it too, after a while. Let them organize and work, undaunted by any temporary defeat. If they fail at first, and if they fail again, let them merely make up their minds to redouble their efforts, and perhaps alter their methods; but let them keep on working.

It is sheer unmanliness and cowardice to shrink from the contest because at first there is failure, or because the work is difficult or repulsive. No man who is worth his salt has any right to abandon the effort to better our politics merely because he does not find it pleasant, merely because it entails associations which to him happen to be disagreeable. Let him keep right on, taking the buffets he gets good-humoredly, and repaying them with heartiness when the chance arises. Let him make up his mind that he will have to face the violent opposition of the spoils politician, and also, too often, the unfair and ungenerous criticism of those who ought to know better. Let him be careful not to show himself so thin-skinned as to mind either; let him fight his way forward, paying only so much regard to both as is necessary to enable him to win in spite of them. He may not, and indeed probably will not, accomplish nearly as much as he would like to, or as he thinks he ought to: but he will certainly accomplish something; and if he can feel that he has helped to elevate the type of representative sent to the municipal, the State, or the national legislature from his district, or to elevate the standard of duty among the public officials in his own ward, he has a right to be profoundly satisfied with what he has accomplished.

Finally, there is one other matter which the man who tries to wake his fellows to higher political action would do well to ponder. It is a good thing to appeal to citizens to work for good government because it will better their estate materially, but it is a far better thing to appeal to them to work for good government because it is right in itself to do so. Doubtless, if we can have clean honest politics, we shall be better off in material matters. A thoroughly pure, upright, and capable administration of the affairs of New York city results in a very appreciable increase of comfort to each citizen. We should have better systems of transportation; we should have cleaner streets, better sewers, and the like. But it is sometimes difficult to show the individual citizen that he will be individually better off in his business and in his home affairs for taking part in politics. I do not think it is always worth while to show that this will always be the case. The citizen should be appealed to primarily on the ground that it is his plain duty, if he wishes to deserve the name of freeman, to do his full share in the hard and difficult work of self-government. He must do his share unless he is willing to prove himself unfit for free institutions, fit only to live under a government where he will be plundered and bullied because he deserves to be plundered and bullied on account of his selfish timidity and short-sightedness. A clean and decent government is sure in the end to benefit our citizens in the material circumstances of their lives; but each citizen should be appealed to, to take part in bettering our politics, not for the sake of any possible improvement it may bring to his affairs, but on the ground that it is his plain duty to do so, and that this is a duty which it is cowardly and dishonorable in him to shirk.

To sum up, then, the men who wish to work for decent politics must work practically, and yet must not swerve from their devotion to a high ideal. They must actually do things, and not merely confine themselves to criticising those who do them. They must work disinterestedly, and appeal to the disinterested element in others, although they must also do work which will result in the material betterment of the community. They must act as Americans through and through, in spirit and hope and purpose, and, while being disinterested, unselfish, and generous in their dealings with others, they must also show that they possess the essential manly virtues of energy, of resolution, and of indomitable personal courage.

IV.
THE COLLEGE GRADUATE AND PUBLIC LIFE[4]

THERE are always, in our national life, certain tendencies that give us ground for alarm, and certain others that give us ground for hope. Among the latter we must put the fact that there has undoubtedly been a growing feeling among educated men that they are in honor bound to do their full share of the work of American public life.

We have in this country an equality of rights. It is the plain duty of every man to see that his rights are respected. That weak good-nature which acquiesces in wrong-doing, whether from laziness, timidity, or indifference, is a very unwholesome quality. It should be second nature with every man to insist that he be given full justice. But if there is an equality of rights, there is an inequality of duties. It is proper to demand more from the man with exceptional advantages than from the

[4] *Atlantic Monthly*, August, 1894.

man without them. A heavy moral obligation rests upon the man of means and upon the man of education to do their full duty by their country. On no class does this obligation rest more heavily than upon the men with a collegiate education, the men who are graduates of our universities. Their education gives them no right to feel the least superiority over any of their fellow-citizens; but it certainly ought to make them feel that they should stand foremost in the honorable effort to serve the whole public by doing their duty as Americans in the body politic. This obligation very possibly rests even more heavily upon the men of means; but of this it is not necessary now to speak. The men of mere wealth never can have and never should have the capacity for doing good work that is possessed by the men of exceptional mental training; but that they may become both a laughing-stock and a menace to the community is made unpleasantly apparent by that portion of the New York business and social world which is most in evidence in the newspapers.

To the great body of men who have had exceptional advantages in the way of educational facilities we have a right, then, to look for good service to the state. The service may be rendered in many different ways. In a reasonable number of cases, the man may himself rise to high political position. That men actually do so rise is shown by the number of graduates of Harvard, Yale, and our other universities who are now taking a prominent part in public life. These cases must necessarily, however, form but a small part of the whole. The enormous majority of our educated men have to make their own living, and are obliged to take up careers in which they must work heart and soul to succeed. Nevertheless, the man of business and the man of science, the doctor of divinity and the doctor of law, the architect, the engineer, and the writer, all alike owe a positive duty to the community, the neglect of which they cannot excuse on any plea of their private affairs. They are bound to follow understandingly the course of public events; they are bound to try to estimate and form judgment upon public men; and they are bound to act intelligently and effectively in support of the principles which they deem to be right and for the best interests of the country.

The most important thing for this class of educated men to realize is that they do not really form a class at all. I have used the word in default of another, but I have merely used it roughly to group together people who have had unusual opportunities of a certain kind. A large number of the people to whom these opportunities are offered fail to take advantage of them, and a very much larger number of those to whom they have not been offered succeed none the less in making them for themselves. An educated man must not go into politics as such; he must go in simply as an American; and when he is once in, he will speedily realize that he must work very hard indeed, or he will be upset by some other American, with no education at all, but with much natural capacity. His education ought to make him feel particularly ashamed of himself if he acts meanly or dishonorably, or in any way falls short of the ideal of good citizenship, and it ought to make him feel that he must show that he has profited by it; but it should certainly give him no feeling of superiority until by actual work he has shown that superiority. In other words, the educated man must realize that he is living in a democracy and under democratic conditions, and that he is entitled to no more respect and consideration than he can win by actual performance.

This must be steadily kept in mind not only by educated men themselves, but particularly by the men who give the tone to our great educational institutions.

These educational institutions, if they are to do their best work, must strain every effort to keep their life in touch with the life of the nation at the present day. This is necessary for the country, but it is very much more necessary for the educated men themselves. It is a misfortune for any land if its people of cultivation take little part in shaping its destiny; but the misfortune is far greater for the people of cultivation. The country has a right to demand the honest and efficient service of every man in it, but especially of every man who has had the advantage of rigid mental and moral training; the country is so much the poorer when any class of honest men fail to do their duty by it; but the loss to the class itself is immeasurable. If our educated men as a whole become incapable of playing their full part in our life, if they cease doing their share of the rough, hard work which must be done, and grow to take a position of mere dilettanteism in our public affairs, they will speedily sink in relation to their fellows who really do the work of governing, until they stand toward them as a cultivated, ineffective man with a taste for bric-a-brac stands toward a great artist. When once a body of citizens becomes thoroughly out of touch and out of temper with the national life, its usefulness is gone, and its power of leaving its mark on the times is gone also.

The first great lesson which the college graduate should learn is the lesson of work rather than of criticism. Criticism is necessary and useful; it is often indispensable; but it can never take the place of action, or be even a poor substitute for it. The function of the mere critic is of very subordinate usefulness. It is the doer of deeds who actually counts in the battle for life, and not the man who looks on and says how the fight ought to be fought, without himself sharing the stress and the danger.

There is, however, a need for proper critical work. Wrongs should be strenuously and fearlessly denounced; evil principles and evil men should be condemned. The politician who cheats or swindles, or the newspaper man who lies in any form, should be made to feel that he is an object of scorn for all honest men. We need fearless criticism; but we need that it should also be intelligent. At present, the man who is most apt to regard himself as an intelligent critic of our political affairs is often the man who knows nothing whatever about them. Criticism which is ignorant or prejudiced is a source of great harm to the nation; and where ignorant or prejudiced critics are themselves educated men, their attitude does real harm also to the class to which they belong.

The tone of a portion of the press of the country toward public men, and especially toward political opponents, is degrading, all forms of coarse and noisy slander being apparently considered legitimate weapons to employ against men of the opposite party or faction. Unfortunately, not a few of the journals that pride themselves upon being independent in politics, and the organs of cultivated men, betray the same characteristics in a less coarse but quite as noxious form. All these journals do great harm by accustoming good citizens to see their public men, good and bad, assailed indiscriminately as scoundrels. The effect is twofold: the citizen learning, on the one hand, to disbelieve any statement he sees in any newspaper, so that the attacks on evil lose their edge; and on the other, gradually acquiring a deep-rooted belief that all public men are more or less bad. In consequence, his political instinct becomes hopelessly blurred, and he grows unable to tell the good representative from the bad. The worst offence that can be committed against the Republic is the offence of the public man who betrays his trust; but second only to it comes the offence of the man who tries to persuade others that an honest and efficient public man is dishonest or unworthy. This is a wrong that can be committed in a great many different ways. Downright foul abuse may be, after all, less dangerous than incessant misstatements, sneers, and those half-truths that are the meanest lies.

For educated men of weak fibre, there lies a real danger in that species of literary work which appeals to their cultivated senses because of its scholarly and pleasant tone, but which enjoins as the proper attitude to assume in public life one of mere criticism and negation; which teaches the adoption toward public men and public affairs of that sneering tone which so surely denotes a mean and small mind. If a man does not have belief and enthusiasm, the chances are small indeed that he will ever do a man's work in the world; and the paper or the college which, by its general course, tends to eradicate this power of belief and enthusiasm, this desire for work, has rendered to the young men under its influence the worst service it could possibly render. Good can often be done by criticising sharply and severely the wrong; but excessive indulgence in criticism is never anything but bad, and no amount of criticism can in any way take the place of active and zealous warfare for the right.

Again, there is a certain tendency in college life, a tendency encouraged by some of the very papers referred to, to make educated men shrink from contact with the rough people who do the world's work, and associate only with one another and with those who think as they do. This is a most dangerous tendency. It is very agreeable to deceive one's self into the belief that one is performing the whole duty of man by sitting at home in ease, doing nothing wrong, and confining one's participation in politics to conversations and meetings with men who have had the same training and look at things in the same way. It is always a temptation to do this, because those who do nothing else often speak as if in some way they deserved credit for their attitude, and as if they stood above their brethren who plough the rough fields. Moreover, many people whose political work is done more or less after this fashion are very noble and very sincere in their aims and aspirations, and are striving for what is best and most decent in public life.

Nevertheless, this is a snare round which it behooves every young man to walk carefully. Let him beware of associating only with the people of his own caste and of his own little ways of political thought. Let him learn that he must deal with the mass of men; that he must go out and stand shoulder to shoulder with his friends of every rank, and face to face with his foes of every rank, and must bear himself well in the hurly-burly. He must not be frightened by the many unpleasant features of the contest, and he must not expect to have it all his own way, or to accomplish too much. He will meet with checks and will make many mistakes; but if he perseveres, he will achieve a measure of success and will do a measure of good such as is never possible to the refined, cultivated, intellectual men who shrink aside from the actual fray.

Yet again, college men must learn to be as practical in politics as they would be in business or in law. It is surely unnecessary to say that by "practical" I do not mean anything that savors in the least of dishonesty. On the contrary, a college man is peculiarly bound to keep a high ideal and to be true to it; but he must work in practical ways to try to realize this ideal, and must not refuse to do anything because he cannot get everything. One especially necessary thing is to know the facts by actual experience, and not to take refuge in mere theorizing. There are always a number of excellent and well-meaning men whom we grow to regard with amused impatience because they waste all their energies on some visionary scheme which, even if it were not visionary, would be useless. When they come to deal with political questions, these men are apt to err from sheer lack of familiarity with the workings of our government. No man ever really learned from books how to manage a governmental system. Books are admirable adjuncts, and the statesman who has carefully studied them is far more apt to do good work than if he had not; but if he has never done anything but study books he will not be a statesman at all. Thus, every young politician should of course read the *Federalist* . It is the greatest book of the kind that has ever been written. Hamilton, Madison, and Jay would have been poorly equipped for writing it if they had not possessed an extensive acquaintance with literature, and in particular if they had not been careful students of political literature; but the great cause of the value of their writings lay in the fact that they knew by actual work and association what practical politics meant. They had helped to shape the political thought of the country, and to do its legislative and executive work, and so they were in a condition to speak understandingly about it. For similar reasons, Mr. Bryce's *American Commonwealth* has a value possessed by no other book of the kind, largely because Mr. Bryce is himself an active member of Parliament, a man of good standing and some leadership in his own party, and a practical politician. In the same way, a life of Washington by Cabot Lodge, a sketch of Lincoln by Carl Schurz, a biography of Pitt by Lord Rosebery, have an added value because of the writers' own work in politics.

It is always a pity to see men fritter away their energies on any pointless scheme; and unfortunately, a good many of our educated people when they come to deal with politics, do just such frittering. Take, for instance, the queer freak of arguing in favor of establishing what its advocates are pleased to call "responsible government" in our institutions, or in other words of grafting certain features of the English parliamentary system upon our own Presidential and Congressional system. This agitation was too largely deficient in body to enable it to last, and it has now, I think, died away; but at one time quite a number of our men who spoke of themselves as students of political history were engaged in treating this scheme as something serious. Few men who had ever taken an active part in politics, or who had studied politics in the way that a doctor is expected to study surgery and medicine, so much as gave it a thought; but very intelligent men did, just because they were misdirecting their energies, and were wholly ignorant that they ought to know practically about a problem before they attempted its solution. The English, or so-called "responsible," theory of parliamentary government is one entirely incompatible with our own governmental institutions. It could not be put into operation here save by absolutely sweeping away the United States Constitution. Incidentally, I may say it would be to the last degree undesirable, if it were practicable. But this is not the point upon which I wish to dwell; the point is that it was wholly impracticable to put it into operation, and that an agitation favoring this kind of government was from its nature unintelligent. The people who wrote about it wasted their time, whereas they could have spent it to great advantage had they seriously studied our institutions and sought to devise practicable and desirable methods of increasing and centring genuine responsibility—for all thinking men agree that there is an undoubted need for a change in this direction.

But of course much of the best work that has been done in the field of political study has been done by men who were not active politicians, though they were careful and painstaking students of the phenomena of politics. The back numbers of our leading magazines afford proof of this. Certain of the governmental essays by such writers as Mr. Lawrence Lowell and Professor A. B. Hart, and especially such books as that on the *Speakers' Powers and Duties*, by Miss Follet, have been genuine and valuable contributions to our political thought. These essays have been studied carefully not only by scholars, but by men engaged in practical politics, because they were written with good judgment and keen insight after careful investigation of the facts, and so deserved respectful attention.

It is a misfortune for any people when the paths of the practical and the theoretical politicians diverge so widely that they have no common standing-ground. When the Greek thinkers began to devote their attention to purely visionary politics of the kind found in Plato's Republic, while the Greek practical politicians simply exploited the quarrelsome little commonwealths in their own interests, then the end of Greek liberty was at hand. No government that cannot command the respectful support of the best thinkers is in an entirely sound condition; but it is well to keep in mind the remark of Frederick the Great, that if he wished to punish a province, he would allow it to be governed by the philosophers. It is a great misfortune for the country when the practical politician and the doctrinaire have no point in common, but the misfortune is, if anything, greatest for the doctrinaire. The ideal to be set before the student of politics and the practical politician alike is the ideal of the Federalist, Each man should realize that he cannot do his best, either in the study of politics or in applied politics unless he has a working knowledge of both branches. A limited number of people can do good work by the careful study of governmental institutions, but they can do it only if they have themselves a practical knowledge of the workings of these institutions. A very large number of people, on the other hand, may do excellent work in politics without much theoretic knowledge of the subject; but without this knowledge they cannot rise to the highest rank, while in any rank their capacity to do good work will be immensely increased if they have such knowledge.

There are certain other qualities, about which it is hardly necessary to speak. If an educated man is not heartily American in instinct and feeling and taste and sympathy, he will amount to nothing in our public life. Patriotism, love of country, and pride in the flag which symbolizes country may be feelings which the race will at some period outgrow, but at present they are very real and strong, and the man who lacks them is a useless creature, a mere incumbrance to the land.

A man of sound political instincts can no more subscribe to the doctrine of absolute independence of party on the one hand than to that of unquestioning party allegiance on the other. No man can accomplish much unless he works in an organization with others, and this organization, no matter how temporary, is a party for the time being. But that man is a dangerous citizen who so far mistakes means for ends as to become servile in his devotion to his party, and afraid to leave it when the party goes wrong. To deify either independence or party allegiance merely as such is a little absurd. It depends entirely upon the motive, the purpose, the result. For the last two years, the Senator who, beyond all his colleagues in the United States Senate, has shown himself independent of party ties is the very man to whom the leading champions of independence in politics most strenuously object. The truth is, simply, that there are times when it may be the duty of a man to break with his party, and there are other times when it may be his duty to stand by his party, even though, on some points, he thinks that party wrong; he must be prepared to leave it when necessary, and he must not sacrifice his influence by leaving it unless it is necessary. If we had no party allegiance, our politics would become mere windy anarchy, and, under present conditions, our government could hardly continue at all. If we had no independence, we should always be running the risk of the most degraded kind of despotism,— the despotism of the party boss and the party machine.

It is just the same way about compromises. Occasionally one hears some well-meaning person say of another, apparently in praise, that he is "never willing to compromise." It is a mere truism to say that, in politics, there has to be one continual compromise. Of course now and then questions arise upon which a compromise is inadmissible. There could be no compromise with secession, and there was none. There should be no avoidable compromise about any great moral question. But only a very few great reforms or great measures of any kind can be carried through without concession. No student of American history needs to be reminded that the Constitution itself is a bundle of compromises, and was adopted only because of this fact, and that the same thing is true of the Emancipation Proclamation.

In conclusion, then, the man with a university education is in honor bound to take an active part in our political life, and to do his full duty as a citizen by helping his fellow-citizens to the extent of his power in the exercise of the rights of self-government. He is bound to rank action far above criticism, and to understand that the man deserving of credit is the man who actually does the things, even though imperfectly, and not the man who confines himself to talking about how they ought to be done. He is bound to have a high ideal and to strive to realize it, and yet he must make up his mind that he will never be able to get the highest good, and that he must devote himself with all his energy to getting the best that he can. Finally, his work must be disinterested and honest, and it must be given without regard to his own success or failure, and without regard to the effect it has upon his own fortunes; and while he must show the virtues of uprightness and tolerance and gentleness, he must also show the sterner virtues of courage, resolution, and hardihood, and the desire to war with merciless effectiveness against the existence of wrong.

V.
PHASES OF STATE LEGISLATION[5]
THE ALBANY LEGISLATURE.

FEW persons realize the magnitude of the interests affected by State legislation in New York. It is no mere figure of speech to call New York the Empire State; and many of the laws most directly and immediately affecting the interests of its citizens are passed at Albany, and not at Washington. In fact, there is at Albany a little home rule parliament which presides over the destinies of a commonwealth more populous than any one of two thirds of the kingdoms of Europe, and one which, in point of wealth, material prosperity, variety of interests, extent of territory, and capacity for expansion, can fairly be said to rank next to the powers of the first class. This little parliament, composed of one hundred and twenty-eight members in the Assembly and thirty-two in the Senate, is, in the fullest sense of the term, a *representative* body; there

[5] The *Century*, January, 1885.

is hardly one of the many and widely diversified interests of the State that has not a mouthpiece at Albany, and hardly a single class of its citizens— not even excepting, I regret to say, the criminal class—which lacks its representative among the legislators. In the three Legislatures of which I have been a member, I have sat with bankers and bricklayers, with merchants and mechanics, with lawyers, farmers, day-laborers, saloon-keepers, clergymen, and prize-fighters. Among my colleagues there were many very good men; there was a still more numerous class of men who were neither very good nor very bad, but went one way or the other, according to the strength of the various conflicting influences acting around, behind, and upon them; and, finally, there were many very bad men. Still, the New York Legislature, taken as a whole, is by no means as bad a body as we would be led to believe if our judgment was based purely on what we read in the great metropolitan papers; for the custom of the latter is to portray things as either very much better or very much worse than they are. Where a number of men, many of them poor, some of them unscrupulous, and others elected by constituents too ignorant to hold them to a proper accountability for their actions, are put into a position of great temporary power, where they are called to take action upon questions affecting the welfare of large corporations and wealthy private individuals, the chances for corruption are always great; and that there is much viciousness and political dishonesty, much moral cowardice, and a good deal of actual bribetaking in Albany, no one who has had any practical experience of legislation can doubt; but, at the same time, I think that the good members generally outnumber the bad, and that there is not often doubt as to the result when a naked question of right or wrong can be placed clearly and in its true light before the Legislature. The trouble is that on many questions the Legislature never does have the right and wrong clearly shown it. Either some bold, clever parliamentary tactician snaps the measure through before the members are aware of its nature, or else the obnoxious features are so combined with good ones as to procure the support of a certain proportion of that large class of men whose intentions are excellent, but whose intellects are foggy. Or else the necessary party organization, which we call the "machine," uses its great power for some definite evil aim.

THE CHARACTER OF THE RERPESENTATIVES.

THE representatives from different sections of the State differ widely in character. Those from the country districts are generally very good men. They are usually well-to-do farmers, small lawyers, or prosperous store-keepers, and are shrewd, quiet, and honest. They are often narrow-minded and slow to receive an idea; but, on the other hand, when they get a good one, they cling to it with the utmost tenacity. They form very much the most valuable class of legislators. For the most part they are native Americans, and those who are not are men who have become completely Americanized in all their ways and habits of thought. One of the most useful members of the last Legislature was a German from a western county, and the extent of his Americanization can be judged from the fact that he was actually an ardent prohibitionist: certainly no one who knows Teutonic human nature will require further proof. Again, I sat for an entire session beside a very intelligent member from northern New York before I discovered that he was an Irishman: all his views of legislation, even upon such subjects as free schools and the impropriety of making appropriations from the treasury for the support of sectarian institutions, were precisely similar to those of his Protestant-American neighbors, though he was himself a Catholic. Now a German or an Irishman from one of the great cities would probably have retained many of his national peculiarities.

It is from these same great cities that the worst legislators come. It is true that there are always among them a few cultivated and scholarly men who are well educated, and who stand on a higher and broader intellectual and moral plane than the country members, but the bulk are very low indeed. They are usually foreigners, of little or no education, with exceedingly misty ideas as to morality, and possessed of an ignorance so profound that it could only be called comic, were it not for the fact that it has at times such serious effects upon our laws. It is their ignorance, quite as much as actual viciousness, which makes it so difficult to procure the passage of good laws or prevent the passage of bad ones; and it is the most irritating of the many elements with which we have to contend in the fight for good government

DARK SIDE OF THE LEGISLATIVE PICTURE.

MENTION has been made above of the bribetaking which undoubtedly at times occurs in the New York Legislature. This is what is commonly called "a delicate subject" with which to deal, and, therefore, according to our usual methods of handling delicate subjects, it is either never discussed at all, or else discussed with the grossest exaggeration; but most certainly there is nothing about which it is more important to know the truth.

In each of the last three legislatures there were a number of us who were interested in getting through certain measures which we deemed to be for the public good, but which were certain to be strongly opposed, some for political and some for pecuniary reasons. Now, to get through any such measure requires genuine hard work, a certain amount of parliamentary skill, a good deal of tact and courage, and above all, a thorough knowledge of the men with whom one has to deal, and of the motives which actuate them. In other words, before taking any active steps, we had to "size up" our fellow-legislators, to find out their past history and present character and associates, to find out whether they were their own masters or were acting under the directions of somebody else, whether they were bright or stupid, etc., etc. As a result, and after very careful study, conducted purely with the object of learning the truth, so that we might work more effectually, we came to the conclusion that about a third of the members were open to corrupt influences in some form or other; in certain sessions the proportion was greater, and in some less. Now it would, of course, be impossible for me or for anyone else to prove in a court of law that these men were guilty, except perhaps in two or three cases; yet we felt absolutely confident that there was hardly a case in which our judgment as to the honesty of any given member was not correct. The two or three exceptional cases alluded to, where legal proof of guilt might have been forthcoming, were instances in which honest men were approached by their colleagues at times when the need for votes was very great; but, even then, it would have been almost impossible to punish the offenders before a court, for it would have merely resulted in his denying what his accuser stated. Moreover, the members who had been approached would have been very reluctant to come forward, for each of them felt ashamed that his character should not have been well enough known to prevent anyone's daring to speak to him on such a subject. And another reason why the few honest men who are approached (for the lobbyist rarely makes a mistake in his estimate of the men who will be apt to take bribes) do not feel like taking action in the matter is that a doubtful lawsuit will certainly follow, which will drag on so long that the public will come to regard all of the participants with equal distrust, while in the end the decision is quite as likely to be against as to be for them. Take the Bradly-Sessions case, for example. This was an incident that occurred at the time of the faction-fight in the Republican ranks over the return of Mr. Conkling to the United States Senate after his resignation from that body. Bradly, an Assemblyman, accused Sessions, a State Senator, of attempting to bribe him. The affair dragged on for an indefinite time; no one was able actually to determine whether it was a case of blackmail on the one hand, or of bribery on the other; the vast majority of people recollected the names of both parties, but totally forgot which it was that was supposed to have bribed the other, and regarded both with equal disfavor; and the upshot has been that the case is now merely remembered as illustrating one of the most unsavory phases of the once-famous Halfbreed-Stalwart fight.

DIFFICULTIES OF PREVENTING AND PUNISHING CORRUPTION.

FROM the causes indicated, it is almost impossible to actually convict a legislator of bribetaking; but at the same time, the character of a legislator, if bad, soon becomes a matter of common notoriety, and no dishonest legislator can long keep his reputation good with honest men. If the constituents wish to know the character of their member, they can easily find it out, and no member will be dishonest if he thinks his constituents are looking at him; he presumes upon their ignorance or indifference. I do not see how bribetaking among legislators can be stopped until the public conscience becomes awake to the matter. Then it will stop fast enough; for just as soon as politicians realize that the people are in earnest in wanting a thing done, they make haste to do it. The trouble is always in rousing the people sufficiently to make them take an *effective* interest,—that is, in making them sufficiently in earnest to be willing to give a little of their time to the accomplishment of the object they have in view.

Much the largest percentage of corrupt legislators come from the great cities; indeed, the majority of the assemblymen from the great cities are "very poor specimens" indeed, while, on the contrary, the congressmen who go from them are generally pretty good men. This fact is only one of the many which go to establish the curious political law that in a great city the larger the constituency which elects a public servant, the more apt that servant is to be a good one; exactly as the Mayor is almost certain to be infinitely superior in character to the average alderman, or the average city judge to the average civil justice. This is because the public servants of comparatively small importance are protected by their own insignificance from the consequences of their bad actions. Life is carried on at such a high pressure in the great cities, men's time is so fully occupied by their manifold and harassing interests and duties, and their knowledge of their neighbors is necessarily so limited, that they are only able to fix in their minds the characters and records of a few prominent men; the others they lump together without distinguishing between individuals. They know whether the aldermen, as a body, are to be admired or despised; but they probably do not even know the name, far less the worth, of the particular alderman who represents their district; so it happens that their votes for aldermen or assemblymen are generally given with very little intelligence indeed, while, on the contrary, they are fully competent to pass and execute judgment upon as prominent an official as a mayor or even a congressman. Hence it follows that the latter have to give a good deal of attention to the wishes and prejudices of the public at large, while a city assemblyman, though he always talks a great deal about the people, rarely, except in certain extraordinary cases, has to pay much heed to their wants. His political future depends far more upon the skill and success with which he cultivates the good-will of certain "bosses," or of certain cliques of politicians, or even of certain bodies and knots of men (such as compose a trade-union, or a collection of merchants in some special business, or the managers of a railroad) whose interests, being vitally affected by Albany legislation, oblige them closely to watch, and to try to punish or reward, the Albany legislators. These politicians or sets of interested individuals generally care very little for a man's honesty so long as he can be depended upon to do as they wish on certain occasions; and hence it often happens that a dishonest man who has sense enough not to excite attention by any flagrant outrage may continue for a number of years to represent an honest constituency.

THE CONSTITUENTS LARGELY TO BLAME.

MOREOVER, a member from a large city can often count upon the educated and intelligent men of his district showing the most gross ignorance and stupidity in political affairs. The much-lauded intelligent voter—the man of cultured mind, liberal education, and excellent intentions—at times performs exceedingly queer antics.

The great public meetings to advance certain political movements irrespective of party, which have been held so frequently during the past few years, have undoubtedly done a vast amount of good; but the very men who attend these public meetings and inveigh against the folly and wickedness of the politicians will sometimes on election day do things which have quite as evil effects as any of the acts of the men whom they very properly condemn. A recent instance of this is worth giving. In 1882 there was in the Assembly a young member from New York, who did as hard and effective work for the city of New York as has ever been done by anyone. It was a peculiarly disagreeable year to be in the Legislature. The composition of that body was unusually bad. The more disreputable politicians relied upon it to pass. some of their schemes and to protect certain of their members from the consequences of their own misdeeds. Demagogic measures were continnally brought forward, nominally in the interests of the laboring classes, for which an honest and intelligent man could not vote, and yet which were jealously watched by, and received the hearty support of, not mere demagogues and agitators, but also a large number of perfectly honest though misguided workingmen, And, finally, certain wealthy corporations attempted, by the most unscrupulous means, to rush through a number of laws in their own interest. The young member of whom we are speaking incurred by his course on these various measures the bitter hostility alike of the politicians, the demagogues, and the members of that most dangerous of all classes, the wealthy criminal class. He had also earned the gratitude of all honest citizens, and he got it—as far as words went. The better class of newspapers spoke well of him; cultured and intelligent men generally— the well-to-do, prosperous people who belong to the different social and literary clubs, and their followers— were loud in his praise. I call to mind one man who lived in his district who expressed great indignation that the politicians should dare to oppose his re-election; when told that it was to be hoped he would help to insure the legislator's return to Albany by himself staying at the polls all day, he answered that he was very sorry, but he unfortunately had an engagement to go quail-shooting on election day! Most respectable people, however, would undoubtedly have voted for and re-elected the young member had it not been for the unexpected political movements that took place in the fall. A citizens' ticket, largely nonpartisan in character, was run for certain local offices, receiving its support from among those who claimed to be, and who undoubtedly were, the best men of both parties. The ticket contained the names of candidates only for municipal offices, and had nothing whatever to do with the election of men to the Legislature; yet it proved absolutely impossible to drill this simple fact through the heads of a great many worthy people, who, when election day came round, declined to vote anything but the citizens' ticket, and persisted in thinking that if no legislative candidate was on the ticket, it was because, for some reason or other, the citizens' committee did not consider any legislative candidate worth voting for. All over the city the better class of candidates for legislative offices lost from this cause votes which they had a right to expect, and in the particular district under consideration the loss was so great as to cause the defeat of the sitting member, or rather to elect him by so narrow a vote as to enable an unscrupulously partisan legislative majority to keep him out of his seat.

It is this kind of ignorance of the simplest political matters among really good citizens, combined with their timidity, which is so apt to characterize a wealthy *bourgeoisie*, and with their short-sighted selfishness in being unwilling to take the smallest portion of time away from their business or pleasure to devote to public affairs, which renders it so easy for corrupt men from the city to keep their places in the Legislature. In the country the case is different. Here the constituencies, who are usually composed of honest though narrow-minded and bigoted individuals, generally keep a pretty sharp lookout on their members, and, as already said, the latter are apt to be fairly honest men. Even when they are not honest, they take good care to act perfectly well as regards all district matters, for most of the measures about which corrupt influences are at work relate to city affairs. The constituents of a country member know well how to judge him for those of his acts which immediately affect themselves; but as regards others they often have no means of forming an opinion, except through the newspapers,—more especially through the great metropolitan newspapers,—and they have gradually come to look upon all statements made by the latter with reference to the honesty or dishonesty of public men with extreme distrust. This is because our newspapers, including those who professedly stand as representatives of the highest culture of the community, have been in the habit of making such constant and reckless assaults upon the characters of even very good public men, as to greatly detract from their influence when they attack one who is really bad. They paint everyone with whom they disagree black. As a consequence the average man, who knows they are partly wrong, thinks they may also be partly right; he concludes that no man is absolutely white, and at the same time that no one is as black as he is painted; and takes refuge in the belief that all alike are gray. It then becomes impossible to rouse him to make an effort either for a good man or against a scoundrel. Nothing helps dishonest politicians as much as this feeling; and among the chief instruments in its production we must number certain of our newspapers who are loudest in asserting that they stand on the highest moral plane. As for the other newspapers, those of frankly "sensational" character, such as the two which at present claim to have the largest circulation in New York, there is small need to characterize them; they form a very great promotive to public corruption and private vice, and are on the whole the most potent of all the forces for evil which are at work in the city.

PERILS OF LEGISLATIVE LIFE.

HOWEVER, there can be no question that a great many men do deteriorate very much morally when they go to Albany. The last accusation most of us would think of bringing against that dear, dull, old Dutch city is that of being a fast place; and yet there are plenty of members coming from out-of-the-way villages or quiet country towns on whom Albany has as bad an effect as Paris sometimes has on wealthy young Americans from the great seaboard cities. Many men go to the Legislature with the set purpose of making money; but many others, who afterwards become bad, go there intending to do good work. These latter may be well-meaning, weak young fellows of some shallow brightness, who expect to make names for themselves; perhaps they are young lawyers, or real-estate brokers, or small shop-keepers; they achieve but little success; they gradually become conscious that their business is broken up, and that they have not enough ability to warrant any expectation of their continuing in public life; some great temptation comes in their way (a corporation which expects to be relieved of perhaps a million dollars of taxes by the passage of a bill can afford to pay high for voters); they fall, and that is the end of them. Indeed, legislative life has temptations enough to make it unadvisable for any weak man, whether young or old, to enter it.

ALLIES OF VICIOUS LEGISLATORS.

THE array of vicious legislators is swelled by a number of men who really at bottom are not bad. Foremost among these are those most hopeless of beings who are handicapped by having some measure which they consider it absolutely necessary for the sake of their own future to "get through." One of these men will have a bill, for instance, appropriating a sum of money from the State Treasury to clear out a river, dam the outlet of a lake, or drain a marsh; it may be, although not usually so, proper enough in itself, but it is drawn up primarily in the interest of a certain set of his constituents who have given him clearly to understand that his continuance in their good graces depends upon his success in passing the bill. He feels that he must get it through at all hazards; the bad men find this out, and tell him he must count on their opposition unless he consents also to help their measures; he resists at first, but sooner or later yields; and from that moment his fate is sealed,—so far as his ability to do any work of general good is concerned.

A still larger number of men are good enough in themselves, but are "owned" by third parties. Usually the latter are politicians who have absolute control of the district machine, or who are, at least, of very great importance in the political affairs of their district. A curious fact is that they are not invariably, though usually, of the same party as the member; for in some places, especially in the lower portions of the great cities, politics become purely a business, and in the squabbles for offices of emolument it becomes important for a local leader to have supporters among all the factions. When one of these supporters is sent to a legislative body, he is allowed to act with the rest of his party on what his chief regards as the unimportant questions of party or public interest, but he has to come in to heel at once when any matter arises touching the said chief's power, pocket, or influence.

Other members will be controlled by some wealthy private citizen who is not in politics, but who has business interests likely to be affected by legislation, and who is therefore, willing to subscribe heavily to the campaign expenses of an individual or of an association so as to insure the presence in Albany of someone who will give him information and assistance.

On one occasion there came before a committee of which I happened to be a member, a perfectly proper bill in the interest of a certain corporation; the majority of the committee, six in number, were thoroughly bad men, who opposed the measure with the hope of being paid to cease their opposition. When I consented to take charge of the bill, I had stipulated that not a penny should be paid to insure its passage. It therefore became necessary to see what pressure could be brought to bear on the recalcitrant members; and, accordingly, we had to find out who were the authors and sponsors of their political being. Three proved to be under the control of local statesmen of the same party as themselves, and of equally bad moral character; one was ruled by a politician of unsavory reputation from a different city; the fifth, a Democrat, was owned by a Republican Federal official; and the sixth by the president of a horse-car company. A couple of letters from these two magnates forced the last members mentioned to change front on the bill with surprising alacrity.

Nowadays, however, the greatest danger is that the member will be a servile tool of the "boss" or "machine" of his own party, in which case he can very rarely indeed be a good public servant.

There are two classes of cases in which corrupt members get money. One is when a wealthy corporation buys through some measure which will be of great benefit to itself, although, perhaps an in-jury to the public at large; the other is when a member introduces a bill hostile to some moneyed interest, with the expectation of being paid to let the matter drop. The latter, technically called a "strike," is much the most common; for, in spite of the outcry against them in legislative matters, corporations are more often sinned against than sinning. It is difficult, for reasons already given, in either case to convict the offending member, though we have very good laws against bribery. The reform has got to come from the people at large. It will be hard to make any very great improvement in the character of the legislators until respectable people become more fully awake to their duties, and until the newspapers become more truthful and less reckless in their statements.

It is not a pleasant task to have to draw one side of legislative life in such dark colors; but as the side exists, and as the dark lines never can be rubbed out until we have manfully acknowledged that they are there and need rubbing out, it seems the falsest of false delicacy to refrain from dwelling upon them. But it would be most unjust to accept this partial truth as being the whole truth. We blame the Legislature for many evils, the ultimate cause for whose existence is to be found in our own shortcomings.

THE OTHER SIDE OF THE PICTURE.

THERE is a much brighter side to the picture, and this is the larger side, too. It would be impossible to get together a body of more earnest, upright, and disinterested men than the band of legislators, largely young men, who during the past three years have averted so much evil and accomplished so much good at Albany. They were able, at least partially, to put into actual practice the theories that had long been taught by the intellectual leaders of the country. And the life of a legislator who is earnest in his efforts faithfully to perform his duty as a public servant, is harassing and laborious to the last degree. He is kept at work from eight to fourteen hours a day; he is obliged to incur the bitterest hostility of a body of men as powerful as they are unscrupulous, who are always on the watch to find out, or to make out, anything in his private or his public life which can be used against him; and he has on his side either a but partially roused public opinion, or else a public opinion roused, it is true, but only blindly conscious of the evil from which it suffers, and alike ignorant and unwilling to avail itself of the proper remedy.

This body of legislators, who, at any rate, worked honestly for what they thought right, were, as a whole, quite unselfish, and were not treated particularly well by their constituents. Most of them soon got to realize the fact that if they wished to enjoy their brief space of political life (and most though not all of them did enjoy it) they would have to make it a rule never to consider, in deciding how to vote upon any question, how their vote would affect their own political prospects. No man can do good service in the Legislature as long as he is worrying over the effect of his actions upon his own future. After having learned this, most of them got on very happily indeed. As a rule, and where no matter of vital principle is involved, a member is bound to represent the views of those who have elected him; but there are times when the voice of the people is anything but the voice of God, and then a conscientious man is equally bound to disregard it.

In the long run, and on the average, the public will usually do justice to its representatives; but it is a very rough, uneven, and long-delayed justice. That is, judging from what I have myself seen of the way in which members were treated by their constituents, I should say that the chances of an honest man being retained in public life were about ten per cent, better than if he were dishonest, other things being equal. This is not a showing very creditable to us as a people; and the explanation is to be found in the shortcomings peculiar to the different classes of our honest and respectable voters,—shortcomings which may be briefly outlined.

SHORTCOMINGS OF THE PEOPLE WHO SHOULD TAKE

PART IN POLITICAL WORK.

THE people of means in all great cities have in times past shamefully neglected their political duties, and have been contemptuously disregarded by the professional politicians in consequence. A number of them will get together in a large hall, will vociferously demand "reform," as if it were some concrete substance which could be handed out to them in slices, and will then disband with a feeling of the most serene self-satisfaction, and the belief that they have done their entire duty as citizens and members of the community. It is an actual fact that four out of five of our wealthy and educated men, of those who occupy what is called good social position, are really ignorant of the nature of a caucus or a primary meeting, and never attend either. Now, under our form of government, no man can accomplish anything by himself; he must work in combination with others; and the men of whom we are speaking will never carry their proper weight in the political affairs of the country until they have formed themselves into some organization, or else, which would be better, have joined some of the organizations already existing. But there seems often to be a certain lack of the ro-buster virtues in our educated men, which makes them shrink from the struggle and the inevitable contact with rough politicians (who must often be rudely handled before they can be forced to behave); while their lack of familiarity with their surroundings causes them to lack discrimination between the politicians who are decent, and those who are not; for in their eyes the two classes both equally unfamiliar, are indistinguishable. Another reason why this class is not of more consequence in politics, is that it is often really out of sympathy— or, at least, its more conspicuous members are— with the feelings and interests of the great mass of the American people; and it is a discreditable fact that it is in this class that what has been most aptly termed the "colonial" spirit still survives. Until this survival of the spirit of colonial dependence is dead, those in whom it exists will serve chiefly as laughing-stocks to the shrewd, humorous, and prejudiced people who form nine tenths of our body-politic, and whose chief characteristics are their intensely American habits of thought, and their surly intolerance of anything like subservience to outside and foreign influences.

From different causes, the laboring classes, even when thoroughly honest at heart, often fail to appreciate honesty in their representatives. They are frequently not well informed in regard to the character of the latter, and they are apt to be led aside by the loud professions of the so-called labor reformers, who are always promising to procure by legislation the advantages which can only come to working men, or to any other men, by their individual or united energy, intelligence, and forethought. Very much has been accomplished by legislation for laboring men, by procuring mechanics' lien laws, factory laws, etc.; and hence it often comes that they think legislation can accomplish all things for them; and it is only natural, for instance, that a certain proportion of their number should adhere to the demagogue who votes for a law to double the rate of wages, rather than to the honest man who opposes it. When people are struggling for the necessaries of existence, and vaguely feel, no matter how wrongly, that they are also struggling against an unjustly ordered system of life, it is hard to convince them of the truth that an ounce of performance on their own part is worth a ton of legislative promises to change in some mysterious manner that life-system.

In the country districts justice to a member is somewhat more apt to be done. When, as is so often the case, it is not done, the cause is usually to be sought for in the numerous petty jealousies and local rivalries which are certain to exist in any small community whose interests are narrow and most of whose members are acquainted with each other; and besides this, our country vote is essentially a Bourbon or Tory vote, being very slow to receive new ideas, very tenacious of old ones, and hence inclined to look with suspicion upon any one who tries to shape his course according to some standard differing from that which is already in existence.

The actual work of procuring the passage of a bill through the Legislature is in itself far from slight. The hostility of the actively bad has to be discounted in advance, and the indifference of the passive majority, who are neither very good nor very bad, has to be overcome. This can usually be accomplished only by stirring up their constituencies; and so, besides the constant watchfulness over the course of the measure through both houses and the continual debating and parliamentary fencing which is necessary, it is also indispensable to get the people of districts not directly affected by the bill alive to its importance, so as to induce their representatives to vote for it. Thus, when the bill to establish a State Park at Niagara was on its passage, it was found that the great majority of the country members were opposed to it, fearing that it might conceal some land-jobbing scheme, and also fearing that their constituents, whose vice is not extravagance, would not countenance so great an expenditure of public money. It was of no use arguing with the members, and instead the country newspapers were flooded with letters, pamphlets were circulated, visits and personal appeals were made, until a sufficient number of these members changed front to enable us to get the lacking votes.

LIFE IN THE LEGISLATURE.

As already said, some of us who usually acted together took a great deal of genuine enjoyment out of our experience at Albany. We liked the excitement and perpetual conflict, the necessity for putting forth all our powers to reach our ends, and the feeling that we were really being of some use in the world; and if we were often both saddened and angered by the viciousness and ignorance of some of our colleagues, yet, in return, the latter many times unwittingly furnished us a good deal of amusement by their preposterous actions and speeches. Some of these are worth repeating, though they can never, in repetition, seem what they were when they occurred. The names and circumstances, of course, have been so changed as to prevent the possibility of the real heroes of them being recognized. It must be understood that they stand for the exceptional and not the ordinary workings of the average legislative intellect. I have heard more sound sense than foolishness talked in Albany, but to record the former would only bore the reader. And we must bear in mind that while the ignorance of some of our representatives warrants our saying that they should not be in the Legislature, it does not at all warrant our condemning the system of government which permits them to be sent there. There is no system so good that it has not some disadvantages. The only way to teach our foreign-born fellow-citizens how to govern themselves, is to give each the full rights possessed by other American citizens; and it is not to be wondered at if they at first show themselves unskilful in the exercise of these rights. It has been my experience moreover in the Legislature that when Hans or Paddy does turn out really well, there are very few native Americans indeed who do better. A very large number of the ablest and most disinterested and public-spirited citizens in New York are by birth Germans; and their names are towers of strength in the community. When I had to name a committee which was to do the most difficult, dangerous, and important work that came before the Legislature at all during my presence in it, I chose three of my four colleagues from among those of my fellow-legislators who were Irish either by birth or descent. One of the warmest and most disinterested friends I have ever had or hope to have in New York politics, is by birth an Irishman, and is also as genuine and good an American citizen as is to be found within the United States.

A good many of the Yankees in the house would blunder time and again; but their blunders were generally merely stupid and not at all amusing, while, on the contrary, the errors of those who were of Milesian extraction always possessed a most refreshing originality.

INCIDENTS OF LEGISLATIVE EXPERIENCE.

IN 1882 the Democrats in the house had a clear majority, but were for a long time unable to effect an organization, owing to a faction-fight in their own ranks between the Tammany and anti-Tammany members, each side claiming the lion's share of the spoils. After a good deal of bickering, the anti-Tammany men drew up a paper containing a series of propositions, and submitted it to their opponents, with the prefatory remark, in writing, that it was an *ultimatum* . The Tammany members were at once summoned to an indignation meeting, their feelings closely resembling those of the famous fish-wife who was called a parallelopipedon. None of them had any very accurate idea as to what the word *ultimatum* meant; but that it was intensively offensive, not to say abusive, in its nature, they did not question for a moment. It was felt that some equivalent and equally strong term by which to call Tammany's proposed counter-address must be found immediately; but, as the Latin vocabulary of the members was limited, it was some time before a suitable term was forth-coming. Finally, by a happy inspiration, some gentlemen of classical education remembered the phrase *ipse dixit*; it was at once felt to be the very phrase required by the peculiar exigencies of the case, and next day the reply appeared, setting forth with well-satisfied gravity that, in response to the County Democracy's "*ultimatum*," Tammany herewith produced her "*ipse dixit* ."

Public servants of higher grade than aldermen or assemblymen sometimes give words a wider meaning than would be found in the dictionary. In many parts of the United States, owing to a curious series of historical associations (which, by the way, it would be interesting to trace), anything foreign and un-English is called "Dutch," and it was in this sense that a member of a recent Congress used the term when, in speaking in favor of a tariff on works of art, he told of the reluctance with which he saw the productions of native artists exposed to competition "with Dutch daubs from Italy"; a sentence pleasing alike from its alliteration and from its bold disregard of geographic trivialties.

Often an orator of this sort will have his attention attracted by some high-sounding word, which he has not before seen, and which he treasures up to use in his next rhetorical flight, without regard to the exact meaning. There was a laboring man's advocate in the last Legislature, one of whose efforts attracted a good deal of attention from his magnificent heedlessness of technical accuracy in the use of similes. He was speaking against the convict contract-labor system, and wound up an already sufficiently remarkable oration with the still more startling ending that the system "was a vital cobra which was swamping the lives of the laboring men." Now, he had evidently carefully put together the sentence beforehand, and the process of mental synthesis by which he built it up must have been curious. "Vital" was, of course, used merely as an adjective of intensity; he was a little uncertain in his ideas as to what a "cobra" was, but took it for granted that it was some terrible manifestation of nature, possibly hostile to man, like a volcano, or a cyclone, or Niagara, for instance; then "swamping" was chosen as describing an operation very likely to be performed by Niagara, or a cyclone, or a cobra; and behold, the sentence was complete.

Sometimes a common phrase will be given a new meaning. Thus, the mass of legislation is strictly local in its character. Over a thousand bills come up for consideration in the course of a session, but a very few of which affect the interests of the State at large. The latter and the more important private bills are, or ought to be, carefully studied by each member; but it is a physical impossibility for any one man to examine the countless local bills of small importance. For these we have to trust to the member for the district affected, and when one comes up the response to any inquiry about it is usually, "Oh, it 's a local bill, affecting so-and-so's district; he is responsible for it." By degrees, some of the members get to use "local" in the sense of unimportant, and a few of the assemblymen of doubtful honesty gradually come to regard it as meaning a bill of no pecuniary interest to themselves. There was a smug little rascal in one of the last legislatures, who might have come out of one of Lever's novels. He was undoubtedly a bad case, but had a genuine sense of humor, and his "bulls" made him the delight of the house. One day I came in late, just as a bill was being voted on, and meeting my friend, hailed him, "Hello, Pat, what's up? what's this they 're voting on?" to which Pat replied, with contemptuous indifference to the subject, but with a sly twinkle in his eye, "Oh, some unimportant measure, sorr; some local bill or other—*a constitutional amendment*!"

The old Dublin Parliament never listened to a better specimen of a bull than was contained in the speech of a very genial and pleasant friend of mine, a really finished orator, who, in the excitement attendant upon receiving Governor Cleveland's message vetoing the five-cent-fare bill, uttered the following sentence: "Mr. Speaker, I recognize the hand that crops out in that veto; *I have heard it before!*"

One member rather astonished us one day by his use of the word "shibboleth." He had evidently concluded that this was merely a more elegant synonym of the good old word shillalah, and in reproving a colleague for opposing a bill to increase the salaries of public laborers, he said, very impressively, "The throuble wid the young man is, that he uses the wurrd economy as a shibboleth, wherewith to strike the working man." Afterwards he changed the metaphor, and spoke of a number of us as using the word "reform" as a shibboleth, behind which to cloak our evil intentions.

A mixture of classical and constitutional misinformation was displayed a few sessions past in the State Assembly when I was a member of the Legislature. It was on the occasion of that annual nuisance, the debate upon the Catholic Protectory item of the Supply Bill. Every year some one who is desirous of bidding for the Catholic vote introduces this bill, which appropriates a sum of varying dimensions for the support of the Catholic Protectory, an excellent institution, but one which has no right whatever to come to the State for support; each year the insertion of the item is opposed by a small number of men, including the more liberal Catholics themselves, on proper grounds, and by a larger number from simple bigotry—a fact which was shown two years ago, when many of the most bitter opponents of this measure cheerfully supported a similar and equally objectionable one in aid of a Protestant institution. On the occasion referred to there were two assemblymen, both Celtic gentlemen, who were rivals for the leadership of the minority; one of them a stout, red-faced man, who may go by the name of the "Colonel," owing to his having seen service in the army; while the other was a dapper, voluble fellow, who had at one time been a civil justice and was called the "Judge." Somebody was opposing the insertion of the item on the ground (perfectly just, by the way) that it was unconstitutional, and he dwelt upon this objection at some length. The Judge, who knew nothing of the constitution, except that it was continually being quoted against all of his favorite projects, fidgeted about for some time, and at last jumped up to know if he might ask the gentleman a question. The latter said, "Yes," and the Judge went on, "I'd like to know if the gintleman has ever personally seen the Catholic Protectoree?" "No, I haven't," said his astonished opponent. "Then, phwat do you mane by talking about its being unconstitootional? It's no more unconstitootional than you are! Then, turning to the house, with slow and withering sarcasm, he added, "The throuble wid the gintleman is that he okkipies what lawyers would call a kind of a quasi-position upon this bill," and sat down amid the applause of his followers.

His rival, the Colonel, felt he had gained altogether too much glory from the encounter, and after the nonplussed countryman had taken his seat, he stalked solemnly over to the desk of the elated Judge, looked at him majestically for a moment, and said, "You'll excuse my mentioning, sorr, that the gintleman who has just sat down knows more law in a wake than you do in a month; and more than that, Mike Shaunnessy, phwat do you mane by quotin' Latin on the flure of this House, *when you don't know the alpha and omayga of the language!*" and back he walked, leaving the Judge in humiliated submission behind him.

The Judge was always falling foul of the Constitution. Once, when defending one of his bills which made a small but wholly indefensible appropriation of State money for a private purpose, he asserted "that the Constitution didn't touch little things like that"; and on another occasion he remarked to me that he "never allowed the Constitution to come between friends."

The Colonel was at that time chairman of a committee, before which there sometimes came questions affecting the interests or supposed interests of labor. The committee was hopelessly bad in its composition, most of the members being either very corrupt or exceedingly inefficient. The Colonel generally kept order with a good deal of dignity; indeed, when, as not infrequently happened, he had looked upon the rye that was flavored with lemon-peel, his sense of personal dignity grew till it became fairly majestic, and he ruled the committee with a rod of iron. At one time a bill had been introduced (one of the several score of preposterous measures that annually make their appearance purely for purposes of buncombe), by whose terms all laborers in the public works of great cities were to receive three dollars a day— double the market price of labor. To this bill, by the way, an amendment was afterwards offered in the house by some gentleman with a sense of humor, which was to make it read that all the inhabitants of great cities were to receive three dollars a day, and the privilege of laboring on the public works if they chose; the original author of the bill questioning doubtfully if the amendment "didn't make the measure too sweeping." The measure was, of course, of no consequence whatever to the genuine laboring men, but was of interest to the professional labor agitators; and a body of the latter requested leave to appear before the committee. This was granted, but on the appointed day the chairman turned up in a condition of such portentous dignity as to make it evident that he had been on a spree of protracted duration. Down he sat at the head of the table, and glared at the committeemen, while the latter, whose faces would not have looked amiss in a rogues' gallery, cowered before him. The first speaker was a typical professional laboring man; a sleek, oily little fellow, with a black mustache, who had never done a stroke of work in his life. He felt confident that the Colonel would favor him,—a confidence soon to be rudely shaken,—and began with a deprecatory smile:

"Humble though I am—"

Rap, rap, went the chairman's gavel, and the following dialogue occurred:

Chairman (with dignity). "What's that you said you were, sir?"

Professional Workingman (decidedly taken aback). "I—I said I was humble, sir?"

Chairman (reproachfully). "Are you an American citizen, sir?"

P. W. "Yes, sir."

Chairman (with emphasis). "Then you're the equal of any man in this State! Then you're the equal of any man on this committee! *Don't let me hear you call yourself humble again! Go on sir!*"

After this warning the advocate managed to keep clear of the rocks until, having worked himself up to quite a pitch of excitement, he incautiously exclaimed, "But the poor man has no friends!" which brought the Colonel down on him at once. Rap, rap, went his gavel, and he scowled grimly at the offender while he asked with deadly deliberation:

"What did you say that time, sir?"

P. W. (hopelessly). "I said the poor man had no friends, sir."

Chairman (with sudden fire). "Then you lied, sir! I am the poor man's friend! so are my colleagues, sir!" (Here the rogues' gallery tried to look benevolent.) "Speak the truth, sir!" (with sudden change from the manner admonitory to the manner mandatory). "Now, you sit down quick, or get out of this somehow!"

This put an end to the sleek gentleman, and his place was taken by a fellow-professional of another type—a great, burly man, who would talk to you on private matters in a perfectly natural tone of voice, but who, the minute he began to speak of the Wrongs (with a capital W) of Labor (with a capital L), bellowed as if he had been a bull of Bashan. The Colonel, by this time pretty far gone, eyed him malevolently, swaying to and fro in his chair. However, the first effect of the fellow's oratory was soothing rather than otherwise, and produced the unexpected result of sending the chairman fast asleep sitting bolt upright. But in a minute or two, as the man warmed up to his work, he gave a peculiarly resonant howl which waked the Colonel up. The latter came to himself with a jerk, looked fixedly at the audience, caught sight of the speaker, remembered having seen him before, forgot that he had been asleep, and concluded that it must have been on some previous day. Hammer, hammer, went the gavel, and—

"I've seen you before, sir!"

"You have not," said the man.

"Don't tell me I lie, sir!" responded the Colonel, with sudden ferocity. "You've addressed this committee on a previous day!"

"I've never—" began the man; but the Colonel broke in again:

"Sit down, sir! The dignity of the chair must be preserved! No man shall speak to this committee twice. The committee stands adjourned." And with that he stalked majestically out of the room, leaving the committee and the delegation to gaze sheepishly into each other's faces.

OUTSIDERS.

AFTER all, outsiders furnish quite as much fun as the legislators themselves. The number of men who persist in writing one letters of praise, abuse, and advice on every conceivable subject is appalling; and the writers are of every grade, from the lunatic and the criminal up. The most difficult to deal with are the men with hobbies. There is the Protestant fool, who thinks that our liberties are menaced by the machinations of the Church of Rome; and his companion idiot, who wants legislation against all secret societies, especially the Masons. Then there are the believers in "isms," of whom the women-suffragists stand in the first rank. Now I have always been a believer in woman's rights, but I must confess I have never seen such a hopelessly impracticable set of persons as the woman-suffragists who came up to Albany to get legislation. They simply would not draw up their measures in proper form; when I pointed out to one of them that their proposed bill was drawn up in direct defiance of certain of the sections of the Constitution of the State he blandly replied that he did not care at all for that, because the measure had been drawn up so as to be in accord with the Constitution of Heaven. There was no answer to this beyond the very obvious one that Albany was in no way akin to Heaven. The ultra-temperance people —not the moderate and sensible ones—are quite as impervious to common sense.

A member's correspondence is sometimes amusing. A member receives shoals of letters of advice, congratulation, entreaty, and abuse, half of them anonymous. Most of these are stupid; but some are at least out of the common.

I had some constant correspondents. One lady in the western part of the State wrote me a weekly disquisition on woman's rights. A Buffalo clergyman spent two years on a one-sided correspondence about prohibition. A gentleman of Syracuse wrote me such a stream of essays and requests about the charter of that city that I feared he would drive me into a lunatic asylum; but he anticipated matters by going into one himself. A New Yorker at regular intervals sent up a request that I would "reintroduce" the Dongan charter, which had lapsed two centuries before. A gentleman interested in a proposed law to protect primaries took to telegraphing daily questions as to its progress —a habit of which I broke him by sending in response telegrams of several hundred words each, which I was careful not to prepay.

There are certain legislative actions which must be taken in a purely Pickwickian sense. Notable among these are the resolutions of sympathy for the alleged oppressed patriots and peoples of Europe. These are generally directed against England, as there exists in the lower strata of political life an Anglophobia quite as objectionable as the Anglomania of the higher social circles.

As a rule, these resolutions are to be classed as simply *bouffe* affairs; they are commonly introduced by some ambitious legislator—often, I regret to say, a native American—who has a large foreign vote in his district. During my term of service in the Legislature, resolutions were introduced demanding the recall of Minister Lowell, assailing the Czar for his conduct towards the Russian Jews, sympathizing with the Land League and the Dutch Boers, etc., etc.; the passage of each of which we strenuously and usually successfully opposed, on the ground that while we would warmly welcome any foreigner who came here, and in good faith assumed the duties of American citizenship, we had a right to demand in return that he should not bring any of his race or national antipathies into American political life. Resolutions of this character are sometimes undoubtedly proper; but in nine cases out of ten they are wholly unjustifiable. An instance of this sort of thing which took place not at Albany may be cited. Recently the Board of Aldermen of one of our great cities received a stinging rebuke, which it is to be feared the aldermanic intellect was too dense fully to appreciate. The aldermen passed a resolution "condemning" the Czar of Russia for his conduct towards his fellow-citizens of Hebrew faith, and "demanding" that he should forthwith treat them better; this was forwarded to the Russian Minister, with a request that it be sent to the Czar. It came back forty-eight hours afterwards, with a note on the back by one of the under-secretaries of the legation, to the effect that as he was not aware that Russia had any diplomatic relations with this particular Board of Aldermen, and as, indeed, Russia was not officially cognizant of their existence, and, moreover, was wholly indifferent to their opinions on any conceivable subject, he herewith returned them their kind communication.[6]

[6] A few years later a member of the Italian Legation "scored" heavily on one of our least pleasant national peculiarities. An Italian had just been lynched in Colorado, and an Italian paper in New York bitterly denounced the Italian Minister for his supposed apathy in the matter. The member of the Legation in question answered that the accusations were most unjust, for the Minister had worked zealously until he found that the deceased "had taken out his naturalization papers, and was entitled to all the privileges of American citizenship."

IN concluding I would say, that while there is so much evil at Albany, and so much reason for our exerting ourselves to bring about a better state of things, yet there is no cause for being disheartened or for thinking that it is hopeless to expect improvement. On the contrary, the standard of legislative morals is certainly higher than it was fifteen years ago or twenty-five years ago. In the future it may either improve or retrograde, by fits and starts, for it will keep pace exactly with the awakening of the popular mind to the necessity of having honest and intelligent representatives in the State Legislature.[7]

I have had opportunity of knowing something about the workings of but a few of our other State legislatures: from what I have seen and heard, I should say that we stand about on a par with those of Pennsylvania, Maryland, and Illinois, above that of Louisiana, and below those of Vermont, Massachusetts, Rhode Island, and Wyoming, as well as below the national legislature at Washington. But the moral status of a legislative body, especially in the West, often varies widely from year to year.

Minister for his supposed apathy in the matter. The member of the Legation in question answered that the accusations were most unjust, for the Minister had worked zealously until he found that the deceased "had taken out his naturalization papers, and was entitled to all the privileges of American citizenship."

> [7] At present, twelve years later, I should say that there was rather less personal corruption in the Legislature; but also less independence and greater subservience to the machine, which is even less responsive to honest and enlightened public opinion.

VI
MACHINE POLITICS IN NEW YORK CITY[8]

IN New York city, as in most of our other great municipalities, the direction of political affairs has been for many years mainly in the hands of a class of men who make politics their regular business and means of livelihood. These men are able to keep their grip only by means of the singularly perfect way in which they have succeeded in organizing their respective parties and factions; and it is in consequence of the clock-work regularity and efficiency with which these several organizations play their parts, alike for good and for evil, that they have been nicknamed by outsiders "machines," while the men who take part in and control, or, as they would themselves say, "run" them, now form a well-recognized and fairly well-defined class in the community, and are familiarly

[8] The *Century*, November, 1886.

known as machine politicians. It may be of interest to sketch in outline some of the characteristics of these men and of their machines, the methods by which and the objects for which they work, and the reasons for their success in the political field.

The terms machine and machine politician are now undoubtedly used ordinarily in a reproachful sense; but it does not at all follow that this sense is always the right one. On the contrary, the machine is often a very powerful instrument for good; and a machine politician really desirous of doing honest work on behalf of the community, is fifty times as useful an ally as is the average philanthropic outsider. Indeed, it is of course true, that any political organization (and absolutely no good work can be done in politics without an organization) is a machine; and any man who perfects and uses this organization is himself, to a certain extent, a machine politician. In the rough, however, the feeling against machine politics and politicians is tolerably well justified by the facts, although this statement really reflects most severely upon the educated and honest people who largely hold themselves aloof from public life, and show a curious incapacity for fulfilling their public duties.

The organizations that are commonly and distinctively known as machines are those belonging to the two great recognized parties, or to their factional subdivisions; and the reason why the word machine has come to be used, to a certain extent, as a term of opprobrium is to be found in the fact that these organizations are now run by the leaders very largely as business concerns to benefit themselves and their followers, with little regard to the community at large. This is natural enough. The men having control and doing all the work have gradually come to have the same feeling about politics that other men have about the business of a merchant or manufacturer; it was too much to expect that if left entirely to themselves they would continue disinterestedly to work for the benefit of others. Many a machine politician who is to-day a most unwholesome influence in our politics is in private life quite as respectable as anyone else; only he has forgotten that his business affects the state at large, and, regarding it as merely his own private concern, he has carried into it the same selfish spirit that actuates in business matters the majority of the average mercantile community. A merchant or manufacturer works his business, as a rule, purely for his own benefit, without any regard whatever for the community at large. The merchant uses all his influence for a low tariff, and the manufacturer is even more strenuously in favor of protection, not at all from any theory of abstract right, but because of self-interest. Each views such a political question as the tariff, not from the standpoint of how it will affect the nation as a whole, but merely from that of how it will affect him personally. If a community were in favor of protection, but nevertheless permitted all the governmental machinery to fall into the hands of importing merchants, it would be small cause for wonder if the latter shaped the laws to suit themselves, and the chief blame, after all, would rest with the supine and lethargic majority which failed to have enough energy to take charge of there own affairs. Our machine politicians, in actual life act in just this same way; their actions are very often dictated by selfish motives, with but little regard for the people at large though, like the merchants, they often hold a very high standard of honor on certain points; they therefore need continually to be watched and opposed by those who wish to see good government. But, after all, it is hardly to be wondered at that they abuse power which is allowed to fall into their hands owing to the ignorance or timid indifference of those who by rights should themselves keep it

In a society properly constituted for true democratic government—in a society such as that seen in many of our country towns, for example— machine rule is impossible. But in New York, as well as in most of our other great cities, the conditions favor the growth of ring or boss rule. The chief causes thus operating against good government are the moral and mental attitudes towards politics assumed by different sections of the voters. A large number of these are simply densely ignorant, and, of course, such are apt to fall under the influence of cunning leaders, and even if they do right, it is by hazard merely. The criminal class in a great city is always of some size, while what may be called the potentially criminal class is still larger. Then there is a great class of laboring men, mostly of foreign birth or parentage, who at present both expect too much from legislation and yet at the same time realize too little how powerfully though indirectly they are affected by a bad or corrupt government. In many wards the overwhelming majority of the voters do not realize that heavy taxes fall ultimately upon them, and actually view with perfect complacency burdens laid by their representatives upon the tax-payers, and, if anything, approve of a hostile attitude towards the latter—having a vague feeling of animosity towards them as possessing more than their proper proportion of the world's good things, and sharing with most other human beings the capacity to bear with philo-sophic equanimity ills merely affecting one's neighbors. When power fully roused on some financial, but still more on some sentimental question, this same laboring class will throw its enormous and usually decisive weight into the scale which it believes inclines to the right; but its members are often curiously and cynically in-different to charges of corruption against favorite heroes or demagogues, so long as these charges do not imply betrayal of their own real or fancied interests. Thus an alderman or assemblyman representing certain wards may make as much money as he pleases out of corporations without seriously jeopardizing his standing with his constituents; but if he once, whether from honest or dishonest motives, stands by a corporation when the interests of the latter are supposed to conflict with those of "the people," it is all up with him. These voters are, moreover, very emotional; they value in a public man what we are accustomed to consider virtues only to be taken into account when estimating private character. Thus, if a man is open-handed and warm-hearted, they consider it as a fair offset to his being a little bit shaky when it comes to applying the eighth commandment to affairs of state. I have more than once heard the statement, "He is very liberal to the poor," advanced as a perfectly satisfactory answer to the charge that a certain public man was corrupt. Moreover, working men, whose lives are passed in one unceasing round of narrow and monotonous toil, are not unnaturally inclined to pay heed to the demagogues and professional labor advocates who promise if elected to try to pass laws to better their condition; they are hardly prepared to understand or approve the American doctrine of government, which is that the state cannot ordinarily attempt to better the condition of a man or a set of men, but can merely see that no wrong is done him or them by anyone else, and that all alike have a fair chance in the struggle for life—a struggle wherein, it may as well at once be freely though sadly acknowl-edged, very many are bound to fail, no matter how ideally perfect any given system of government may be.

Of course it must be remembered that all these general statements are subject to an immense number of individual exceptions; there are tens of thousands of men who work with their hands for their daily bread and yet put into actual practice that sublime virtue of disinterested adherence to the right, even when it seems likely merely to benefit others, and those others better off than they themselves are; for they vote for honesty and cleanliness, in spite of great temptation to do the opposite, and in spite of their not seeing how any immediate benefit will result to themselves.

REASONS FOR THE NEGLECT OF PUBLIC DUTIES BY RESPECTABLE MEN IN EASY CIRCUMSTANCES.

THIS class is composed of the great bulk of the men who range from well-to-do up to very rich; and of these the former generally and the latter almost universally neglect their political duties, for the most part rather pluming themselves upon their good conduct if they so much as vote on election day. This largely comes from the tremendous wear and tension of life in our great cities. Moreover, the men of small means with us are usually men of domestic habits; and this very devotion to home, which is one of their chief virtues, leads them to neglect their public duties. They work hard, as clerks, mechanics, small tradesmen, etc., all day long, and when they get home in the evening they dislike to go out. If they do go to a ward meeting, they find themselves isolated, and strangers both to the men whom they meet and to the matter on which they have to act; for in the city a man is quite as sure to know next to nothing about his neighbors as in the country he is to be intimately acquainted with them. In the country the people of a neighborhood, when they assemble in one of their local conventions, are already well acquainted, and therefore able to act together with effect; whereas in the city, even if the ordinary citizens do come out, they are totally unacquainted with one another, and are as helplessly unable to oppose the disciplined ranks of the professional politicians as is the case with a mob of freshmen in one of our colleges when in danger of being hazed by the sophomores. Moreover, the pressure of competition in city life is so keen that men often have as much as they can do to attend to their own affairs, and really hardly have the leisure to look after those of the public. The general tendency everywhere is toward the specialization of functions, and this holds good as well in politics as elsewhere.

The reputable private citizens of small means thus often neglect to attend to their public duties because to do so would perhaps interfere with their private business. This is bad enough, but the case is worse with the really wealthy, who still more generally neglect these same duties, partly because not to do so would interfere with their pleasure, and partly from a combination of other motives, all of them natural but none of them creditable. A successful merchant, well dressed, pompous, self-important, unused to any life outside of the counting-room, and accustomed because of his very success to be treated with deferential regard, as one who stands above the common run of humanity, naturally finds it very unpleasant to go to a caucus or primary where he has to stand on an equal footing with his groom and day-laborers, and indeed may discover that the latter, thanks to their faculty for combination, are rated higher in the scale of political importance than he is himself. In all the large cities of the North the wealthier, or, as they would prefer to style themselves, the "upper" classes, tend distinctly towards the bourgeois type; and an individual in the bourgeois stage of development, while honest, industrious, and virtuous, is also not unapt to be a miracle of timid and short-sighted selfishness. The commercial classes are only too likely to regard everything merely from the standpoint of "Does it pay?" and many a merchant does not take any part in politics because he is short-sighted enough to think that it will pay him better to attend purely to making money, and too selfish to be willing to undergo any trouble for the sake of abstract duty; while the younger men of this type are too much engrossed in their various social pleasures to be willing to give their time to anything else. It is also unfortunately true, especially throughout New England and the Middle States, that the general tendency among people of culture and high education has been to neglect and even to look down upon the rougher and manlier virtues, so that an advanced state of intellectual development is too often associated with a certain effeminacy of character. Our more intellectual men often shrink from the raw coarseness and the eager struggle of political life as if they were women. Now, however refined and virtuous a man may be, he is yet entirely out of place in the American body-politic unless he is himself of sufficiently coarse fibre and virile character to be more angered than hurt by an insult or injury; the timid good form a most useless as well as a most despicable portion of the community. Again, when a man is heard objecting to taking part in politics because it is "low," he may be set down as either a fool or a coward: it would be quite as sensible for a militiaman to advance the same statement as an excuse for refusing to assist in quelling a riot. Many cultured men neglect their political duties simply because they are too delicate to have the element of "strike back" in their natures, and because they have an unmanly fear of being forced to stand up for their own rights when threatened with abuse or insult. Such are the conditions which give the machine men their chance; and they have been able to make the most possible out of this chance,—first, because of the perfection to which they have brought their machinery, and, second, because of the social character of their political organizations.

ORGANIZATION AND WORK OF THE MACHINES.

THE machinery of any one of our political bodies is always rather complicated; and its politicians invariably endeavor to keep it so, because, their time being wholly given to it, they are able to become perfectly familiar with all its workings, while the average outsider becomes more and more helpless in proportion as the organization is less and less simple. Besides some others of minor importance, there are at present in New York three great political organizations, *viz* ., those of the regular Republicans, of the County Democracy,[9] and of Tammany Hall, that of the last being perhaps the most perfect, viewed from a machine standpoint. Although with wide differences in detail, all these bodies are organized upon much the same general plan; and one description may be taken in the rough, as applying to all. There is a large central committee, composed of numerous delegates from the different assembly districts, which decides upon the various questions affecting the party as a whole in the county and city; and then there are the various organizations in the assembly districts themselves, which are the real sources of strength, and with which alone it is necessary to deal. There are different rules for the admission to the various district primaries and caucuses of the voters belonging to the respective parties; but in almost every case the real work is done and the real power held by a small knot of men, who in turn pay a greater or less degree of fealty to a single boss.

The mere work to be done on election day and in preparing for it forms no slight task. There is an association in each assembly or election district, with its president, secretary, treasurer, executive committee, etc.; these call the primaries and caucuses, arrange the lists of the delegates to the various nominating conventions, raise funds for

[9] Since succeeded every year or two by some other anti-Tammany Democratic organization or organizations.

campaign purposes, and hold themselves in communication with their central party organizations. At the primaries in each assembly district a full set of delegates is chosen to nominate assemblymen and aldermen, while others are chosen to go to the State, county, and congressional conventions. Before election day many thousands of complete sets of the party ticket are printed, folded, and put together, or, as it is called, "bunched." A single bundle of these ballots is then sent to every voter in the district, while thousands are reserved for distribution at the polls. In every election precinct—there are probably twenty or thirty in each assembly district—a captain and from two to a dozen subordinates are appointed.[10] These have charge of the actual giving out of the ballots at the polls. On election day they are at their places long before the hour set for voting; each party has a wooden booth, looking a good deal like a sentry-box, covered over with flaming posters containing the names of their nominees, and the "workers" cluster around these as centres. Every voter as he approaches is certain to be offered a set of tickets; usually these sets are "straight," that is, contain all the nominees of one party, but frequently crooked work will be done, and some one candidate will get his own ballots bunched with the rest of those of the opposite party. Each

> [10] All this has been changed, vastly for the better, by the ballot reform laws, under which the State distributes the printed ballots; and elections are now much more honest than formerly.

captain of a district is generally paid a certain sum of money, greater or less according to his ability as a politican or according to his power of serving the boss or machine. Nominally this money goes in paying the subordinates and in what are vaguely termed "campaign expenses," but as a matter of fact it is in many instances simply pocketed by the recipient; indeed, very little of the large sums of money annually spent by candidates to bribe voters actually reaches the voters supposed to be bribed. The money thus furnished is procured either by subscriptions from rich outsiders, or by assessments upon the candidates themselves; formerly much was also obtained from office-holders, but this is now prohibited by law. A great deal of money is also spent in advertising, placarding posters, paying for public meetings, and organizing and uniforming members to take part in some huge torchlight procession—this last particular form of spectacular enjoyment being one peculiarly dear to the average American political mind. Candidates for very lucrative positions are often assessed really huge sums, in order to pay for the extravagant methods by which our canvasses are conducted. Before a legislative committee of which I was a member, the Register of New York County blandly testified under oath that he had forgotten whether his expenses during his canvass had been over or under fifty thousand dollars. It must be remembered that even now—and until recently the evil was very much greater—the rewards paid to certain public officials are out of all proportion to the services rendered; and in such cases the active managing politicians feel that they have a right to exact the heaviest possible toll from the candidate, to help pay the army of hungry heelers who do their bidding. Thus, before the same committee the County Clerk testified that his income was very nearly eighty thousand a year, but with refreshing frankness admitted that his own position was practically merely that of a figure-head, and that all the work was done by his deputy, on a small fixed salary. As the County Clerk's term is three years, he should nominally have received nearly a quarter of a million dollars; but as a matter of fact two thirds of the money probably went to the political organizations with which he was connected. The enormous emoluments of such officers are, of course, most effective in debauching politics. They bear no relation whatever to the trifling quantity of work done, and the chosen candidate readily recognizes what is the exact truth,—namely, that the benefit of his service is expected to enure to his party allies, and not to the citizens at large. Thus, one of the county officers who came before the above-mentioned committee, testified with a naive openness which was appalling, in answer to what was believed to be a purely formal question as to whether he performed his public duties faithfully, that he did so perform them whenever they did not conflict with his political duties!—meaning thereby, as he explained, attending to his local organizations, seeing politicians, fixing primaries, bailing out those of his friends (apparently by no means few in number) who got hauled up before a justice of the peace, etc., etc. This man's statements were valuable because, being a truthful person and of such dense ignorance that he was at first wholly unaware his testimony was in any way remarkable, he really tried to tell things as they were; and it had evidently never occurred to him that he was not expected by everyone to do just as he had been doing,—that is, to draw a large salary for himself, to turn over a still larger fund to his party allies, and conscientiously to endeavor, as far as he could, by the free use of his time and influence, to satisfy the innumerable demands made upon him by the various small-fry politicians.[11]

" HEELERS."

THE "heelers," or "workers," who stand at the polls, and are paid in the way above described, form a large part of the rank and file composing each organization. There are, of course, scores of them in each assembly district association, and, together with the almost equally numerous class of federal, State, or local paid office-holders (except in so far as these last have been cut out by the operations of the civil-service reform laws), they form the bulk of the men by whom the machine is run, the bosses of great and small degree chiefly merely oversee the work and supervise the deeds

> [11] As a consequence of our investigation the committee, of which I was chairman, succeeded in securing the enactment of laws which abolished these enormous salaries.

of their henchmen. The organization of a party in our city is really much like that of an army. There is one great central boss, assisted by some trusted and able lieutenants; these communicate with the different district bosses, whom they alternately bully and assist. The district boss in turn has a number of half-subordinates, half-allies, under him; these latter choose the captains of the election districts, etc., and come into contact with the common heelers. The more stupid and ignorant the common heelers are, and the more implicitly they obey orders, the greater becomes the effectiveness of the machine. An ideal machine has for its officers men of marked force, cunning and unscrupulous, and for its common soldiers men who may be either corrupt or moderately honest, but who must be of low intelligence. This is the reason why such a large proportion of the members of every political machine are recruited from the lower grades of the foreign population. These henchmen obey unhesitatingly the orders of their chiefs, both at the primary or caucus and on election day, receiving regular rewards for so doing, either in employment procured for them or else in money outright. Of course it is by no means true that these men are all actuated merely by mercenary motives. The great majority entertain also a real feeling of allegiance towards the party to which they belong, or towards the political chief whose fortunes they follow; and many work entirely without pay and purely for what they believe to be right. Indeed, an experienced politician always greatly prefers to have under him men whose hearts are in their work and upon whose unbribed devotion he can rely; but unfortunately he finds in most cases that their exertions have to be seconded by others which are prompted by motives far more mixed.

All of these men, whether paid or not, make a business of political life and are thoroughly at home among the obscure intrigues that go to make up so much of it; and consequently they have quite as much the advantage when pitted against amateurs as regular soldiers have when matched against militiamen. But their numbers, though absolutely large, are, relatively to the entire community, so small that some other cause must be taken into consideration in order to account for the commanding position occupied by the machine and the machine politicians in public life. This other determining cause is to be found in the fact that all these machine associations have a social as well as a political side, and that a large part of the political life of every leader or boss is also identical with his social life.

THE SOCIAL SIDE OF MACHINE POLITICS.

THE political associations of the various districts are not organized merely at the approach of election day; on the contrary, they exist throughout the year, and for the greater part of the time are to a great extent merely social clubs. To a large number of the men who belong to them they are the chief social rallying-point. These men congregate in the association building in the evening to smoke, drink beer, and play cards, precisely as the wealthier men gather in the clubs whose purpose is avowedly social and not political—such as the Union, University, and Knickerbocker. Politics thus becomes a pleasure and relaxation as well as a serious pursuit. The different members of the same club or association become closely allied with one another, and able to act together on occasions with unison and *esprit de corps;* and they will stand by one of their own number for reasons precisely homologous to those which make a member of one of the upper clubs support a fellow-member if the latter happens to run for office. "He is a gentleman, and shall have my vote," says the swell club man. "He's one of the boys, and I'm for him," replies the heeler from the district party association. In each case the feeling is social rather than political, but where the club man influences one vote the heeler controls ten. A rich merchant and a small tradesman alike find it merely a bore to attend the meetings of the local political club; it is to them an irksome duty which is shirked whenever possible. But to the small politicians and to the various workers and hangers-on, these meetings have a distinct social attraction, and the attendance is a matter of preference. They are in congenial society and in the place where by choice they spend their evenings, and where they bring their friends and associates; and naturally all the men so brought together gradually blend their social and political ties, and work with an effectiveness impossible to the outside citizens whose social instincts interfere, instead of coinciding with their political duties. If an ordinary citizen wishes to have a game of cards or a talk with some of his companions, he must keep away from the local headquarters of his party; whereas, under similar circumstances, the professional politician must go there. The man who is fond of his home naturally prefers to stay there in the evenings, rather than go out among the noisy club frequenters, whose pleasure it is to see each other at least weekly, and who spend their evenings discussing neither sport, business, nor scandal, as do other sections of the community, but the equally monotonous subject of ward politics.

The strength of our political organizations arises from their development as social bodies; many of the hardest workers in their ranks are neither officeholders nor yet paid henchmen, but merely members who have gradually learned to identify their fortunes with the party whose hall they have come to regard as the headquarters in which to spend the most agreeable of their leisure moments. Under the American system it is impossible for a man to accomplish anything by himself; he must associate himself with others, and they must throw their weight together. This is just what the social functions of the political clubs enable their members to do. The great and rich society clubs are composed of men who are not apt to take much interest in politics anyhow, and never act as a body. The great effect produced by a social organization for political purposes is shown by the career of the Union League Club; and equally striking proof can be seen by every man who attends a ward meeting. There is thus, however much to be regretted it may be, a constant tendency towards the concentration of political power in the hands of those men who by taste and education are fitted to enjoy the social side of the various political organizations.

THE LIQUOR-SELLER IN POLITICS.

IT is this that gives the liquor-sellers their enormous influence in politics. Preparatory to the general election of 1884, there were held in the various districts of New York ten hundred and seven primaries and political conventions of all parties, and of these no less than six hundred and thirty-three took place in liquorsaloons,—a showing that leaves small ground for wonder at the low average grade of the nominees. The reason for such a condition of things is perfectly evident: it is because the liquorsaloons are places of social resort for the same men who turn the local political organizations into social clubs. Bar-tenders form perhaps the nearest approach to a leisure class that we have at present on this side of the water. Naturally they are on semi-intimate terms with all who frequent their houses. There is no place where more gossip is talked than in bar-rooms, and much of this gossip is about politics,—that is, the politics of the ward, not of the nation. The tariff and the silver question may be alluded to and civil-service reform may be incidentally damned, but the real interest comes in discussing the doings of the men with whom they are personally acquainted: why Billy so-and-so, the alderman, has quarrelled with his former chief supporter; whether "old man X" has really managed to fix the delegates to a given convention; the reason why one faction bolted at the last primary; and if it is true that a great downtown boss who has an intimate friend of opposite political faith running in an up-town district has forced the managers of his own party to put up a man of straw against him. The bar-keeper is a man of much local power, and is, of course, hail-fellow-well-met with his visitors, as he and they can be of mutual assistance to one another. Even if of different politics, their feelings towards each other are influenced purely by personal considerations; and, indeed, this is true of most of the smaller bosses as regards their dealings among themselves, for, as one of them once remarked to me with enigmatic truthfulness, "there are no politics in politics" of the lower sort—which, being interpreted, means that a professional politician is much less apt to be swayed by the fact of a man's being a Democrat or a Republican than he is by his being a personal friend or foe. The liquor-saloons thus become the social head-quarters of the little knots or cliques of men who take most interest in local political affairs; and by an easy transition they become the political head-quarters when the time for preparing for the elections arrives; and, of course, the good-will of the owners of the places is thereby propitiated,—an important point with men striving to control every vote possible.

The local political clubs also become to a certain extent mutual benefit associations. The men in them become pretty intimate with one another; and in the event of one becoming ill, or from any other cause thrown out of employment, his fellow-members will very often combine to assist him through his troubles, and quite large sums are frequently raised for such a purpose. Of course, this forms an additional bond among the members, who become closely knit together by ties of companionship, self-interest, and mutual interdependence. Very many members of these associations come into them without any thought of advancing their own fortunes; they work very hard for their party, or rather for the local body bearing the party name, but they do it quite disinterestedly, and from a feeling akin to that which we often see make other men devote their time and money to advancing the interests of a yacht club or racing stable, although no immediate benefit can result therefrom to themselves. One such man I now call to mind who is by no means well off, and is neither an office-seeker nor an office-holder, but who regularly every year spends about fifty dollars at election time for the success of the party, or rather the wing of the party, to which he belongs. He has a personal pride in seeing his pet candidates rolling up large majorities. Men of this stamp also naturally feel most enthusiasm for, or animosity against, the minor candidates with whom they are themselves acquainted. The names at the head of the ticket do not, to their minds, stand out with much individuality; and while such names usually command the normal party support, yet very often there is an infinitely keener rivalry among the smaller politicians over candidates for local offices. I remember, in 1880, a very ardent Democratic ward club, many of the members of which in the heat of a contest for an assemblyman cooly swapped off quite a number of votes for President in consideration of votes given to their candidate for the State Legislature; and in 1885, in my own district, a local Republican club that had a member running for alderman, performed a precisely similar feat in relation to their party's candidate for governor. A Tammany State Senator openly announced in a public speech that it was of vastly more importance to Tammany to have one of her own men Mayor of New York than it was to have a Democratic President of the United States. Very many of the leaders of the rival organizations, who lack the boldness to make such a frankly cynical avowal of what their party feeling really amounts to, yet in practice, both as regards mayor and as regards all other local offices which are politically or pecuniarily of importance, act exactly on the theory enunciated by the Tammany statesman; and, as a consequence, in every great election not only is it necessary to have the mass off the voters waked up to the importance of the principles that are at stake, but, unfortunately, it is also necessary to see that the powerful local leaders are convinced that it will be to their own interest to be faithful to the party ticket. Often there will be intense rivalry between two associations or two minor bosses; and one may take up and the other oppose the cause of a candidate with an earnestness and hearty good-will arising by no means from any feeling for the man himself, but from the desire to score a triumph over the opposition. It not unfrequently happens that a perfectly good man, who would not knowingly suffer the least impropriety in the conduct of his canvass, is supported in some one district by a little knot of politicians of shady character, who have nothing in common with him at all, but who wish to beat a rival body that is opposing him, and who do not for a moment hesitate to use every device, from bribery down, to accomplish their ends. A curious incident of this sort came to my knowledge while happening to inquire how a certain man became a Republican. It occurred a good many years ago, and thanks to our election laws it could not now be repeated in all its details; but affairs similar in kind occur at every election. I may preface it by stating that the man referred to, whom we will call X, ended by pushing himself up in the world, thanks to his own industry and integrity, and is now a well-to-do private citizen and as good a fellow as anyone would wish to see. But at the time spoken of he was a young laborer, of Irish birth, working for his livelihood on the docks and associating with his Irish and American fellows. The district where he lived was overwhelmingly Democratic, and the contests were generally merely factional. One small politician, a saloonkeeper named Larry, who had a great deal of influence, used to enlist on election day, by pay and other compensation, the services of the gang of young fellows to which X belonged. On one occasion he failed to reward them for their work, and in other ways treated them so shabbily as to make them very angry, more especially X, who was their leader. There was no way to pay Larry off until the next election; but they determined to break his influence utterly then, and as the best method for doing this they decided to "vote as far away from him" as possible, or, in other words, to strain every nerve to secure the election of all the candidates most opposed to those whom Larry favored. After due consultation, it was thought that this could be most surely done by supporting the Republican ticket. Most of the other bodies of young laborers, or, indeed, of young roughs, made common cause with X and his friends. Everything was kept very quiet until election day, neither Larry nor the few Republicans having an inkling of what was going on. It was a rough district, and usually the Republican booths were broken up and their ballot-distributers driven off early in the day; but on this occasion, to the speechless astonishment of everybody, things went just the other way. The Republican ballots were distributed most actively, the opposing workers were bribed, persuaded, or frightened away, all means fair and foul were tried, and finally there was almost a riot,—the outcome being that the Republicans actually obtained a majority in a district where they had never before polled ten per cent of the total vote. Such a phenomenon attracted the attention of the big Republican leaders, who after some inquiry found it was due to X. To show their gratitude and to secure so useful an ally permanently (for this was before the days of civil-service reform), they procured him a lucrative place in the New York Post-office; and he, in turn, being a man of natural parts, at once seized the opportunity, set to work to correct the defects of his early education, and is now what I have described him to be.

BOSS METHODS.

A POLITICIAN who becomes an influential local leader or boss is, of course, always one with a genuine talent for intrigue and organization. He owes much of his power to the rewards he is able to dispense. Not only does he procure for his supporters positions in the service of the State or city,—as in the custom-house, sheriff's office, etc.,—but he is also able to procure positions for many on horse railroads, the elevated roads, quarry works, etc. Great corporations are peculiarly subject to the attacks of demagogues, and they find it much to their interest to be on good terms with the leader in each district who controls the vote of the Assemblyman and Alderman; and therefore the former is pretty sure that a letter of recommendation from him on behalf of any applicant for work will receive most favorable consideration. The leader is also continually helping his henchmen out of difficulties, pecuniary and otherwise; he lends them a dollar or two now and then, helps out, when possible, such of their kinsmen as get into the clutches of the law, gets a hold over such of them as have done wrong and are afraid of being exposed, and learns to mix judicious bullying with the rendering of service.

But, in addition to all this, the boss owes very much of his commanding influence to his social relations with various bodies of his constituents; and it is his work as well as his pleasure to keep up these relations. No débutante during her first winter in society has a more exacting round of social duties to perform than has a prominent ward politician. In every ward there are numerous organizations, primarily social in character, but capable of being turned to good account politically. The Amalgamated Hack-drivers' Union, the Hibernian Republican Club, the West Side Young Democrats, the Jefferson C. Mullin Picnic Assotion,—there are twenty such bodies as these in every district, and with, at any rate, the master spirits in each and all it is necessary for the boss to keep on terms of intimate and, indeed, rather boisterous friendship. When the Jefferson C. Mullin society goes on a picnic, the average citizen scrupulously avoids its neighborhood; but the boss goes, perhaps with his wife, and, moreover, enjoys himself heartily, and is hail-fellow-well-met with the rest of the picnickers, who, by the way, may be by no means bad fellows; and when election day comes round, the latter, in return, no matter to what party they may nominally belong, enthusiastically support their friend and guest, on social, not political, grounds. The boss knows every man in his district who can control any number of votes: an influential saloon-keeper, the owner of a large livery stable, the leader among a set of horse-car drivers, a foreman in a machine-shop who has a taste for politics,—with all alike he keeps up constant and friendly relations. Of course this fact does not of itself make the boss a bad man; there are several such I could point out who are ten times over better fellows than are the mild-mannered scholars of timorous virtue who criticise them. But on the whole the qualities tending to make a man a successful local political leader under our present conditions are not apt to be qualities that make him serve the public honestly or disinterestedly; and in the lower wards, where there is a large vicious population, the condition of politics is often fairly appalling, and the boss of the dominant party is generally a man of grossly immoral public and private character, as anyone can satisfy himself by examining the testimony taken by the last two or three legislative committees that have investigated the affairs of New York city. In some of these wards many of the social organizations with which the leaders are obliged to keep on good terms are composed of criminals, or of the relatives and associates of criminals. The testimony mentioned above showed some strange things. I will take at random a few instances that occur to me at the moment. There was one case of an assemblyman who served several terms in the Legislature, while his private business was to carry on corrupt negotiations between the Excise Commissioners and owners of low haunts who wished licenses. The president of a powerful semi-political association was by profession a burglar; the man who received the goods he stole was an alderman. Another alderman was elected while his hair was still short from a term in State Prison. A school trustee had been convicted of embezzlement, and was the associate of criminals. A prominent official in the Police Department was interested in disreputable houses and gambling saloons, and was backed politically by their proprietors.

BEATING THE MACHINE.

IN the better wards the difficulty comes in drilling a little sense and energy into decent people: they either do not care to combine or else refuse to learn how. In one district we did at one time and for a considerable period get control of affairs and elect a set of almost ideal delegates and candidates to the various nominating and legislative bodies, and in the end took an absolutely commanding although temporary position in State and even in national politics.

This was done by the efforts of some twenty or thirty young fellows who devoted a large part of their time to thoroughly organizing and getting out the respectable vote. The moving spirits were all active, energetic men, with common sense, whose motives were perfectly disinterested. Some went in from principle; others, doubtless, from good-fellowship or sheer love of the excitement always attendant upon a political struggle. Our success was due to our absolute freedom from caste spirit. Among our chief workers were a Columbia College professor, a crack oarsman from the same institution, an Irish quarryman, a master carpenter, a rich young merchant, the owner of a small cigar store, the editor of a little German newspaper, and a couple of employees from the post-office and custom-house, who worked directly against their own seeming interests. One of our important committees was composed of a prominent member of a Jewish synagogue, of the son of a noted Presbyterian clergyman, and of a young Catholic lawyer. We won some quite remarkable triumphs, for the first time in New York politics carrying primaries against the machine, and as the result of our most successful struggle completely revolutionizing the State Convention held to send delegates to the National Republican Convention of 1884, and returning to that body, for the first and only time it was ever done, a solid delegation of Independent Republicans. This was done, however, by sheer hard work on the part of a score or so of men; the mass of our good citizens, even after the victories which they had assisted in winning, understood nothing about how they were won. Many of them actually objected to organizing, apparently having a confused idea that we could always win by what one of their number called a "spontaneous uprising," to which a quiet young fellow in our camp grimly responded that he had done a good deal of political work in his day, but that he never in his life had worked so hard and so long as he did to get up the "spontaneous" movement in which we were then engaged.

CONCLUSIONS.

IN conclusion, it may be accepted as a fact, however unpleasant, that if steady work and much attention to detail are required, ordinary citizens, to whom participation in politics is merely a disagreeable duty, will always be beaten by the organized army of politicians to whom it is both duty, business, and pleasure, and who are knit together and to outsiders by their social relations. On the other hand, average citizens do take a spasmodic interest in public affairs; and we should therefore so shape our governmental system that the action required by the voters should be as simple and direct as possible, and should not need to be taken any more often than is necessary. Governmental power should be concentrated in the hands of a very few men, who would be so conspicuous that no citizen could help knowing all about them; and the elections should not come too frequently. Not one decent voter in ten will take the trouble annually to inform himself as to the character of the host of petty candidates to be balloted for, but he will be sure to know all about the mayor, comptroller, etc. It is not to his credit that we can only rely, and that without much certainty, upon his taking a spasmodic interest in the government that affects his own well-being; but such is the case, and accordingly we ought, as far as possible, to have a system requiring on his part intermittent and not sustained action.

VII
SIX YEARS OF CIVIL SERVICE REFORM[12]

NO question of internal administration is so important to the United States as the question of Civil Service reform, because the spoils system, which can only be supplanted through the agencies which have found expression in the act creating the Civil Service Commission, has been for seventy years the most potent of all the forces tending to bring about the degradation of our politics. No republic can permanently endure when its politics are corrupt and base; and the spoils system, the application in political life of the degrading doctrine that to the victor belong the spoils, produces corruption and degradation. The man who is in politics for the offices might just as well be in politics for the money he can get for his vote, so far as the general good is concerned. When the then Vice-President of the United States, Mr. Hendricks,

[12] *Scribner's Magazine*, August, 1895.

said that he "wished to take the boys in out of the cold to warm their toes," thereby meaning that he wished to distribute offices among the more active heelers, to the rapturous enthusiasm of the latter, he uttered a sentiment which was morally on the same plane with a wish to give "the boys" five dollars apiece all around for their votes, and fifty dollars apiece when they showed themselves sufficiently active in bullying, bribing, and cajoling other voters. Such a sentiment should bar any man from public life, and will bar him whenever the people grow to realize that the worst enemies of the Republic are the demagogue and the corruptionist. The spoils-monger and spoils-seeker invariably breed the bribe-taker and bribe-giver, the embezzler of public funds and the corrupter of voters. Civil Service reform is not merely a movement to better the public service. It achieves this end too; but its main purpose is to raise the tone of public life, and it is in this direction that its effects have been of incalculable good to the whole community.

For six years, from May, 1889, to May, 1895, I was a member of the National Civil Service Commission, and it seems to me to be of interest to show exactly what has been done to advance the law and what to hinder its advancement during these six years, and who have been the more prominent among its friends and foes. I wish to tell "the adventures of Philip on his way through the world," and show who robbed him, who helped him, and who passed him by. It would take too long to give the names of all our friends, and it is not worth while to more than allude to most of our foes and to most of those who were indifferent to us; but a few of the names should be preserved and some record made of the fights that have been fought and won and of the way in which, by fits and starts, and with more than one set-back, the general advance has been made.

Of the Commission itself little need be said. When I took office the only Commissioner was Mr. Charles Lyman, of Connecticut, who resigned when I did. Honorable Hugh S. Thompson, ex-Governor of South Carolina, was made Commissioner at the same time that I was, and after serving for three years resigned. He was succeeded by Mr. George D. Johnston, of Louisiana, who was removed by the President in November, 1893, being replaced by Mr. John R. Procter, the former State Geologist of Kentucky, who is still serving. The Commission has never varied a hand's-breadth from its course throughout this time; and Messrs. Thompson, Procter, Lyman, and myself were always a unit in all important questions of policy and principle. Our aim was always to procure the extension of the classified service as rapidly as possible, and to see that the law was administered thoroughly and fairly. The Commission does not have the power that it should, and in many instances there have been violations or evasions of the law in particular bureaus or departments which the Commission was not able to prevent. In every case, however, we made a resolute fight, and gave the widest publicity to the wrong-doing. Often, even where we have been unable to win the actual fight in which we were engaged, the fact of our having made it, and the further fact that we were ready to repeat it on provocation, has put a complete stop to the repetition of the offence. As a consequence, while there have been plenty of violations and evasions of the law, yet their proportion was really very small, taking into account the extent of the service. In the aggregate it is doubtful if one per cent, of all the employees have been dismissed for political reasons. In other words, where under the spoils system a hundred men would have been turned out, under the Civil Service Law, as administered under our supervision, ninety-nine men were kept in.

In the administration of the law very much depends upon the Commission. Good heads of departments and bureaus will administer it well anyhow; but not only the bad men, but also the large class of men who are weak rather than bad, are sure to administer the law poorly unless kept well up to the mark. The public should exercise a most careful scrutiny over the appointment and over the acts of Civil Service Commissioners, for there is no office the effectiveness of which depends so much upon the way in which the man himself chooses to construe his duties. A Commissioner can keep within the letter of the law and do his routine work and yet accomplish absolutely nothing in the way of securing the observance of the law. The Commission, to do useful work, must be fearless and vigilant. It must actively interfere whenever wrong is done, and must take all the steps that can be taken to secure the punishment of the wrong-doer and to protect the employee threatened with molestation.

This course was consistently followed by the Commission throughout my connection with it. I was myself a Republican from the North. Messrs. Thompson and Procter were from the South, and were both Democrats who had served in the Confederate armies; and it would be impossible for anyone to desire as associates two public men with higher ideals of duty, or more resolute in their adherence to those ideals It is unnecessary to say that in all our dealings there was no single instance wherein the politics of any person or the political significance of any action was so much as taken into account in any case that arose. The force of the Commission itself was all chosen through the competitive examinations, and included men of every party and from every section of the country; and I do not believe that in any public or private office of the size it would be possible to find a more honest, efficient, and coherent body of workers.

From the beginning of the present system each President of the United States has been its friend, but no President has been a radical Civil Service reformer. Presidents Arthur, Harrison, and Cleveland have all desired to see the service extended, and to see the law well administered. No one of them has felt willing or able to do all that the reformers asked, or to pay much heed to their wishes save as regards that portion of the service to which the law actually applied. Each has been a sincere party man, who has felt strongly on such questions as those of the tariff, of finance, and of our foreign policy, and each has been obliged to conform more or less closely to the wishes of his party associates and fellow party leaders; and, of course, these party leaders, and the party politicians generally, wished the offices to be distributed as they had been ever since Andrew Jackson became President. In consequence the offices outside the protection of the law have still been treated, under every administration, as patronage, to be disposed of in the interest of the dominant party. An occasional exception was made here and there. The postmaster at New York, a Republican, was retained by President Cleveland in his first administration, and the postmaster of Charleston, a Democrat, was retained by President Harrison; but, with altogether insignificant exceptions, the great bulk of the non-classified places have been changed for political reasons by each administration, the office-holders politically opposed to the administration being supplanted or succeeded by political adherents of the administration.

Where the change has been complete it does not matter much whether it was made rapidly or slowly. Thus, the fourth-class postmasterships were looted more rapidly under the administration of President Harrison than under that of President Cleveland, and the consular service more rapidly under President Cleveland than under President Harrison; but the final result was the same in both cases. Indeed, I think that the brutality which accompanied the greater speed was in some ways of service to the country, for it directed attention to the iniquity and folly of the system, and emphasized, in the minds of decent citizens, the fact that appointments and removals for political reasons in places where the duties are wholly nonpolitical cannot be defended by any man who looks at public affairs from the proper standpoint.

The advance has been made purely on two lines, that is, by better enforcement of the law, and by inclusion under the law, or under some system similar in its operations, of a portion of the service previously administered in accordance with the spoils theory. Under President Arthur the first classification was made, which included 14,000 places. Under President Cleveland, during his first term, the limits of the classified service were extended by the inclusion of 7000 additional places. During President Harrison's term the limit was extended by the inclusion of about eight thousand places; and hitherto during President Cleveland's second term, by the inclusion of some six thousand places; in addition to which the natural growth of the service has been such that the total number of offices now classified is over forty thousand. Moreover, the Secretary of the Navy under President Harrison, introduced into the navy yards a system of registration of laborers, which secures the end desired by the Commission; and Secretary Herbert has continued this system. It only rests, however, upon the will of the Secretary of the Navy; and as we cannot expect always to have secretaries as clear-sighted as Messrs. Tracy and Herbert, it is most desirable that this branch of the service should be put directly under the control of the Commission.

The Cabinet officers, though often not Civil Service reformers to start with, usually become such before their terms of office expire. This was true, without exception, of all the Cabinet officers with whom I was personally brought into contact while on the Commission. Moreover, from their position and their sense of responsibility they are certain to refrain from violating the law themselves and to try to secure at least a formal compliance with its demands on the part of their subordinates. In most cases it is necessary, however, to goad them continually to see that they do not allow their subordinates to evade the law; and it is very difficult to get either the President or the head of a department to punish these subordinates when they have evaded it. There is not much open violation of the law, because such violation can be reached through the courts; but in the small offices and small bureaus there is often a chance for an unscrupulous head of the office or bureau to persecute his subordinates who are politically opposed to him into resigning, or to trump up charges against them on which they can be dismissed. If this is done in a sufficient number of cases, men of the opposite political party think that it is useless to enter the examinations; and by staying out they leave the way clear for the offender to get precisely the men he wishes for the eligible registers. Cases like this continually occur, and the Commission has to be vigilant in detecting and exposing them, and in demanding their punishment by the head of the office. The offender always, of course, insists that he has been misunderstood, and in most cases he can prepare quite a specious defence. As he is of the same political faith as the head of the department, and as he is certain to be backed by influential politicians, the head of the department is usually loath to act against him, and, if possible, will let him off with, at most, a warning not to repeat the offence. In some departments this kind of evasion has never been tolerated; and where the Commission has the force under its eye, as in the departments at Washington, the chance of injustice is minimized. Nevertheless, there have been considerable abuses of this kind, notably in the custom-houses and post-offices, throughout the time I have been at Washington. So far as the Post-Office Department was concerned the abuses were more flagrant under President Harrison's Postmaster-General, Mr. Wanamaker; but in the Treasury Department they were more flagrant under President Cleveland's Secretary of the Treasury, Mr. Carlisle.

Congress has control of the appropriations for the Commission, and as it cannot do its work without an ample appropriation the action of Congress is vital to its welfare. Many, even of the friends of the system in the country at large, are astonishingly ignorant of who the men are who have battled most effectively for the law and for good government in either the Senate or the Lower House. It is not only necessary that a man shall be good and possess the desire to do decent things, but it is also necessary that he shall be courageous, practical, and efficient, if his work is to amount to anything. There is a good deal of rough-and-tumble fighting in Congress, as there is in all our political life, and a man is entirely out of place in it if he does not possess the virile qualities, and if he fails to show himself ready and able to hit back when assailed. Moreover, he must be alert, vigorous, and intelligent if he is going to make his work count. The friends of the Civil Service Law, like the friends of all other laws, would be in a bad way if they had to rely solely upon the backing of the timid good. During the last six years there have been, as there always are, a number of men in the House who believe in the Civil Service Law, and who vote for it if they understand the question and are present when it comes up, but who practically count for very little one way or the other, because they are timid or flighty, or are lacking in capacity for leadership or ability to see a point and to put it strongly before their associates.

There is need of further legislation to perfect and extend the law and the system; but Congress has never been willing seriously to consider a proposition looking to this extension. Bills to provide for the appointment of fourth-class postmasters have been introduced by Senator Lodge and others, but have never come to anything. Indeed, but once has a measure of this kind been reported from committee and fought for in either House. This was in the last session of the 53d Congress, when

Senators Morgan and Lodge introduced bills to reform the consular service. They were referred to Senator Morgan's Committee on Foreign Affairs, and were favorably reported. Senator Lodge made a vigorous fight for them in the Senate, but he received little support, and was defeated, Senator Gorman leading the opposition.

On the other hand, efforts to repeal the law, or to destroy it by new legislation, have uniformly been failures, and have rarely gone beyond committee. Occasionally, in an appropriation bill or some other measure, an amendment will be slipped through, adding forty or fifty employees to the classified service, or providing that the law shall not apply to them; but nothing important has ever been done in this way. But once has there been a resolute attack made on the law by legislation. This was in the 53d Congress, when Mr. Bynum, of Indiana, introduced in the House, and Mr. Vilas, of Wisconsin, pushed in the Senate, a bill to reinstate the Democratic railway mail clerks, turned out before the classification of the railway mail service in the early days of Mr. Harrison's administration.

The classification of the railway mail service was ordered by President Cleveland less than two months before the expiration of his first term of office as President. It was impossible for the Com-mission to prepare and hold the necessary examinations and establish eligible registers prior to May 1, 1889. President Harrison had been inaugurated on March 4th, and Postmaster-General Wanamaker permitted the spoilsmen to take advantage of the necessary delay and turn out half of the employees who were Democrats, and replace them by Republicans. This was an outrageous act, deserving the severe condemnation it received; but it was perfectly legal. During the four years of Mr. Cleveland's first term a clean sweep was made of the railway mail service; the employees who were almost all Republicans, were turned out, and Democrats were put in their places. The result was utterly to demoralize the efficiency of the service. It had begun to recover from this when the change of administration took place in 1889. The time was too short to allow of a clean sweep, but the Republicans did all they could in two months, and turned out half of the Democrats. The law then went into effect, and since that time there have been no more removals for partisan purposes in that service. It has now recovered from the demoralization into which it was thrown by the two political revolutions, and has reached a higher standard of efficiency than ever before. What was done by the Republicans in this service was repeated, on a less scale, by the Democrats four years later in reference to the classification of the small free-delivery post-offices. This classification was ordered by President Harrison two months before his term of office expired; but in many of the offices it was impossible to hold examinations and prepare eligible registers until after the inauguration of President Cleveland, and in a number of cases the incoming postmasters, who were appointed prior to the time when the law went into effect, took advantage of the delay to make clean sweeps of their offices. In one of these offices, where the men were changed in a body, the new appointees hired the men whom they replaced, at $35 a month apiece, to teach them their duties; in itself a sufficient comment on the folly of the spoils system.

Mr. Bynum's bill provided for the reinstatement of the Democrats who were turned out by the Republicans just before the classification of the railway mail service. Of course such a bill was a mere partisan measure. There was no more reason for reinstating the Democrats thus turned out than for reinstating the Republicans who had been previously turned out that these same Democrats might get in, or for reinstating the Republicans in the free-delivery offices who had been turned out just before these offices were classified. If the bill had been enacted into law it would have been a most serious blow to the whole system, for it would have put a premium upon legislation of the kind; and after every change of parties we should have seen the passing of laws to reinstate masses of Republicans or Democrats, as the case might be. This would have meant a return to the old system under a new form of procedure. Nevertheless, Mr. Bynum's bill received the solid support of his party. Not a Democratic vote was cast against it in the House, none even of the Massachusetts Democrats being recorded against it. In the Senate it was pushed by Mr. Vilas. By a piece of rather sharp parliamentary procedure he nearly got it through by unanimous consent. That it failed was owing entirely to the vigilance of Senator Lodge. Senator Vilas asked for the passage of the bill, on the ground that it was one of small importance, upon which his committee were agreed. When it was read the words "classified civil service" caught Senator Lodge's ear, and he insisted upon an explanation. On finding out what the bill was he at once objected to its consideration. Under this objection it could not then be considered. If it could have been brought to a vote it would undoubtedly have passed; but it was late in the session, the calendars were crowded with bills, and it was impossible to get it up in its regular order. Another effort was made, and was again frustrated by Senator Lodge, and the bill then died a natural death.

In the final session of the 53d Congress a little incident occurred which deserves to be related in full, not for its own importance, but because it affords an excellent example of the numerous cases which test the real efficiency of the friends of the reform in Congress. It emphasizes the need of having, to watch over the interests of the law, a man who is willing to fight, who knows the time to fight, and who knows how to fight. The secretary of the Commission was, in the original law of 1883, allowed a salary of $1600 a year. As the Commission's force and work have grown, the salary in successive appropriation bills for the last ten years has been provided for at the rate of $2000 a year. Many of the clerks under the secretary now receive $1800, so that it would be of course an absurdity to reduce him in salary below his subordinates. Scores of other officials of the Government, including, for instance, the President's private secretary, the First Assistant Postmaster-General, the First Assistant Secretary of State, etc., have had their salaries increased in successive appropriation bills over the sum originally provided, in precisely the same way that the salary of the secretary of the Commission was increased. The 53d Congress was Democratic, as was the President, Mr. Cleveland, and the secretary of the Commission was himself a Democrat, who had been appointed to the position by Mr. Cleveland during his first term as President. The rules of the House provide that there shall be no increase of salary beyond that provided in existing law in any appropriation bill. When the appropriation for the Civil Service Commission came up in the House, Mr. Breckinridge, of Kentucky, made the point of order that to give $2000 to the secretary of the Commission was to increase his salary by $400 over that provided in the original law of 1883, and was therefore out of order. He also produced a list of twenty or thirty other officers, including the President's private secretary, the First Assistant Postmaster-General, etc., whose salaries were similarly increased. He withdrew his point of order as regards these persons, but adhered to it as regards the secretary of the Commission. The chairman of the Committee of the Whole, Mr. O'Neill, of Massachusetts, sustained the point of order; and not one person made any objection or made any fight, and the bill was put through the House with the secretary's salary reduced.

Now, the point of order was probably ill taken anyhow. The existing law was and had been for ten years that the salary was $2000. But, in any event, had there been a single Congressman alert to the situation and willing to make a fight he could have stopped the whole movement by at once making a similar point of order against the President's private secretary, against the First Assistant Postmaster-General, the Assistant Secretary of State, and all the others involved. The House would of course have refused to cut down the salaries of all of these officials, and a resolute man, willing to insist that they should all go or none, could have saved the salary of the secretary of the Civil Service Commission. There were plenty of men who would have done this if it had been pointed out to them; but no one did so, and Mr. Breckinridge's point of order was sustained, and the salary of the secretary reduced by $400. When it got over to the Senate, however, the Civil Service reformers had allies who needed but little coaching. In the first place, the subcommittee of the Committee on Appropriations, composed of Messrs. Teller, Cockrell, and Allison, to which the Civil Service Commission section of the Appropriation bill was referred, restored the salary to $2000; but Senator Gorman succeeded in carrying, by a bare majority, the Appropriations Committee against it, and it was reported to the full Senate still at $1600. The minute it got into the full Senate, however, Senator Lodge had a fair chance at it, and it was known that he would receive ample support. All that he had to do was to show clearly the absolute folly of the provision thus put in by Mr. Breckinridge, and kept in by Mr. Gorman, and to make it evident that he intended to fight it resolutely. The opposition collapsed at once; the salary was put back at $2000, and the bill became a law in that form.

Whether bad legislation shall be choked and good legislation forwarded depends largely upon the composition of the committees on Civil Service reform of the Senate and the Lower House. The make-up of these committees is consequently of great importance. They are charged with the duty of investigating complaints against the Commission, and it is of course very important that if ever the Commission becomes corrupt or inefficient its shortcomings should be unsparingly exposed in Congress. On the other hand, it is equally important that the falsity of untruthful charges advanced against it should be made public. In the 51st, 52d, and 53d Congresses a good deal of work was done by the Civil Service Committee of the House, and none at all by the corresponding committee of the Senate. The three chairmen of the House committee were Mr. Lehlbach, Mr. Andrew, and Mr. De Forest. All three were able and consci-entious men and stanch supporters of the law. The chairman in the 52d Congress, Mr. John F. Andrew, was throughout his whole term of service one of the ablest, most fearless, and most effective champions of the cause of the reform in the House. Among the other members of the committee, in different Congresses, who stood up valiantly for the reform, were Mr. Hopkins, of Illinois, Mr. Butterworth, of Ohio, Mr. Boatner, of Louisiana, and Mr. Dargan and Mr. Brawley, of South Carolina. Occasionally there have been on the committee members who were hostile to the reform, such as Mr. Alderson, of West Virginia; but these have not been men carrying weight in the House. The men of intelligence and ability who once familiarize themselves with the workings of the system, as they are bound to do if they are on the committee, are sure to become its supporters. In both the 51st and the 52d Congresses charges were made against the Commission, and investigations were held into its actions and into the workings of the law by the House committee. In each case, in its report the committee not only heartily applauded the conduct of the Commission, but no less heartily approved the workings of the law, and submitted bills to increase the power of the Commission and to render the law still more wide-reaching and drastic. These bills, unfortunately, were never acted on in the House.

The main fight in each session comes on the Appropriation bill. There is not the slightest danger that the law will be repealed, and there is not much danger that any President will suffer it to be so laxly administered as to deprive it of all value; though there is always need to keep a vigilant lookout for fear of such lax administration. The danger-point is in the appropriations. The first Civil Service Commission, established in the days of President Grant, was starved out by Congress refusing to appropriate for it. A hostile Congress could repeat the same course now; and, as a matter of fact, in every Congress resolute efforts are made by the champions of foul government and dishonest politics to cut off the Commission's supplies. The bolder men, who come from districts where little is known of the law, and where there is no adequate expression of intelligent and honest opinion on the subject, attack it openly. They are always joined by a number who make the attack covertly under some point of order, or because of a nominal desire for economy. These are quite as dangerous as the others, and deserve exposure. Every man interested in decent government should keep an eye on his Congressman and see how he votes on the question of appropriations for the Commission.

The opposition to the reform is generally well led by skilled parliamentarians, and they fight with the vindictiveness natural to men who see a chance of striking at the institution which has baffled their ferocious greed. As a rule, the rank and file are composed of politicians who could not rise in public life because of their attitude on any public question, and who derive most of their power from the skill with which they manipulate the patronage of their districts. These men have a gift at office-mongering, just as other men have a peculiar knack in picking pockets; and they are joined by all the honest dull men, who vote wrong out of pure ignorance, and by a very few sincere and intelligent, but wholly misguided people. Many of the spoils leaders are both efficient and fearless, and able to strike hard blows. In consequence, the leaders on the side of decency must themselves be men of ability and force, or the cause will suffer. For our good fortune, we have never yet lacked such leaders.

The Appropriation committees, both in the House and Senate, almost invariably show a friendly disposition toward the law. They are composed of men of prominence, who have a sense of the responsibilities of their positions and an earnest desire to do well for the country and to make an honorable record for their party in matters of legislation. They are usually above resorting to the arts of low cunning or of sheer demagogy to which the foes of the reform system are inevitably driven, and in consequence they can be relied upon to give, if not what is needed, at least enough to prevent any retrogression. It is in the open House and in Committee of the Whole that the fight is waged. The most dangerous fight occurs in Committee of the Whole, for there the members do not vote by aye and no, and in consequence a mean politician who wishes ill to the law, but is afraid of his constituents, votes against it in committee, but does not dare to do so when the ayes and noes are called in the House. One result of this has been that more than once the whole appropriation has been stricken out in Committee of the Whole, and then voted back again by substantial majorities by the same men sitting in open House.

In the debate on the appropriation the whole question of the workings of the law is usually discussed, and those members who are opposed to it attack not only the law itself, but the Commission which administers it. The occasion is, therefore, invariably seized as an opportunity for a pitched battle between the friends and foes of the system, the former trying to secure such an increase of appropriation as will permit the Commission to extend its work, and the latter striving to abolish the law outright by refusing all appropriations. In the 51st and 52d Congresses, Mr. Lodge, of Massachusetts, led the fight for the reform in the Lower House. He was supported by such party leaders as Messrs. Reed, of Maine, and McKinley, of Ohio, among the Republicans, and Messrs. Wilson, of West Virginia, and Sayers, of Texas, among the Democrats. Among the other champions of the law on the floor of the House were Messrs. Hopkins and Butterworth, Mr. Greenhalge, of Massachusetts, Mr. Henderson, of Iowa, Messrs. Payne, Tracey, and Coombs, of New York. I wish I had the space to chronicle the names of all, and to give a complete list of those who voted for the law. Among the chief opponents of it were Messrs. Spinola, of New York, Enloe, of Tennessee, Stock-dale, of Mississippi, Grosvenor, of Ohio, and Bowers, of California. The task of the defenders of the law was, in one way easy, for they had no arguments to meet, the speeches of their adversaries being invariably divisible into mere declamation and direct misstatement of facts. In the Senate, Senators Hoar, of Massachusetts, Allison, of Iowa, Hawley, of Connecticut, Wolcott, of Colorado, Perkins, of California, Cockerel, of Missouri, and Butler, of South Carolina, always supported the Commission against unjust attack. Senator Gorman was naturally the chief leader of the assaults upon the Commission. Senators Harris, Plumb, Stewart, and Ingalls were among his allies.

In each session the net result of the fight was an increase in the appropriation for the Commission. The most important increase was that obtained in the first session of the 53d Congress. On this occasion Mr. Lodge was no longer in the House, having been elected to the Senate. The work of the Commission had grown so that it was impossible to perform it without a great increase of force; and it would have been impossible to have put into effect the extensions of the classified service had this increase not been allowed. In the House the Committee on Appropriations, of which Mr. Sayers was chairman, allowed the increase, but it was stricken out in the House itself after an acrimonious debate, in which the cause of the law was sustained by Messrs. Henderson and Hopkins, Mr. McCall, of Massachusetts, Mr. Coombs, Mr. Crain, of Texas, Mr. Storer, of Ohio, and many others, while the spoils-mongers were led by Messrs. Stock-dale and Williams, of Mississippi, Pendelton, of West Virginia, Fithian, of Illinois, and others less important.

When the bill went over to the Senate, however, Mr. Lodge, well supported by

Messrs. Allison, Cockrell, Wolcott, and Teller, had the provision for the increase of appropriation for the Commission restored and increased, thereby adding by one half to the efficiency of the Commission's work. Had it not been for this the Commission would have been quite unable to have undertaken the extensions recently ordered by President Cleveland.

It is noteworthy that the men who have done most effective work for the law in Washington in the departments, and more especially in the House and Senate, are men of spotless character, who show by their whole course in public life that they are not only able and resolute, but also devoted to a high ideal. Much of what they have done has received little comment in public, because much of the work in committee, and some of the work in the House, such as making or combating points of order, and pointing out the danger or merit of certain bills, is not of a kind readily understood or appreciated by an outsider; yet no men have deserved better of the country, for there is in American public life no one other cause so fruitful of harm to the body-politic as the spoils system, and the legislators and administrative officers who have done the best work toward its destruction merit a peculiar meed of praise from all well-wishers of the Republic.

I have spoken above of the good that would come from a thorough and intelligent knowledge as to who were the friends and who were the foes of the law in Washington. Departmental officers, the heads of bureaus, and, above all, the Commissioners themselves, should be carefully watched by all friends of the reform. They should be supported when they do well, and condemned when they do ill; and attention should be called not only to what they do, but to what they fail to do. To an even greater extent, of course, this applies to the President. As regards the Senators and Congressmen also there is urgent need of careful supervision by the friends of the law. We need criticism by those who are unable to do their part in action; but the criticism, to be useful, must be both honest and intelligent, and the critics must remember that the system has its stanch friends and bitter foes among both party men and men of no party— among Republicans, Democrats, and Independents. Each Congressman should be made to feel that it is his duty to support the law, and that he will be held to account if he fails to support it. Especially is it necessary to concentrate effort in working for each step of reform. In legislative matters, for instance, there is need of increase of appropriations for the Commission, and there is a chance of putting through the bill to reform the Consular service. This has received substantial backing in the Senate, and has the support of the majority of the Foreign Affairs Committee. Instead of wasting efforts by a diffuse support of eight or ten bills, it would be well to bend every energy to securing the passage of the Consular bill; and to do this it is necessary to arouse not only the Civil Service Reform Associations, but the Boards of Trade throughout the country, and to make the Congressmen and Senators feel individually the pressure from those of their constituents who are resolved no longer to tolerate the peculiarly gross manifestation of the spoils system which now obtains in the consular service, with its attendant discredit to the national honor abroad.

People sometimes grow a little down-hearted about the reform. When they feel in this mood it would be well for them to reflect on what has actually been gained in the past six years. By the inclusion of the railway mail service, the smaller free-delivery offices, the Indian School service, the Internal Revenue service, and other less important branches, the extent of the public service which is under the protection of the law has been more than doubled, and there are now nearly fifty thousand employees of the Federal Government who have been withdrawn from the degrading influences that rule under the spoils system. This of itself is a great success and a great advance, though, of course, it ought only to spur us on to renewed effort. In the fall of 1894 the people of the State of New York, by a popular vote, put into their constitution a provision providing for a merit system in the affairs of the State and its municipalities; and the following spring the great city of Chicago voted, by an overwhelming majority, in favor of applying in its municipal affairs the advanced and radical Civil Service Reform Law, which had already passed the Illinois Legislature. Undoubtedly, after every success there comes a moment of reaction. The friends of the reform grow temporarily lukewarm, or, because it fails to secure everything they hoped, they neglect to lay proper stress upon all that it does secure. Yet, in spite of all rebuffs, in spite of all disappointments and opposition, the growth of the principle of Civil Service reform has been continually more rapid, and every year has taken us measurably nearer that ideal of pure and decent government which is dear to the heart of every honest American citizen.

VIII
ADMINISTERING THE NEW YORK POLICE FORCE[13]

IN New York, in the fall of 1894, Tammany Hall was overthrown by a coalition composed partly of the regular republicans, partly of anti-Tammany democrats, and partly of independents. Under the latter head must be included a great many men who in national politics habitually act with one or the other of the two great parties, but who feel that in municipal politics good citizens should act independently. The tidal wave, which was running high against the democratic party, was undoubtedly very influential in bringing about the anti-Tammany victory; but the chief factor in producing the result was the wide-spread anger and disgust felt by decent citizens at the corruption which, under the sway of Tammany, had honey-combed every department of the city government, but especially the police force. A few well-meaning

[13] *Atlantic Monthly*, September, 1897.

people have at times tried to show that this corruption was not really so very great. In reality it would be difficult to overestimate the utter rottenness of many branches of the city administration. There were a few honorable and high-minded Tammany officials, and there were a few bureaus which were administered with more or less efficiency, although dishonestly. But the corruption had become so wide-spread as seriously to impair the work of administration, and to bring us back within measurable distance of the days of Tweed.

The chief centre of corruption was the Police Department. No man not intimately acquainted with both the lower and humbler sides of New York life—for there is a wide distinction between the two—can realize how far this corruption extended. Except in rare instances, where prominent politicians made demands which could not be refused, both promotions and appointments towards the close of Tammany rule were made almost solely for money, and the prices were discussed with cynical frankness. There was a well-recognized tariff of charges, ranging from two or three hundred dollars for appointment as a patrolman, to twelve or fifteen thousand dollars for promotion to the position of captain. The money was reimbursed to those who paid it by an elaborate system of blackmail. This was chiefly carried on at the expense of gamblers, liquor sellers, and keepers of disorderly houses; but every form of vice and crime contributed more or less, and a great many respectable people who were ignorant or timid were black-mailed under pretence of forbidding or allowing them to violate obscure ordinances and the like. From top to bottom the New York police force was utterly demoralized by the gangrene of such a system, where venality and blackmail went hand in hand with the basest forms of low ward politics, and where the policeman, the ward politician, the liquor seller, and the criminal alternately preyed on one another and helped one another to prey on the general public.

In May,1895, I was made president of the newly appointed police board, whose duty it was to cut out the chief source of civic corruption in New York by cleansing the police department. The police board consisted of four members. All four of the new men were appointed by Mayor Strong, the reform Mayor, who had taken office in January.

With me, was associated, as treasurer of the Board, Mr. Avery D. Andrews. He was a democrat and I a republican, and there were questions of national politics on which we disagreed widely; but such questions could not enter into the administration of the New York police, if that administration was to be both honest and efficient; and as a matter of fact, during my two years' service, Mr. Andrews and I worked in absolute harmony on every important question of policy which arose. The prevention of blackmail and corruption, the repression of crime and violence, safeguarding of life and property, securing honest elections, and rewarding efficient and punishing inefficient police service, are not, and cannot properly be made, questions of party difference. In other words, such a body as the police force of New York can be wisely and properly administered only upon a nonpartisan basis, and both Mr. Andrews and myself were quite incapable of managing it on any other. There were many men who helped us in our work; and among them all, the man who helped us most, by advice and counsel, by stalwart, loyal friendship, and by ardent championship of all that was good against all that was evil, was Jacob A. Riis, the author of *How the Other Half Lives* .

Certain of the difficulties we had to face were merely those which confronted the entire reform administration in its management of the municipality. Many worthy people expected that this reform administration would work an absolute revolution, not merely in the government, but in the minds of the citizens as a whole; and felt vaguely that they had been cheated because there was not an immediate cleansing of every bad influence in civic or social life. Moreover, the different bodies forming the victorious coalition felt the pressure of conflicting interests and hopes. The mass of effective strength was given by the republican organization, and not only all the enrolled party workers, but a great number of well-meaning republicans who had no personal interest at stake, expected the administration to be used to further the fortunes of their own party. Another great body of the administration's supporters took a diametrically opposite view, and believed that the administration should be administered without the least reference whatever to party. In theory they were quite right, and I cordially sympathized with them; but as a matter of fact the victory could not have been won by the votes of this class of people alone, and it was out of the question to put these theories into complete effect. Like all other men who actually try to do things instead of confining themselves to saying how they should be done, the members of the new city government were obliged to face the facts and to do the best they could in the effort to get some kind of good result out of the conflicting forces. They had to disregard party so far as was possible; and yet they could not afford to disregard all party connections so utterly as to bring the whole administration to grief.

In addition to these two large groups of supporters of the administration, there were other groups, also possessing influence who expected to receive recognition distinctly as democrats, but as anti-Tammany democrats; and such members of any victorious coalition are always sure to overestimate their own services, and to feel ill-treated.

It is of course an easy thing to show on paper that the municipal administration should have been administered without the slightest reference to national party lines, and if the bulk of the people saw things with entire clearness the truth would seem so obvious as to need no demonstration. But as a matter of fact the bulk of the people who voted the new administration into power neither saw this nor realized it, and in politics, as in life generally, conditions must be faced as they are, and not as they ought to be. The regular democratic organization, not only in the city but in the State, was completely under the dominion of Tammany Hall and its allies, and they fought us at every step with wholly unscrupulous hatred. In the State and the city alike the democratic campaign was waged against the reform administration in New York. The Tammany officials who were still left in power in the city, headed by the comptroller, Mr. Fitch, did everything in their power to prevent the efficient administration of the government. The democratic members of the Legislature acted as their faithful allies in all such efforts. Whatever was accomplished by the reform administration— and a very great deal was accomplished—was due to the action of the republican majority in the constitutional convention, and especially to the republican Governor, Mr. Morton, and the republican majority in the Legislature, who enacted laws giving to the newly chosen Mayor, Mr. Strong, the great powers necessary for properly administering his office. Without these laws the Mayor would have been very nearly powerless. He certainly could not have done a tenth part of what actually was done.

Now, of course, the republican politicians who gave Mayor Strong all these powers, in the teeth of violent democratic opposition to every law for the betterment of civic conditions in New York, ought not, under ideal conditions, to have expected the slightest reward. They should have been contented with showing the public that their only purpose was to serve the public, and that the republican party wished no better reward than the consciousness of having done its duty by the State and the city. But as a whole they had not reached such a standard. There were some who had reached it; there were others who, though perfectly honest, and wishing to see good government prosper, yet felt that somehow it ought to be combined with party advantage of a tangible sort; and finally, there were yet others who were not honest at all and cared nothing for the victory unless it resulted in some way to their own personal advantage. In short, the problem presented was of the kind which usually is presented when dealing with men as a mass. The Mayor and his administration had to keep in touch with the republican party or they could have accomplished nothing; and on the other hand there was much that the republican machine asked which they could not do, because a surrender on certain vital points meant the abandonment of the effort to obtain good administration.

The undesirability of breaking with the republican organization was shown by what happened in the administration of the police department. This being the great centre of power was the especial object of the republican machine leaders. Toward the close of Tammany rule, of the four Police Commissioners, two had been machine republicans, whose actions were in no wise to be distinguished from those of their Tammany colleagues; and immediately after the new board was appointed to office the machine got through the Legislature the so-called bi-partisan or Lexow law, under which the department is at present administered; and a more foolish or vicious law was never enacted by any legislative body. It modelled the government of the police force somewhat on the lines of the Polish parliament, and it was avowedly designed to make it difficult to get effective action. It provided for a four-headed board, so that it was difficult to get a majority anyhow; but, lest we should get such a majority, it gave each member power to veto the actions of his colleagues in certain very important matters; and, lest we should do too much when we were unanimous, it provided that the chief, our nominal subordinate, should have entirely independent action in the most important matters, and should be practically irremovable, except for proved corruption; so that he was responsible to nobody. The Mayor was similarly hindered from removing any Police Commissioner, so that when one of our colleagues began obstructing the work of the board, and thwarting its effort to reform the force, the Mayor in vain strove to turn him out. In short, there was a complete divorce of power and responsibility, and it was exceedingly difficult either to do anything, or to place anywhere, the responsibility for not doing it.

If, by any reasonable concessions, if, indeed, by the performance of any act not incompatible with our oaths of office, we could have stood on good terms with the machine, we would certainly have made the effort, even at the cost of sacrificing many of our ideals; and in almost any other department we could probably have avoided a break, but in the police force such a compromise was not possible. What was demanded of us usually took some such form as the refusal to enforce certain laws, or the protection of certain law-breakers, or the promotion of the least fit men to positions of high power and grave responsibility; and on such points it was not possible to yield. We were obliged to treat all questions that arose purely on their merits, without reference to the desires of the politicians. We went into this course with our eyes open, for we knew the trouble it would cause us personally, and, what was far more important, the way in which our efforts for reform would consequently be hampered. However, there was no alternative, and we had to abide by the result. We had counted the cost before we adopted our course, and we followed it resolutely to the end. We could not accomplish all that we should have liked to accomplish for we were shackled by preposterous legislation, and by the opposition and intrigues of the basest machine politicians, which cost us the support, sometimes of one, and sometimes of both, of our colleagues. Nevertheless, the net result of our two years of work was that we did more to increase the efficiency and honesty of the police department than had ever previously been done in its history.

But a decent people will have to show by emphatic action that they are in the majority if they wish this result to be permanent; for under such a law as the "bipartisan" law it is almost impossible to keep the department honest and efficient for any length of time; and the machine politicians, by their opposition outside the board, and by the aid of any tool or ally whom they can get on the board, can always hamper and cripple the honest members of the board, no matter how resolute and able the latter may be, if they do not have an aroused and determined public opinion behind them.

Besides suffering, in aggravated form, from the difficulties which beset the course of the entire administration, the police board had to encounter— and honest and efficient police boards must always encounter—certain special and peculiar difficulties. It is not a pleasant thing to deal with criminals and purveyors of vice. It is very rough work, and it cannot always be done in a nice manner. The man with the night stick, the man in the blue coat with the helmet, can keep order and repress open violence on the streets; but most kinds of crime and vice are ordinarily carried on furtively and by stealth, perhaps at night, perhaps behind closed doors. It is possible to reach them only by the employment of the man in plain clothes, the detective. Now the function of the detective is primarily that of the spy, and it is always easy to arouse feeling against a spy. It is absolutely necessary to employ him. Ninety per cent, of the most dangerous criminals and purveyors of vice cannot be reached in any other way. But the average citizen who does not think deeply fails to realize the necessity for any such employment. In a vague way he desires vice and crime put down; but, also in a vague way, he objects to the only possible means by which they can be put down. It is easy to mislead him into denouncing what is necessarily done in order to carry out the very policy for which he is clamoring. The Tammany officials of New York, headed by the Comptroller, made a systematic effort to excite public hostility against the police for their warfare on vice. The law-breaking liquor seller, the keeper of disorderly houses, and the gambler, had been influential allies of Tammany, and head contributors to its campaign chest. Naturally Tammany fought for them; and the effective way in which to carry on such a fight was to portray with gross exaggeration and misstatement the methods necessarily employed by every police force which honestly endeavors to do its work. The methods are unpleasant, just as the methods employed in any surgical operation are unpleasant; and the Tammany champions were able to arouse more or less feeling against the police board for precisely the same reason that a century ago it was easy to arouse what were called "doctors' mobs" against surgeons who cut up dead bodies. In neither case is the operation attractive, and it is one which readily lends itself to denunciation; but in both cases it is necessary if there is a real intention to get at the disease. Tammany of course found its best allies in the sensational newspapers. Of all the forces that tend for evil in a great city like New York, probably none are so potent as the sensational papers. Until one has had experience with them it is difficult to realize the reckless indifference to truth or decency displayed by papers such as the two that have the largest circulation in New York City. Scandal forms the breath of the nostrils of such papers, and they are quite as ready to create as to describe it. To sustain law and order is humdrum, and does not readily lend itself to flaunting woodcuts; but if the editor will stoop, and make his subordinates stoop, to raking the gutters of human depravity, to upholding the wrong-doer, and furiously assailing what is upright and honest, he can make money, just as other types of pander make it. The man who is to do honorable work in any form of civic politics must make up his mind (and if he is a man of properly robust character he will make it up without difficulty) to treat the assaults of papers like these with absolute indifference, and to go his way unheeded. Indeed he will have to make up his mind to be criticised, sometimes justly, and more often unjustly, even by decent people; and he must not be so thin-skinned as to mind such criticism overmuch.

In administering the police force we found, as might be expected, that there was no need of genius, nor indeed of any very unusual qualities. What was needed was exercise of the plain, ordinary virtues, of a rather commonplace type, which all good citizens should be expected to possess. Common sense, common honesty, courage, energy, resolution, readiness to learn, and a desire to be as pleasant with everybody as was compatible with a strict performance of duty—these were the qualities most called for. We soon found that, in spite of the wide-spread corruption which had obtained in the New York police department, the bulk of the men were heartily desirous of being honest. There were some who were incurably dishonest, just as there were some who had remained decent in spite of terrific temptation and pressure; but the great mass came in between. Although not possessing the stamina to war against corruption when the odds seemed well-nigh hopeless, they were nevertheless heartily glad to be decent and to welcome the change to a system under which they were rewarded for doing well, and punished for doing ill.

Our methods for restoring order and discipline were simple, and indeed so were our methods for securing efficiency. We made frequent personal inspections, especially at night, turning up anywhere, at any time. We thus speedily got an idea of whom among our upper subordinates we could trust and whom we could not. We then proceeded to punish those guilty of shortcomings, and to reward those who did well, refusing to pay any heed whatever in either case to anything except the man' s own character and record. A very few of these promotions and dismissals sufficed to show our subordinates that at last they were dealing with superiors who meant what they said, and that the days of political "pull" were over while we had the power. The effect was immediate. The decent men took heart, and those who were not decent feared longer to offend. The morale of the entire force improved steadily. A similar course was followed in reference to the relations between the police and citizens generally. There had formerly been much complaint of the brutal treatment by police of innocent citizens. This was stopped peremptorily by the simple expedient of dismissing from the force the first two or three men who were found guilty of brutality. On the other hand we made the force understand that in the event of any emergency requiring them to use their weapons against either a mob or an individual criminal, the police board backed them up without reservation. Our sympathy was for the friends, and not the foes, of order. If a mob threatened violence we were glad to have the mob hurt. If a criminal showed fight we expected the officer to use any weapon that was necessary to overcome him on the instant; and even, if it became necessary, to take life. All that the board required was to be convinced that the necessity really existed. We did not possess a particle of that maudlin sympathy for the criminal, disorderly, and lawless classes which is such a particularly unhealthy sign of social development; and we were bound that the improvement in the fighting efficiency of the police should go hand in hand with the improvement in their moral tone.

To break up the system of blackmail and corruption was less easy. It was not at all difficult to protect decent people in their rights, and this was accomplished at once. But the criminal who is blackmailed has a direct interest in paying the blackmailer, and it is not easy to get information about it. Nevertheless, we put a complete stop to most of the blackmail by the simple process of rigorously enforcing the laws, not only against crime, but against vice.

It was the enforcement of the liquor law which caused most excitement. In New York we suffer from the altogether too common tendency to make any law which a certain section of the community wants, and then to allow that law to be more or less of a dead-letter if any other section of the community objects to it. The multiplication of laws by the Legislature, and their partial enforcement by the executive authorities, go hand in hand, and offer one of the many serious problems with which we are confronted in striving to better civic conditions. New York State felt that liquor should not be sold on Sunday. The larger part of New York City wished to drink liquor on Sunday. Any man who studies the social condition of the poor knows that liquor works more ruin than any other one cause. He knows also, however, that it is simply impracticable to extirpate the habit entirely, and that to attempt too much often merely results in accomplishing too little; and he knows, moreover, that for a man alone to drink whiskey in a bar-room is one thing, and for men with their families to drink light wines or beer in respectable restaurants is quite a different thing. The average citizen, who doesn't think at all, and the average politician of the baser sort, who only thinks about his own personal advantage, find it easiest to disregard these facts, and to pass a liquor law which will please the temperance people, and then trust to the police department to enforce it with such laxity as to please the intemperate.

The results of this pleasing system were evident in New York when our board came into power. The Sunday liquor law was by no means a dead letter in New York City. On the contrary no less than eight thousand arrests for its violation had been made under the Tammany regime the year before we came in. It was very much alive; but it was only executed against those who either had no political pull, or who refused to pay money. The liquor business does not stand on the same footing with other occupations. It always tends to produce criminality in the population at large, and lawbreaking among the saloonkeepers themselves. It is absolutely necessary to supervise it rigidly, and impose restrictions upon the traffic. In large cities the traffic cannot be stopped; but the evils can at least be minimized.

In New York the saloonkeepers have always stood high among professional politicians. Nearly two thirds of the political leaders of Tammany Hall have, at one time or another, been in the liquor business. The saloon is the natural club and meeting place for the ward heelers and leaders, and the bar-room politician is one of the most common and best recognized factors, in local political government. The saloonkeepers are always hand in glove with the professional politicians, and occupy toward them a position such as is not held by any Other class of men. The influence they wield in local politics has always been very great, and until our board took office no man ever dared seriously to threaten them for their flagrant violations of the law. The powerful and influential saloonkeeper was glad to see his neighbors closed, for it gave him business. On the other hand, a corrupt police captain, or the corrupt politician who controlled him, could always extort money from a saloonkeeper by threatening to close him and let his neighbor remain open. Gradually the greed of corrupt police officials and of corrupt politicians, grew by what it fed on, until they began to blackmail all but the very most influential liquor sellers; and as liquor sellers were very numerous, and the profits of the liquor business great, the amount collected was enormous.

The reputable saloonkeepers themselves found this condition of blackmail and political favoritism almost intolerable. The law which we found on the statute books had been put on by a Tammany Legislature three years before we took office. A couple of months after we took office, Mr. J. P. Smith, the editor of the liquor-dealers' organ, *The Wine and Spirit Gazette*, gave out the following interview, which is of such an extraordinary character that I insert it almost in full:

"Governor Flower, as well as the Legislature of1892, was elected upon distinct pledges that relief would be given by the Democratic party to the liquor dealers, especially of the cities of the State. In accordance with this promise a Sunday-opening clause was inserted in the excise bill of1892. Governor Flower then said that he could not approve the Sunday-opening clause; whereupon the Liquor Dealers' Association, which had charge of the bill, struck the Sunday-opening clause out. After Governor Hill had been elected for the second term I had several interviews with him on that very subject He told me, "You know I am the friend of the liquor dealers and will go to almost any length to help them and give them relief; but do not ask me to recommend to the Legislature the passage of the law opening the saloons on Sunday. I cannot do it, for it will ruin the Democratic party in the State." He gave the same interview to various members of the State Liquor Dealers" Association, who waited upon him for the purpose of getting relief from the blackmail of the police, stating that the lack of having the Sunday question properly regulated was at the bottom of the trouble. Blackmail had been brought to such a state of perfection, and had become so oppressive to the liquor dealers themselves, that they communicated first with Governor Hill and then with Mr. Croker. The *Wine and Spirit Gazette* had taken up the subject because of gross discrimination made by the police in the enforcement of the Sunday-closing law. The paper again and again called upon the police commissioners to either uniformly enforce the law or uniformly disregard it. A committee of the Central Association of Liquor Dealers of this city then took up the matter and called upon Police Commissioner Martin. *An agreementwas then made between the leaders of Tammany Hall and the liquor dealers, according to which the monthly blackmail paid to the police should be discontinued in return for political support* .[15] 'In other words, the retail dealers should bind themselves to solidly support the Tammany ticket in consideration of the discontinuance of the monthly blackmail by the police. This agreement was carried out. Now what was the consequence? If the liquor dealer, after the monthly blackmail ceased, showed any signs of independence, the Tammany Hall district leader would give the tip to the police captain, and that man would be pulled and arrested on the following Sunday."

Continuing, Mr. Smith inveighed against the law, but said:

"The (present) police commissioners are honestly endeavoring to have the law impartially carried out. They are no respectors of persons. And our information from all classes of liquor-dealers is that the rich and the poor, the influential and the uninfluential, are required equally to obey the law."

There is really some difficulty in commenting upon the statements of this interview, statements which were never denied.

The law was not in the least a dead-letter; it was enforced, but it was corruptly and partially enforced. It was a prominent factor in the Tammany scheme of government. It afforded a most effective means for blackmailing a large portion of the liquor sellers and for the wholesale corruption of the police department. The high Tammany officials and police captains and patrolmen blackmailed and bullied the small liquor sellers without a pull, and turned them into abject slaves of Tammany Hall. On the other hand, the wealthy and politically influential liquor sellers controlled the police, and made or marred captains, sergeants, and patrolmen at their pleasure. In some of the precincts most of the saloons were closed; in others almost all were open. The rich and powerful liquor seller violated the law at will, unless he had fallen under the ban of the police or the ward boss, when he was not allowed to violate it at all.

Under these circumstances the new police board had one of two courses to follow. We could either instruct the police to allow all the saloonkeepers to become law-breakers, or else we could instruct them to allow none to be law-breakers. We followed the latter course, because we had some regard for our oaths of office. For two or three months we had a regular fight, and on Sundays had to employ half the force to enforce the liquor law; for the Tammany legislators had drawn the law so as to make it easy of enforcement for purposes of blackmail, but not easy of enforcement generally, certain provisions being deliberately inserted with the intention to make it difficult of universal execution. However, when once the liquor sellers and their allies understood that we had not the slightest intention of being bullied, threatened or @@@ out of following the course which we down, resistance practically ceased. During the year after we took office the number of arrests for violation of the Sunday liquor law sank to about one half of what they had been during the last year of the Tammany rule; and yet the saloons were practically closed, whereas under Tammany most of them had been open. We adopted no new methods, save in so far as honesty could be called a new method. We did not enforce the law with unusual severity; we merely enforced it against the man with a pull, just as much as against the man without a pull. We refused to discriminate in favor of influential law-breakers. The professional politicians of low type, the liquor sellers, the editors of some German newspapers, and the sensational press generally, attacked us with a ferocity which really verged on insanity.

We went our way without regarding this opposition, and gave a very wholesome lesson to the effect that a law should not be put on the statute books if it was not meant to be enforced, and that even an excise law could be honestly enforced in New York if the public officials so desired. The rich brewers and liquor sellers, who had made money hand over fist by violating the excise law with the corrupt connivance of the police, raved with anger, and every corrupt politician and newspaper in the city gave them clamorous assistance; but the poor man, and notably the poor man's wife and children, benefited very greatly by what we did. The hospital surgeons found that their Monday labors were lessened by nearly one half, owing to the startling diminution in cases of injury due to drunken brawls; the work of the magistrates who sat in the city courts on Monday for the trial of the offenders of the preceding twenty-four hours was correspondingly decreased; while many a tenement-house family spent Sunday in the country because for the first time the head of the family could not use up his money in getting drunk. The one all-important element in good citizenship in our country is obedience to law, and nothing is more needed than the resolute enforcement of law. This we gave.

There was no species of mendacity to which our opponents did not resort in the effort to break us down in our purpose. For weeks they eagerly repeated the tale that the saloons were as wide open as ever; but they finally abandoned this when the counsel for the Liquor Dealers' Association admitted in open court, at the time when we secured the conviction of thirty of his clients and thereby brought the fight to an end, that over nine tenths of the liquor dealers had been rendered bankrupt because we had stopped that illegal trade which gave them the best portion of their revenue. They then took the line that by devoting our attention to enforcing the liquor law we permitted crime to increase. This, of course, offered a very congenial field for newspapers like the *World*, which exploited it to the utmost; all the more readily since the mere reiteration of the falsehood tended to encourage criminals, and so to make it not a falsehood. For a time the cry was not without influence, even with decent people, especially if they belonged to the class of the timid rich; but it simply wasn't true, and so this bubble went down stream with the others. For six or eight months the cry grew, first louder, then lower; and then it died away. A commentary upon its accuracy was furnished toward the end of our administration; for in February1897, the Judge who addressed the grand jury of the month was able to congratulate them upon the fact that there was at that time less crime in New York relatively to the population than ever before; and this held true for our two years' service.

In re-organizing the force the Board had to make, and did make, more promotions, more appointments, and more dismissals than had ever before been made in the same length of time. We were so hampered by the law that we were not able to dismiss many of the men whom we should have dismissed, but we did turn out 200 men—more than four times as many as had ever been turned out in the same length of time before; all of them being dismissed after formal trial, and after having been given full opportunity to be heard in their own defence. We appointed about 1700 men all told—again more than four times as many as ever before; for we were allowed a large increase of the police force by law. We made130 promotions; more than had been made in the six preceding years.

All this work was done in strictest accord with what we have grown to speak of as the principles of civil service reform. In making dismissals we paid heed merely to the man's efficiency and past record, refusing to consider outside pressure; under the old regime no policeman with sufficient influence behind him was ever dismissed, no matter what his offence. In making promotions we took into account not only the man's general record, his faithfulness, industry and vigilance, but also his personal prowess as shown in any special feat of daring, whether in the arresting of criminals or in the saving of life—for the police service is military in character, and we wished to encourage the military virtues. In making appointments we found that it was practicable to employ a system of rigid competitive examinations, which, as finally perfected, combined a very severe physical examination with a mental examination such as could be passed by any man who had attended one of our public schools. Of course there was also a rigid investigation of character. Theorists have often sneered at civil service reform as "impracticable;" and I am very far from asserting that written competitive examinations are always applicable, or that they may not sometimes be merely stop-gaps, used only because they are better than the methods of appointing through political endorsement; but most certainly the system worked admirably in the Police Department. We got the best lot of recruits for patrolmen that had ever been obtained in the history of the force, and we did just as well in our examinations for matrons and police surgeons. The uplifting of the force was very noticeable, both physically and mentally. The best men we got were those who had served for three years or so in the Army or Navy. Next to these came the railroad men. One noticeable feature of the work was that we greatly raised the proportion of native-born, until, of the last hundred appointed, ninety-four per cent, were Americans by birth. Not once in a hundred times did we know the politics of the appointee, and we paid as little heed to this as to their religion.

Another of our important tasks was seeing that the elections were carried on honestly. Under the old Tammany rule the cheating was gross and flagrant, and the police were often deliberately used to facilitate fraudulent practices at the polls. This came about in part from the very low character of the men put in as election officers. By conducting a written examination of the latter, and supplementing this by a careful inquiry into their character, in which we invited any decent outsiders to assist, we very distinctly raised their calibre. To show how necessary our examinations were, I may mention that before each election held under us we were obliged to reject, for moral or mental shortcomings, over a thousand of the men whom the regular party organizations, exercising their legal rights, proposed as election officers. We then merely had to make the police thoroughly understand that their sole duty was to guarantee an honest election, and that they would be punished with the utmost rigor if they interfered with honest citizens on the one hand, or failed to prevent fraud and violence on the other. The result was that the elections of 1895 and 1896 were by far the most honest and orderly ever held in New York City.

There were a number of other ways in which we sought to reform the police force, less important, and nevertheless very important. We paid particular heed to putting a premium on specially meritorious conduct, by awarding certificates of honorable mention, and medals, where we were unable to promote. We introduced a system of pistol practice by which, for the first time, the policemen were brought to a reasonable standard of efficiency in handling their revolvers. The Bertillion system for the identification of criminals was introduced. A bicycle squad was organized with remarkable results, this squad speedily becoming a kind of *corps d'elite*, whose individual members distinguished themselves not only by their devotion to duty, but by repeated exhibitions of remarkable daring and skill. One important bit of reform was abolishing the tramp lodging-houses, which had originally been started in the police stations, in a spirit of unwise philanthropy. These tramp lodging-houses, not being properly supervised, were mere nurseries for pauperism and crime, tramps and loafers of every shade thronging to the city every winter to enjoy their benefits. We abolished them, a municipal lodging-house being substituted. Here all homeless wanderers were received, forced to bathe, given night-clothes before going to bed, and made to work next morning and in addition the were so closely supervised that habitual tramps and vagrants were speedily detected and apprehended.

There was a striking increase in the honesty of the force, and there was a like increase in its efficiency. When we took office it is not too much to say that the great majority of the citizens of New York were firmly convinced that no police force could be both honest and efficient. They felt it to be part of the necessary order of things that a policeman should be corrupt, and they were convinced that the most efficient way of warring against certain forms of crime—notably crimes against person and property—was by enlisting the service of other criminals, and of purveyors of vice generally, giving them immunity in return for their aid. Before we took power the ordinary purveyor of vice was allowed to ply his or her trade un-molested, partly in consideration of paying blackmail to the police, partly in consideration of giving information about any criminal who belonged to the unprotected classes. We at once broke up this whole business of blackmail and protection, and made war upon all criminals alike, instead of getting the assistance of half in warring on the other half. Nevertheless, so great was the improvement in the spirit of the force, that, although deprived of their former vicious allies, they actually did better work than ever before against those criminals who threatened life and property. Relatively to the population, fewer crimes of violence occurred during our administration of the Board than in any previous two years of the city's history in recent times; and the total number of arrests of criminals increased, while the number of cases in which no arrest followed the commission of crime decreased. The detective bureau nearly doubled the number of arrests made compared with the year before we took office; obtaining, moreover, 365 convictions of felons and 215 convictions for misdemeanors, as against 269 and 105 respectively for the previous year. At the same time every attempt at riot or disorder was summarily checked, and all gangs of violent criminals brought into immediate subjection; while on the other hand the immense mass meetings and political parades were handled with such care that not a single case of clubbing of any innocent citizen was reported.

The result of our labors was of value to the city, for we gave the citizens better protection than they had ever before received, and at the same time cut out the corruption which was eating away civic morality. We showed conclusively that it was possible to combine both honesty and efficiency in handling the police. We were attacked with the most bitter animosity by every sensational newspaper and every politician of the baser sort, not because of our shortcomings, but because of what we did that was good. We enforced the laws as they were on the statute books, we broke up blackmail, we kept down the spirit of disorder, and repressed rascality, and we administered the force with an eye single to the welfare of the city. In doing this we encountered, as we had expected, the venemous opposition of all men whose interest it was that corruption should continue, or who were of such dull morality that they were not willing to see honesty triumph at the cost of strife.

IX
THE VICE-PRESIDENCY AND THE CAMPAIGN OF 1896[16]

THE Vice-President is an officer unique in his character and functions, or to speak more properly, in his want of functions while he remains Vice-President, and in his possibility of at any moment ceasing to be a functionless official and becoming the head of the whole nation. There is no corresponding position in any constitutional government. Perhaps the nearest analogue is the heir apparent in a monarchy. Neither the French President nor the British Prime Minister has a substitute, ready at any moment to take his place, but exercising scarcely any authority until his place is taken. The history of such an office is interesting, and the personality of the incumbent for the time being may at any moment become of vast importance.

The founders of our government—the men who

[16] *Review of Reviews*, September, 1896.

did far more than draw up the Declaration of Independence, for they put forth the National Constitution—in many respects builded very wisely of set purpose. In some cases they built wiser than they knew. In yet other instances they failed entirely to achieve objects for which they had endeavored to provide by a most elaborate and ingenious governmental arrangement. They distrusted what would now be called pure Democracy, and they dreaded what we would now call party government.

Their distrust of Democracy induced them to construct the electoral college for the choice of a President, the original idea being that the people should elect their best and wisest men who in turn should, untrammeled by outside pressure, elect a President. As a matter of fact the functions of the electorate have now by time and custom become of little more importance than those of so many letter-carriers. They deliver the electoral votes of their states just as a letter-carrier delivers his mail. But in the presidential contest this year it may be we shall see a partial return to the ideals of the men of 1789; for some of the electors on the Bryan-Sewall-Watson ticket may exercise a choice between the vice-presidential candidates.

The distrust felt by the founders of the constitution for party government took shape in the scheme to provide that the majority party should have the foremost place, and the minority party the second place, in the national executive. The man who received the greatest number of electoral votes was made President, and the man who received the second greatest number was made Vice-President, on a theory somewhat akin to that by which certain reformers hope to revolutionize our system of voting at the present day. In the early days under the present constitution this system resulted in the choice of Adams for President and of his anti-type Jefferson as Vice-President, the combination being about as incongruous as if we should now see Mc-Kinley President and either Bryan or Watson Vice-President. Even in theory such an arrangement is very bad, because under it the Vice-President might readily be, and as a matter of fact was, a man utterly opposed to all the principles to which the President was devoted, so that the arrangement provided in the event of the death of the President, not for a succession, but for a revolution. The system was very soon dropped, and each party nominated its own candidates for both positions. But it was many years before all the members of the electoral college of one party felt obliged to cast the same votes for both President and Vice-President, and consequently there was a good deal of scrambling and shifting in taking the vote. When, however, the parties had crystallized into Democratic and Whig, a score of years after the disappearance of the Federalists, the system of party voting also crystallized. Each party then as a rule nominated one man for President and one for Vice-President, these being voted for throughout the nation. This system in turn speedily produced strange results, some of which remain to this day. There are and must be in every party factions. The victorious faction may crush out and destroy the others, or it may try to propitiate at least its most formidable rival. In consequence, the custom grew of offering the vice-presidency as a consolation prize, to be given in many cases to the very men who were most bitterly opposed to the nomination of the successful candidate for President. Sometimes this consolation prize was awarded for geographical reasons, sometimes to bring into the party men who on points of principle might split away because of the principles of the presidential candidate himself, and at other times it was awarded for merely factional reasons to some faction which did not differ in the least from the dominant faction in matters of principles, but had very decided views on the question of offices.

The presidency being all important, and the vice-presidency of comparatively little note, the entire strength of the contending factions is spent in the conflict over the first, and very often a man who is most anxious to take the first place will not take the second, preferring some other political position. It has thus frequently happened that the two candidates have been totally dissimilar in character and even in party principle, though both running on the same ticket. Very odd results have followed in more than one instance.

A striking illustration of the evils sometimes springing from this system is afforded by what befell the Whigs after the election and death of the elder Harrison. Translated into the terms of the politics of continental Europe of to-day, Harrison's adherents represented a union between the right and the extreme left against the centre. That is the regular Whigs who formed the bulk of his supporters were supplemented by a small body of extremists who in their political principles were even more alien to the Whigs than were the bulk of the regular Democrats, but who themselves hated these regular Democrats with the peculiar ferocity so often felt by the extremist for the man who goes far, but not quite far enough. In consequence, the President represented Whig principles, the Vice-President represented a rather extreme form of the very principles to which the Whigs were most opposed. The result was that when Harrison died the presidency fell into the hands of a man who had but a corporal's guard of supporters in the nation, and who proceeded to oppose all the measures of the immense majority of those who elected him.

A somewhat similar instance was afforded in the case of Lincoln and Johnson. Johnson was put on the ticket largely for geographical reasons, and on the death of Lincoln he tried to reverse the policy of the party which had put him in office. An instance of an entirely different kind is afforded by Garfield and Arthur. The differences between these two party leaders were mainly merely factional. Each stood squarely on the platform of the party, and all the principles advocated by one were advocated by the other; yet the death of Garfield meant a complete overturn in the *personnel* of the upper Republican officials, because Arthur had been nominated expressly to placate the group of party leaders who most objected to the nomination of Garfield. Arthur made a very good President, but the bitterness caused by his succession to power nearly tore the party in twain. It will be noted that most of these evils arose from the fact that the Vice—President under ordinary circumstances possesses so little real power. He presides over the Senate and he has in Washington a position of marked social importance, but his political weight as Vice-President is almost *nil* . There is always a chance that he may become President. As this is only a chance it seems quite impossible to persuade politicians to give it proper weight. This certainly does not seem right. The Vice-President should, so far as possible, represent the same views and principles which have secured the nomination and election of the President, and he should be a man standing well in the councils of the party, trusted by his fellow party leaders, and able in the event of any accident to his chief to take up the work of the latter just where it was left. The Republican party has this year nominated such a man in the person of Mr. Hobart. But nominations of this kind have by no means always been the rule of recent years. No change of parties, for instance, could well produce a greater revolution in policy than would have been produced at almost any time during the last three years if Mr. Cleveland had died and Mr. Stevenson had succeeded him.

One sure way to secure this desired result would undoubtedly be to increase the power of the Vice-President. He should always be a man who would be consulted by the President on every great party question. It would be very well if he were given a seat in the Cabinet. It might be well if, in addition to his vote in the Senate in the event of a tie, he should be given a vote, on ordinary occasions, and perchance on occasions a voice in the debates. A man of the character of Mr. Hobart is sure to make his weight felt in an administration, but the power of thus exercising influence should be made official rather than personal.

The present contest offers a striking illustration of the way in which the Vice-President ought and ought not to be nominated, and to study this it is necessary to study not only the way in which the different candidates were nominated, but at least in outline the characters of the candidates themselves.

For the first time in many years, indeed for the first time since parties have fairly crystallized along their present lines, there are three parties running, two of which support the same presidential candidate but different candidates for the vice-presidency. Each one of these parties has carried several states during the last three or four years. Each party has a right to count upon a number of electoral votes as its own. Closely though the Democratic and Populistic parties have now approximated in their principles as enunciated in the platforms of Chicago and St. Louis, they yet do differ on certain points, and neither would have any chance of beating the Republicans without the help of the other. The result has been a coalition, yet each party to the coalition has retained enough of its jealous individuality to make it refuse to accept the candidate of the other for the second position on the ticket.

The Republican party stands on a normal and healthy party footing. It has enunciated a definite set of principles entirely in accord with its past actions. It has nominated on this platform a President and Vice-President, both of whom are thorough-going believers in all the party principles set forth in the platform upon which they stand. Mr. McKinley believes in sound finance,—that is, in a currency based upon gold and as good as gold. So does Mr. Hobart. Mr. McKinley believes in a protective tariff. So does Mr. Hobart. Mr. McKinley believes in the only method of preserving orderly liberty,—that is, in seeing that the laws are enforced at what-ever cost. So does Mr. Hobart. In short, Mr. Hobart stands for precisely the same principles that are represented by Mr. McKinley. He is a man of weight in the community, who has had wide experience both in business and in politics. He is taking an active part in the campaign, and he will be a power if elected to the vice-presidency. All the elements which have rallied behind Mr. McKinley are just as heartily behind Mr. Hobart. The two represent the same forces, and they stand for a party with a coherent organization and a definite purpose, to the carrying out of which they are equally pledged.

It will be a matter of much importance to the nation that the next Vice-President should stand for some settled policy. It is an unhealthy thing to have the Vice-President and President represented by principles so far apart that the succession of one to the place of the other means a change as radical as any possible party overturn. The straining and dislocation of our governmental institutions was very great when Tyler succeeded Harrison and Johnson succeeded Lincoln. In each case the majority of the party that had won the victory felt that it had been treated with scandalous treachery, for Tyler grew to be as repulsive to the Whigs as Polk himself, and the Republicans could scarcely have hated Seymour more than they hated Johnson. The Vice-President has a threefold relation. First to the administration; next as presiding officer in the Senate, where he should be a man of dignity and force; and third in his social position, for socially he ranks second to the President alone. Mr. Morton was in every way an admirable Vice-President under General Harrison, and had he succeeded to the presidential chair there would have been no break in the great policies which were being pushed forward by the administration. But during Mr. Cleveland's two incumbencies Messrs. Hendricks and Stevenson have represented, not merely hostile factions, but principles and interests from which he was sundered by a gulf quite as great as that which divided him from his normal party foes. Mr. Sewall would make a colorless Vice-President, and were he at any time to succeed Mr. Bryan in the White House would travel Mr. Bryan's path only with extreme reluctance and under duress. Mr. Watson would be a more startling, more attractive, and more dangerous figure, for if he got the chance he would lash the nation with a whip of scorpions, while Mr. Bryan would be content with the torture of ordinary thongs.

Finally, Mr. Hobart would typify as strongly as Mr. McKinley himself what was best in the Republican party and in the nation, and would stand as one of the known champions of his party on the very questions at issue in the present election. He is a man whose advice would be sought by all who are prominent in the administration. In short, he would be the kind of man whom the electors are certain to choose as Vice-President if they exercise their choice rationally.

The men who left the Republican party because of the nomination of McKinley would have left it just as quickly if Hobart had been nominated. They do not believe in sound finance, and though many of the bolters object to anarchy and favor protection, they feel that in this crisis their personal desires must be repressed and that they are conscientiously bound to support the depreciated dollar even at the cost of incidentally supporting the principles of a low tariff and the doctrine that a mob should be allowed to do what it likes with immunity. There are many advocates of clipped or depreciated money who are rather sorry to see the demand for such currency coupled with a demand for more lawlessness and an abandonment by the government of the police functions which are the essential attributes of civilization; but they have overcome their reluctance, feeling that on the whole it is more important that the money of the nation should be unsound than that its laws should be obeyed. People who feel this way are just as much opposed to Mr. Hobart as to Mr. McKinley. They object to the platform upon which the two men stand, and they object as much to the character of one man as to the character of the other. They are repelled by McKinley's allegiance to the cause of sound money, and find nothing to propitiate them in Hobart's uncompromisingly honest attitude on the same question. There is no reason whatever why any voter who would wish to vote against the one should favor the other, or *vice versa* .

When we cross the political line all this is changed. On the leading issue of the campaign the entire triangle of candidates are a unit. Mr. Bryan, the nominee for the presidency, and Messrs. Sewall and Watson, the nominees for the vice-presidency, are almost equally devoted adherents of the light-weight dollar and of a currency which shall not force a man to repay what he has borrowed, and shall punish the wrong-headed laborer, who expects to be paid his wages in money worth something, as heavily as the business man or farmer who is so immoral as to wish to pay his debts. All three are believers in that old-world school of finance which appears under such protean changes of policy, always desiring the increase of the circulating medium, but differing as to the means, which in one age takes the form of putting base metal in with the good, or of clipping the good, and in another assumes the guise of fiat money, or the free coinage of silver. On this currency question they are substantially alike, agreeing (as one of their adherents picturesquely put it, in arguing in favor of that form of abundant currency which has as its highest exponent the money of the late Confederacy) that "the money which was good enough for the soldiers of Washington is good enough for us." As a matter of fact the soldiers of Washington were not at all grateful for the money which the loudmouthed predecessors of Mr. Bryan and his kind then thought "good enough" for them. The money with which the veterans of Washington were paid was worth two cents on the dollar, and as yet neither Mr. Bryan, Mr. Sewall, nor Mr. Watson has advocated a two-cent copper dollar. Still, they are striving toward this ideal, and in their advocacy of the fifty cent dollar they are one.

But beyond this they begin to differ. Mr. Sewall distinctly sags behind the leader of the spike team, Mr. Bryan, and still more distinctly behind his rival, or running mate, or whatever one may choose to call him, the Hon. Thomas Watson. There is far more regard for the essential fitness of things in a ticket which contains Mr. Bryan and Mr. Watson than one which contains Mr. Bryan and Mr. Sewall. Mr. Watson is a man of Mr. Bryan's type, only a little more so. But Mr. Sewall is of a different type, and possesses many attributes which must make association with him exceedingly painful, not merely to Mr. Watson, but to Mr. Bryan himself. He is a well-to-do man. Indeed in many communities he would be called a rich man. He is a banker, a railroad man, a shipbuilder, and has been successful in business. Now if Mr. Bryan and Mr. Watson really stand for any principle it is hostility to this kind of success. Thrift, industry, and business energy are qualities which are quite incompatible with true Populistic feeling. Payment of debts, like the suppression of riots, is abhorrent to the Populistic mind. Such conduct strikes the Populist as immoral. Mr. Bryan made his appearance in Congress with two colleagues elected on the same ticket, one of whom stated to the present writer that no honest man ever earned $5000 a year; that whoever got that amount stole it. Mr. Sewall has earned many times $5000 a year. He is a prosperous capitalist. Populism never prospers save where men are unprosperous, and your true Populist is especially intolerant of business success. If a man is a successful business man he at once calls him a plutocrat.

He makes only one exception. A miner or speculator in mines may be many times a millionaire and yet remain in good standing in the Populist party. The Populist has ineradicably fixed in his mind the belief that silver is a cheap metal, and that silver money is, while not fiat money, still a long step toward it. Silver is connected in his mind with scaling down debts, the partial repudiation of obligations, and other measures aimed at those odious moneyed tyrants who lend money to persons who insist upon borrowing, or who have put their ill-gotten gains in saving banks and kindred wicked institutions for the encouragement of the vice of thrift. These pleasurable associations quite outweigh, with the Populist, the fact that the silver man himself is rich. He is even for the moment blind to the further fact that these prosilver men, like Senator Stewart, Governor Altgeld, and their compeers, strenuously insist that the obligations to themselves shall be liquidated in gold; indeed this particular idiosyncrasy of the silver leaders is not much frowned upon by the bulk of the Populists, because it has at least the merit of savoring strongly of "doing" one's creditors. Not even the fact that rich silver mine owners may have earned their money honestly can outweigh the other fact that they champion a species of currency which will make most thrifty and honest men poorer, in the minds of the truly logical Populist.

But Mr. Sewall has no fictitious advantage in the way of owing his wealth to silver. He has made his money precisely as the most loathed reprobate of Wall Street—or of New York, which the average Populist regards as synonymous with Wall Street—has made his. The average Populist does not draw fine distinctions. There are in New York, as in other large cities, scoundrels of great wealth who have made their money by means skilfully calculated to come just outside the line of criminality. There are other men who have made their money exactly as the successful miner or farmer makes his,—that is, by the exercise of shrewdness, business daring, energy and thrift. But the Populist draws no line of division between these two classes. They have made money, and that is enough. One may have built railroads and the other have wrecked them, but they are both railroad men in his eyes, and that is all. One may have swindled his creditors, and the other built up a bank which has been of incalculable benefit to all who have had dealings with it, but to the Populist they are both gold bugs, and as such noxious. Mr. Sewall is the type of man the contemplation of which usually throws a Populist orator into spasms. But it happens that he believes in free silver, just as other very respectable men believe in spirit rapping, or the faith-cure, or Buddhism, or pilgrimages to Lourdes, or the foot of a graveyard rabbit. There are very able men and very lovely women who believe in each or all of these, and there are a much larger number who believe in free silver. Had they lived in the days of Sparta they would have believed in free iron, iron coin being at that time the cheapest circulating medium, the adoption of which would give the greatest expansion of the currency. But they have been dragged on by the slow procession of the centuries, and now they only believe in free silver. It is a belief which is compatible with all the domestic virtues, and even occasionally with very good capacities as a public servant. Mr. Sewall doubtless stands as one of these men. He can hardly be happy, planted firmly as he is, on the Chicago platform. In the minds of most thrifty, hard-working men, who are given to thinking at all about public questions, the free-silver plank is very far from being the most rotten of the many rotten planks put together with such perverted skill by the Chicago architects. A platform which declares in favor of free and unlimited rioting and which has the same strenuous objection to the exercise of the police power by the general government that is felt in the circles presided over by Herr Most, Eugene V. Debs, and all the people whose pictures appear in the detective bureaus of our great cities, cannot appeal to persons who have gone beyond the unpolished-stone period of civilization.

The men who object to what they style "government by injunction" are, as regards the essential principles of government, in hearty sympathy with their remote skin-clad ancestors who lived in caves, fought one another with stone-headed axes, and ate the mammoth and woolly rhinocerous. They are interesting as representing a geological survival, but they are dangerous whenever there is the least chance of their making the principles of this agesburied past living factors in our present life. They are not in sympathy with men of good minds and sound civic morality. It is not a nice thing to wish to pay one's debts in coins worth fifty cents on the dollar, but it is a much less nice thing to wish to plunge one's country into anarchy by providing that the law shall only protect the lawless and frown scornfully on the law-abiding. There is a good deal of mushy sentiment in the world, and there are always a certain number of people whose minds are weak and whose emotions are strong and who effervesce with sympathy toward any man who does wrong, and with indignation against any man who chastises the criminal for having done wrong. These emotionalists, moreover, are always reinforced by that large body of men who themselves wish to do wrong, and who are not sentimental at all, but, on the contrary, very practical. It is rarely that these two classes control a great political party, but at Chicago this became an accomplished fact.

Furthermore, the Chicago convention attacked the Supreme Court. Again this represents a species of atavism,—that is, of recurrence to the ways of thought of remote barbarian ancestors. Savages do not like an independent and upright judiciary. They want the judge to decide their way, and if he does not, they want to behead him. The Populists experience much the same emotions when they realize that the judiciary stands between them and plunder.

Now on all these points Mr. Sewall can hardly feel complete sympathy with his temporary allies. He is very anxious that the Populists shall vote for him for Vice-President, and of course he feels a kindly emotion toward those who do intend to vote for him. He would doubtless pardon much heresy of political belief in any member of the electoral college who feels that Sewall is his friend, not Watson,—Codlin, not Short. He has, of course, a vein of the erratic in his character, or otherwise he would not be in such company at all, and would have no quality that would recommend him to them. But on the whole his sympathies must lie with the man who saves money rather than with the man who proposes to take away the money when it has been saved, and with the policeman who arrests a violent criminal rather than with the criminal. Such sympathy puts him at a disadvantage in the Populist camp. He is loud in his professions of belief in the remarkable series of principles for which he is supposed to stand, but his protestations ring rather hollow. The average supporter of Bryan doubtless intends to support Sewall, for he thinks him an unimportant tail to the Bryan kite. But, though unimportant, he regards him with a slight feeling of irritation, as being at the best a rather ludicrous contrast to the rest of the kite. He contributes no element of strength to the Bryan ticket, for other men who work hard and wish to enjoy the fruits of their toil simply regard him as a renegade, and the average Populist, or Populistic Democrat, does not like him, and accepts him simply because he fears not doing so may jeopardize Bryan's chances. He is in the uncomfortable position always held by the respectable theorist who gets caught in a revolutionary movement and has to wedge nervously up into the front rank with the gentlemen who are not troubled by any of his scruples, and who really do think that it is all very fine and glorious. In fact Mr. Sewall is much the least picturesque and the least appropriate figure on the platform or platforms upon which Mr. Bryan is standing.

Mr. Watson, whose enemies now call him a Georgia cracker, is in reality a far more suitable companion for Mr. Bryan in such a contest. It must be said, however, that if virtue always received its reward Mr. Watson and not Mr. Bryan would stand at the head of the ticket. In the language of mathematicians Mr. Watson merely represents Mr. Bryan raised several powers. The same is true of the Populist as compared to the Democratic platform. Mr. Bryan may affect to believe that free silver does represent the ultimate goal, and that his friends do not intend to go further in the direction of fiat money. Mr. Watson's friends, the middle-of-the-road Populists, are much more fearless and much more logical. They are willing to accept silver as a temporary makeshift, but they want a currency based on corn and cotton next, and ultimately a currency based on the desires of the people who issue it. The statesmanlike utterance of that great financier, Mr. Bryan's chief rival for the nomination and at present his foremost supporter, Mr. Bland, to the effect that he would "wipe out the national debt as with a sponge," meets with their cordial approval as far as it goes, but they object to the qualification before the word "debt." In wiping out debts they do not wish to halt merely at the national debt. The Populists indorsed Bryan as the best they could get; but they hated Sewall so that they took the extraordinary step of nominating the Vice-President before the President so as to make sure of a really acceptable man in the person of Watson.

With Mr. Bryan denunciation of the gold bug and the banker is largely a mere form of intellectual entertainment; but with Mr. Watson it represents an almost ferocious conviction. Someone has said that Mr. Watson like Mr. Tillman, is an embodied retribution on the South for having failed to educate the cracker, the poor white who gives him his strength. It would ill beseem any dweller in cities of the North, especially any dweller in the city of Tammany, to reproach the South with having failed to educate anybody. But Mr. Watson is certainly an awkward man for a community to develop. He is infinitely more in earnest than is Mr. Bryan. Mr. Watson's followers belong to that school of southern Populists who honestly believe that the respectable and commonplace people who own banks, railroads, dry-goods stores, factories, and the like, are persons with many of the mental and social attributes that unpleasantly distinguished Heliogabalus, Nero, Caligula, and other worthies of later Rome. Not only do they believe this, but they say it with appalling frankness. They are very sincere as a rule, or at least the rank and file are.

They are also very suspicious. They distrust anything they cannot understand; and as they understand but little this opens a very wide field for distrust. They are apt to be emotionally religious. If not, they are then at least atheists of an archaic type. Refinement and comfort they are apt to consider quite as objectionable as im morality. That a man should change his clothes in the evening, that he should dine at any other hour than noon, impress these good people as being symptoms of depravity instead of merely trivial. A taste for learning and cultivated friends, and a tendency to bathe frequently, cause them the deepest suspicion. A well-to-do man they regard with jealous distrust, and if they cannot be well-to-do themselves, at least they hope to make matters uncomfortable for those that are. They possess many strong, rugged virtues, but they are quite impossible politically, because they always confound the essentials and the nonessentials, and though they often make war on vice, they rather prefer making war upon prosperity and refinement.

Mr. Watson was in a sense born out of place when he was born in Georgia, for in Georgia the regular Democracy, while it has accepted the principles of the Populists, has made war on their *personnel*, and in every way strives to press them down. Far better for Mr. Watson would it have been could he have been born in the adjacent State of South Carolina, where the Populists swallowed the Democrats with a gulp. Senator Tillman, the great Populist or Democratic orator from South Carolina, possesses an untrammelled tongue any middle-of-the-road man would envy: and moreover Mr. Tillman's brother has been frequently elected to Congress upon the issue that he never wore either an overcoat or an undershirt, an issue which any Populist statesman finds readily comprehensible, and which he would recognize at first glance as being strong before the people. It needs a certain amount of mental subtlety to appreciate that it is for one's interest to support a man because he is honest and has broad views about coast defenses and the navy, and other similar subjects; but it does not need any mind at all to have one's prejudices stirred in favor of a statesman whose claim to the title rests upon his indifference to the requirements of civilized dress.

Altogether Mr. Watson, with his sincerity, his frankness, his extreme suspiciousness, his distrust of anything he cannot understand, and the feeling he encourages against all the elegancies and decencies of civilized life, is an interesting personage. He represents the real thing, while Bryan after all is more or less a sham and a compromise. Mr. Watson would, at a blow, destroy all banks and bankers, with a cheerful, albeit vague, belief that thereby he was in some abstruse way benefiting the people at large. And he would do this with the simple sincerity and faith of an African savage who tries to benefit his tribe by a sufficiency of human sacrifices. But Mr. Bryan would be beset by ugly doubts when he came to put into effect all the mischievous beliefs of his followers, and Mr. Sewall would doubtless be frankly miserable if it ever became necessary for him to take a lead in such matters. Mr. Watson really ought to be the first man on the ticket, with Mr. Bryan second; for he is much the superior in boldness, in thoroughgoing acceptance of his principles according to their logical conclusions, and in sincerity of faith. It is impossible not to regret that the Democrats and Populists should not have put forward in the first place the man who genuinely represents their ideas.

However, it is even doubtful whether Mr. Watson will receive the support to which he is entitled as a vice-presidential candidate. In the South the Populists have been so crushed under the heel of the Democrats, and have bitten that heel with such eager venom, that they dislike entering into a coalition with them; but in the south the Democrats will generally control the election machinery. In the far West, and generally in those States where the Populist wing of the new alliance is ascendant, the Populists have no especial hatred of the Demo crats. They know that their principles are sub stantially identical, and they think it best to support the man who seems to represent the majority faction among the various factions that stand behind Bryan.

As a consequence of this curious condition of affairs there are several interesting possibilities open. The electoral college consists of the men elected at the polls in the various States to record the decrees of the majorities in those States, and it has grown to be an axiom of politics that they must merely register the will of the men who elected them. But it does seem possible that in the present election some of the electors may return to the old principles of a century ago and exercise at least a limited discretion in casting their votes. In a State like Nebraska, for instance, it looks as. though it would be possible that the electoral ticket on the anti-Republican side would be composed of four Bryan and Watson men and four Bryan and Sewall men. Now in the event of Bryan having more votes than McKinley—that is, in the event of the country showing strong Bedlamite tendencies next November—it might be that a split between Sewall and Watson would give a plurality to Hobart, and in such event it is hardly conceivable that some of the electors would not exercise their discretion by changing their votes. If they did not, we might then again see a return to the early and profoundly interesting practice of our fathers and witness a President chosen by one party and a Vice-President by the other.

I wish it to be distinctly understood, however, that these are merely interesting speculations as to what might occur in a hopelessly improbable contingency. I am a good American, with a profound belief in my countrymen, and I have no idea that they will deliberately lower themselves to a level beneath that of a South American Republic, by voting for the farrago of sinister nonsense which the Populistic-Democratic politicians at Chicago chose to set up as embodying the principles of their party, and for the amiable and windy demagogue who stands upon that platform. Many entirely honest and intelligent men have been misled by the silver talk, and have for the moment joined the ranks of the ignorant, the vicious and the wrongheaded. These men of character and capacity are blinded by their own misfortunes, or their own needs, or else they have never fairly looked into the matter for themselves, being, like most men, whether in "gold" or "silver" communities, content to follow the opinion of those they are accustomed to trust. After full and fair inquiry these men, I am sure, whether they live in Maine, in Tennessee, or in Oregon, will come out on the side of honest money. The shiftless and vicious and the honest but hopelessly ignorant and puzzle-headed voters cannot be reached; but the average farmer, the average business man, the average workman— in short, the average American—will always stand up for honesty and decency when he can once satisfy himself as to the side on which they are to be found.

X
HOW NOT TO HELP OUR POORER BROTHER[17]

AFTER the publication of my article in the September *Review of Reviews* on the vice-presidential candidates, I received the following very manly, and very courteous, letter from the Honorable Thomas Watson, then the candidate with Mr. Bryan on the Populist ticket for Vice-President. I publish it with his permission:

HON. THEODORE ROOSEVELT:

It pains me to be misunderstood by those whose good opinion I respect, and upon reading your trenchant article in the September number of the *Review of Reviews* the impulse was strong to write to you.

When you take your stand for honester government and for juster laws in New York, as you have so courageously done, your motives must be the same as mine— for you do not need the money

[17] *Review of Reviews*, January, 1897.

your office gives you. I can understand, instinctively, what you feel—what your motives are. You merely obey a law of your nature which puts you into mortal combat with what you think is wrong. You fight because your own sense of self-respect and self-loyalty compels you to fight. Is not this so?

If in Georgia and throughout the South we have conditions as intolerable as those that surround you in New York, can you not realize why I make war upon them?

Tammany itself has grown great because mistaken leaders of the southern Democracy catered to its Kellys and Crokers and feared to defy them.

The first "roast" I ever got from the Democratic press of this State followed a speech I had made denouncing Tammany, and denouncing the craven leaders who obeyed Tammany.

It is astonishing how one honest man may honestly misjudge another.

My creed does *not* lead me to dislike the men who run a bank, a factory, a railroad or a foundry. I do *not* hate a man for owning a bond, and having a bank account, or having cash loaned at interest.

Upon the other hand, I think each should make all the profit in business he fairly can; but I do believe that the banks should not exercise the sovereign power of issuing money, and I do believe that all special privileges granted, and all exemption from taxation, work infinite harm. I *do* believe that the wealth of the Republic is practically free from federal taxation, and that the burdens of government fall upon the shoulders of those least able to bear them.

If you could spend an evening with me among my books and amid my family, I feel quite sure you would not again class me with those who make war upon the "decencies and elegancies of civilized life." And if you could attend one of my great political meetings in Georgia, and see the good men and good women who believe in Populism, you would not continue to class them with those who vote for candidates upon the "no undershirt" platform.

In other words, if you understood me and mine your judgment of us would be different.

The "cracker" of the South is simply the man who did not buy slaves to do his work. He did it all himself—like a man. Some of our best generals in war, and magistrates in peace, have come from the "cracker" class. As a matter of fact, however, my own people, from my father back to Revolutionary times, were slave owners and land owners. In the first meeting held in Georgia to express sympathy with the Boston patriots my great-great-grandfather bore a prominent part, and in the first State legislature ever convened in Georgia one of my ancestors was the representative of his county.

My grandfather was wealthy, and so was my father. My boyhood was spent in the idleness of a rich man's son. It was not till I was in my teens that misfortune overtook us, sent us homeless into the world, and deprived me of the thorough collegiate training my father intended for me.

At sixteen years of age I thus had to commence life moneyless, and the weary years I spent among the poor, the kindness I received in their homes, and the acquaintance I made with the hardship of their lives, gave me that profound sympathy for them which I yet retain—though I am no longer poor myself.

Pardon the liberty I take in intruding this letter upon you. I have followed your work in New York with admiring sympathy, and have frequently written of it in my paper. While hundreds of miles separate us, and our tasks and methods have been widely different, I must still believe that we have much in common, and that the ruling force which actuates us both is to challenge wrong and to fight the battles of good government.

Very respectfully yours,

THOS. E. WATSON.

Thompson, GA., August, 30, 1896.

I intended to draw a very sharp line between Mr. Watson and many of those associated with him in the same movement; and certain of the sentences which he quotes as if they were meant to apply to him were, on the contrary, meant to apply generally to the agitators who proclaimed both him and Mr. Bryan as their champions, and especially to many of the men who were running on the Populist tickets in different States. To Mr. Watson's own sincerity and courage I thought I had paid full tribute, and if I failed in any way I wish to make good that failure. I was in Washington when Mr. Watson was in Congress, and I know how highly he was esteemed personally by his colleagues, even by those differing very widely from him in matters of principle. The staunchest friends of order and decent government fully and cordially recognized Mr. Watson's honesty and good faith—men, for instance, like Senator Lodge of Massachusetts, and Representative Bellamy Storer of Ohio. Moreover, I sympathize as little as Mr. Watson with denunciation of the "cracker," and I may mention that one of my forefathers was the first Revolutionary Governor of Georgia at the time that Mr. Watson's ancestor sat in the first Revolutionary legislature of the State. Mr. Watson himself embodies not a few of the very attributes the lack of which we feel so keenly in many of our public men. He is brave, he is earnest, he is honest, he is disinterested. For many of the wrongs which he wishes to remedy, I, too, believe that a remedy can be found, and for this purpose I would gladly strike hands with him. All this makes it a matter of the keenest regret that he should advocate certain remedies that we deem even worse than the wrongs complained of, and should strive in darkling ways to correct other wrongs, or rather inequalities and sufferings, which exist, not because of the shortcomings of society, but because of the existence of human nature itself.

There are plenty of ugly things about wealth and its possessors in the present age, and I suppose there have been in all ages. There are many rich people who so utterly lack patriotism, or show such sordid and selfish traits of character, or lead such mean and vacuous lives, that all right-minded men must look upon them with angry contempt; but, on the whole, the thrifty are apt to be better citizens than the thriftless; and the worst capitalist cannot harm laboring men as they are harmed by demagogues. As the people of a State grow more and more intelligent the State itself may be able to play a larger and larger part in the life of the community, while at the same time individual effort may be given freer and less restricted movement along certain lines; but it is utterly unsafe to give the State more than the minimum of power just so long as it contains masses of men who can be moved by the pleas and denunciations of the average Socialist leader of today. There may be better schemes of taxation than those at present employed; it may be wise to devise inheritance taxes, and to impose regulations on the kinds of business which can be carried on only under the especial protection of the State; and where there is a real abuse by wealth it needs to be, and in this country generally has been, promptly done away with; but the first lesson to teach the poor man is that, as a whole, the wealth in the community is distinctly beneficial to him; that he is better off in the long run because other men are well off; and that the surest way to destroy what measure of prosperity he may have is to paralyze industry and the well-being of those men who have achieved success.

I am not an empiricist; I would no more deny that sometimes human affairs can be much bettered by legislation than I would affirm that they can always be so bettered. I would no more make a fetish of unrestricted individualism than I would admit the power of the State offhand and radically to reconstruct society. It may become necessary to interfere even more than we have done with the right of private contract, and to shackle cunning as we have shackled force. All I insist upon is that we must be sure of our ground before trying to get any legislation at all, and that we must not expect too much from this legislation, nor refuse to better ourselves a little because we cannot accomplish everything at a jump. Above all, it is criminal to excite anger and discontent without proposing a remedy, or only proposing a false remedy. The worst foe of the poor man is the labor leader, whether philanthropist or politician, who tries to teach him that he is a victim of conspiracy and injustice, when in reality he is merely working out his fate with blood and sweat as the immense majority of men who are worthy of the name always have done and always will have to do.

The difference between what can and what cannot be done by law is well exemplified by our experience with the negro problem, an experience of which Mr. Watson must have ample practical knowledge. The negroes were formerly held in slavery. This was a wrong which legislation could remedy, and which could not be remedied except by legislation. Accordingly they were set free by law. This having been done, many of their friends believed that in some way, by additional legislation, we could at once put them on an intellectual, social, and business equality with the whites. The effort has failed completely. In large sections of the country the negroes are not treated as they should be treated, and politically in particular the frauds upon them have been so gross and shameful as to awaken not merely indignation but bitter wrath; yet the best friends of the negro admit that his hope lies, not in legislation, but in the constant working of those often unseen forces of the national life which are greater than all legislation.

It is but rarely that great advances in general social well-being can be made by the adoption of some far-reaching scheme, legislative or otherwise; normally they come only by gradual growth, and by incessant effort to do first one thing, then another, and then another. Quack remedies of the universal cure-all type are generally as noxious to the body politic as to the body corporal.

Often the head-in-the-air social reformers, because people of sane and wholesome minds will not favor their wild schemes, themselves decline to favor schemes for practical reform. For the last two years there has been an honest effort in New York to give the city good government, and to work intelligently for better social conditions, especially in the poorest quarters. We have cleaned the streets; we have broken the power of the ward boss and the saloon-keeper to work injustice; we have destroyed the most hideous of the tenement houses in which poor people are huddled like swine in a sty; we have made parks and play-grounds for the children in the crowded quarters; in every possible way we have striven to make life easier and healthier, and to give man and woman a chance to do their best work; while at the same time we have warred steadily against the pauper-producing, maudlin philanthropy of the free soup-kitchen and tramp lodging-house kind. In all this we have had practically no help from either the parlor socialists or the scarcely more noxious beer-room socialists who are always howling about the selfishness of the rich and their unwillingness to do anything for those who are less well off.

There are certain labor unions, certain bodies of organized labor—notably those admirable organizations which include the railway conductors, the locomotive engineers and the firemen—which to my mind embody almost the best hope that there is for healthy national growth in the future; but bitter experience has taught men who work for reform in New York that the average labor leader, the average demagogue who shouts for a depreciated currency, or for the overthrow of the rich, will not do anything to help those who honestly strive to make better our civic conditions. There are immense numbers of workingmen to whom we can appeal with perfect confidence; but too often we find that a large proportion of the men who style themselves leaders of organized labor are influenced only by sullen short-sighted hatred of what they do not understand, and are deaf to all appeals, whether to their national or to their civic patriotism.

What I most grudge in all this is the fact that sincere and zealous men of high character and honest purpose, men like Mr. Watson, men and women such as those he describes as attending his Populist meetings, or such as are to be found in all strata of our society, from the employer to the hardest-worked day laborer, go astray in their methods, and are thereby prevented from doing the full work for good they ought to. When a man goes on the wrong road himself he can do very little to guide others aright, even though these others are also on the wrong road. There are many wrongs to be righted; there are many measures of relief to be pushed; and it is a pity that when we are fighting what is bad and championing what is good, the men who ought to be our most effective allies should deprive themselves of usefulness by the wrong-headedness of their position. Rich men and poor men both do wrong on occasions, and whenever a specific instance of this can be pointed out all citizens alike should join in punishing the wrong-doer. Honesty and right-mindedness should be the tests; not wealth or poverty.

In our municipal administration here in New York we have acted with an equal hand toward wrong-doers of high and low degree. The Board of Health condemns the tenement-house property of the rich landowner, whether this landowner be priest or layman, banker or railroad president, lawyer or manager of a real estate business; and it pays no heed to the intercession of any politician, whether this politician be Catholic or Protestant, Jew or Gentile. At the same time the Police De partment promptly suppresses, not only the criminal, but the rioter. In other words, we do strict justice. We feel we are defrauded of help to which we are entitled when men who ought to assist in any work to better the condition of the people decline to aid us because their brains are turned by dreams only worthy of a European revolutionist.

Many workingmen look with distrust upon laws which really would help them; laws for the intelligent restriction of immigration, for instance. I have no sympathy with mere dislike of immigrants; there are classes and even nationalities of them which stand at least on an equality with the citizens of native birth, as the last election showed. But in the interest of our workingmen we must in the end keep out laborers who are ignorant, vicious, and with low standards of life and comfort, just as we have shut out the Chinese.

Often labor leaders and the like denounce the present conditions of society, and especially of our political life, for shortcomings which they themselves have been instrumental in causing. In our cities the misgovernment is due, not to the misdeeds of the rich, but to the low standard of honesty and morality among citizens generally; and nothing helps the corrupt politician more than substituting either wealth or poverty for honesty as the standard by which to try a candidate. A few months ago a socialistic reformer in New York was denouncing the corruption caused by rich men because a certain judge was suspected of giving information in advance as to a decision in a case involving the interests of a great corporation. Now this judge had been elected some years previously, mainly because he was supposed to be a representative of the "poor man"; and the socialistic reformer himself, a year ago, was opposing the election of Mr. Beaman as judge because he was one of the firm of Evarts & Choate, who were friends of various millionaires and were counsel for various corporations. But if Mr. Beaman had been elected judge no human being, rich or poor, would have dared so much as hint at his doing anything improper.

Something can be done by good laws; more can be done by honest administration of the laws; but most of all can be done by frowning resolutely upon the preachers of vague discontent; and by upholding the true doctrine of self-reliance, self-help, and self-mastery. This doctrine sets forth many things. Among them is the fact that though a man can occasionally be helped when he stumbles, yet that it is useless to try to carry him when he will not or cannot walk; and worse than useless to try to bring down the work and reward of the thrifty and intelligent to the level of the capacity of the weak, the shiftless, and the idle. It further shows that the maudlin philanthropist and the maudlin sentimentalist are almost as noxious as the demagogue, and that it is even more necessary to temper mercy with justice than justice with mercy.

The worst lesson that can be taught a man is to rely upon others and to whine over his sufferings. If an American is to amount to anything he must rely upon himself, and not upon the State; he must take pride in his own work, instead of sitting idle to envy the luck of others; he must face life with resolute courage, win victory if he can, and accept defeat if he must, without seeking to place on his fellow-men a responsibility which is not theirs.

Let me say in conclusion, that I do not write in the least from the standpoint of those whose association is purely with what are called the wealthy classes. The men with whom I have worked and associated most closely during the last couple of years here in New York, with whom I have shared what is at least an earnest desire to better social and civic conditions (neither blinking what is evil nor being misled by the apostles of a false remedy), and with whose opinions as to what is right and practical my own in the main agree, are not capitalists, save as all men who by toil earn, and with prudence save, money are capitalists. They include reporters on the daily papers, editors of magazines, as well as of newspapers, principals in the public schools, young lawyers, young architects, young doctors, young men of business, who are struggling to rise in their profession by dint of faithful work, but who give some of their time to doing what they can for the city, and a number of priests and clergymen; but as it happens the list does not include any man of great wealth, or any of those men whose names are in the public mind identified with great business corporations. Most of them have at one time or another in their lives faced poverty and know what it is; none of them are more than well-to-do. They include Catholics and Protestants, Jews, and men who would be regarded as heterodox by professors of most recognized creeds; some of them were born on this side, others are of foreign birth; but they are all Americans, heart and soul, who fight out for themselves the battles of their own lives, meeting sometimes defeat and sometimes victory. They neither forget that man does owe a duty to his fellows, and should strive to do what he can to increase the well-being of the community; nor yet do they forget that in the long run the only way to help people is to make them help themselves. They are prepared to try any properly guarded legislative remedy for ills which they believe can be remedied; but they perceive clearly that it is both foolish and wicked to teach the average man who is not well off that some wrong or injustice has been done him, and that he should hope for redress elsewhere than in his own industry, honesty, and intelligence.

XI
THE MONROE DOCTRINE[18]

THE Monroe Doctrine should not be considered from any purely academic standpoint, but as a broad, general principle of living policy. It is to be justified not by precedent merely, but by the needs of the nation and the true interests of Western civilization. It, of course, adds strength to our position at this moment to show that the action of the national authorities is warranted by the actions of their predecessors on like occasions in time past, and that the line of policy we are now pursuing is that which has been pursued by all our statesmen of note since the republic grew sufficiently powerful to make what it said of weight in foreign affairs. But even if in time past we had been as blind to the national honor and welfare as are the men who at the present day champion the anti-American side of the Venezulan question, it would now be necessary for statesmen

[18] The Bachelor of Arts, March, 1896.

who were both far-sighted and patriotic to enunciate the principles for which the Monroe Doctrine stands. In other words, if the Monroe Doctrine did not already exist it would be necessary forthwith to create it.

Let us first of all clear the question at issue by brushing away one or two false objections. Lord Salisbury at first put in emphatic words his refusal in any way to recognize the Monroe Doctrine as part of the law of nations or as binding upon Great Britain. Most British statesmen and publicists followed his lead; but recently a goodly number have shown an inclination to acquiesce in the views of Lord Salisbury's colleague, Mr. Chamberlain, who announces, with bland indifference to the expressed opinion of his nominal chief, that England does recognize the existence of the Monroe Doctrine and never thought of ignoring it. Lord Salisbury himself has recently shown symptoms of changing ground and taking this position; while Mr. Balfour has gone still farther in the right direction, and the Liberal leaders farther yet. It is not very important to us how far Lord Salisbury and Mr. Chamberlain may diverge in their views, although, of course, in the interests of the English-speaking peoples and of peace between England and the United States, we trust that Mr. Chamberlain's position will be sustained by Great Britain. But the attitude of our own people is important, and it would be amusing, were it not unpleasant, to see, that many Americans, whose Americanism is of the timid and flabby type, have been inclined eagerly to agree with Lord Salisbury. A very able member of the New York bar remarked the other day that he had not yet met the lawyer who agreed with Secretary Olney as to the legal interpretation of the Monroe Doctrine. This remark was chiefly interesting as showing the lawyer's own limitations. It would not have been made if he had met the Justices of the Supreme Court, for instance; but even on the unfounded supposition that his remark was well grounded, it would have had little more significance than if he had said that he had not yet met a dentist who agreed with Mr. Olney. The Monroe Doctrine is not a question of law at all. It is a question of policy. It is a question to be considered not only by statesmen, but by all good citizens. Lawyers, as lawyers, have absolutely nothing whatever to say about it. To argue that it cannot be recognized as a principle of international law, is a mere waste of breath. Nobody cares whether it is or is not so recognized, any more than any one cares whether the Declaration of Independence and Washington's farewell address are so recognized.

The Monroe Doctrine may be briefly defined as forbidding European encroachment on American soil. It is not desirable to define it so rigidly as to prevent our taking into account the varying degrees of national interest in varying cases. The United States has not the slightest wish to establish a universal protectorate over other American States, or to become responsible for their mis-deeds. If one of them becomes involved in an ordinary quarrel with a European power, such quarrel must be settled between them by any one of the usual methods. But no European State is to be allowed to aggrandize itself on American soil at the expense of any American State. Furthermore, no transfer of an American colony from one European State to another is to be permitted, if, in the judgment of the United States, such transfer would be hostile to its own interests.

John Quincy Adams, who, during the presidency of Monroe, first clearly enunciated the doctrine which bears his chief's name, asserted it as against both Spain and Russia. In the clearest and most emphatic terms he stated that the United States could not acquiesce in the acquisition of new territory within the limits of any independent American State, whether in the Northern or Southern Hemisphere, by any European power. He took this position against Russia when Russia threatened to take possession of what is now Oregon. He took this position as against Spain when, backed by other powers of Continental Europe, she threatened to reconquer certain of the Spanish-American States.

This is precisely and exactly the position the United States has now taken in reference to England and Venezuela. It is idle to contend that there is any serious difference in the application of the doctrine to the two sets of questions. An American may, of course, announce his opposition to the Monroe Doctrine, although by so doing he forfeits all title to far-seeing and patriotic devotion to the interests of his country. But he cannot argue that the Monroe Doctrine does not apply to the present case, unless he argues that the Monroe Doctrine has no existence whatsoever. In fact, such arguments are, on their face, so absurd that they need no refutation, and can be relegated where they belong—to the realm of the hairsplitting schoolmen. They have no concern either for practical politicians or for historians with true historic insight.

We have asserted the principles which underlie the Monroe Doctrine, not only against Russia and Spain, but also against France, on at least two different occasions. The last and most important was when the French conquered Mexico and made it into an Empire. It is not necessary to recall to any one the action of our Government in the matter as soon as the Civil War came to an end. Suffice it to say that, under threat of our interposition, the French promptly abandoned Maximilian, and the latter's Empire fell. Long before this, however, and a score of years before the Doctrine was christened by the name Monroe even the timid statesmen of the Jeffersonian era embodied its principle in their protest against the acquisition of Louisiana, by France, from Spain. Spain at that time held all of what is now the Great West. France wished to acquire it. Our statesmen at once announced that they would regard as hostile to America the transfer of the territory in question from a weak to a strong European power. Under the American pressure the matter was finally settled by the sale of the territory in question to the United States. The principle which our statesmen then announced was in kind precisely the same as that upon which we should now act if Germany sought to acquire Cuba from Spain, or St. Thomas from the Danes. In either of these events it is hardly conceivable that the United

States would hesitate to interfere, if necessary, by force of arms; and in so doing the national authorities would undoubtedly be supported by the immense majority of the American people, and, indeed, by all save the men of abnormal timidity or abnormal political shortsightedness.

Historically, therefore, the position of our representatives in the Venezuelan question is completely justified. It cannot be attacked on academic grounds. The propriety of their position is even more easily defensible.

Primarily, our action is based on national self-interest. In other words, it is patriotic. A certain limited number of persons are fond of decrying patriotism as a selfish virtue, and strive with all their feeble might to inculcate in its place a kind of milk-and-water cosmopolitanism. These good people are never men of robust character or of imposing personality, and the plea itself is not worth considering. Some reformers may urge that in the ages' distant future patriotism, like the habit of monogamous marriage, will become a needless and obsolete virtue; but just at present the man who loves other countries as much as he does his own is quite as noxious a member of society as the man who loves other women as much as he loves his wife. Love of country is an elemental virtue, like love of home, or like honesty or courage. No country will accomplish very much for the world at large unless it elevates itself. The useful member of a community is the man who first and foremost attends to his own rights and his own duties, and who therefore becomes better fitted to do his share in the common duties of all. The useful member of the brotherhood of nations is that nation which is most thoroughly saturated with the national idea, and which realizes most fully its rights as a nation and its duties to its own citizens. This is in no way incompatible with a scrupulous regard for the rights of other nations, or a desire to remedy the wrongs of suffering peoples.

The United States ought not to permit any great military powers, which have no foothold on this continent, to establish such foothold; nor should they permit any aggrandizement of those who already have possessions on the continent. We do not wish to bring ourselves to a position where we shall have to emulate the European system of enormous armies. Every true patriot, every man of statesman-like habit, should look forward to the day when not a single European power will hold a foot of American soil. At present it is not necessary to take the position that no European power shall hold American territory; but it certainly will become necessary, if the timid and selfish "peace at any price" men have their way, and if the United States fails to check at the outset European aggrandizement on this continent.

Primarily, therefore, it is to the interest of the citizens of the United States to prevent the further colonial growth of European powers in the Western Hemisphere. But this is also to the interest of all the people of the Western Hemisphere. At best, the inhabitants of a colony are in a cramped and unnatural state. At the worst, the establishment of a colony prevents any healthy popular growth. Some time in the dim future it may be that all the English-speaking peoples will be able to unite in some kind of confederacy. However desirable this would be, it is, under existing conditions, only a dream. At present the only hope for a colony that wishes to attain full moral and mental growth, is to become an independent State, or part of an independent State. No English colony now stands on a footing of genuine equality with the parent State. As long as the Canadian remains a colonist, he remains in a position which is distinctly inferior to that of his cousins, both in England and in the United States. The Englishman at bottom looks down on the Canadian, as he does on any one who admits his inferiority, and quite properly, too. The American, on the other hand, with equal propriety, regards the Canadian with the good-natured condescension always felt by the freeman for the man who is not free. A funny instance of the English attitude toward Canada was shown after Lord Dun-raven's inglorious *fiasco* last September, when the Canadian yachtsman, Rose, challenged for the America cup. The English journals repudiated him on the express ground that a Canadian was not an Englishman and not entitled to the privileges of an Englishman. In their comments, many of them showed a dislike for Americans which almost rose to hatred. The feeling they displayed for the Canadians was not one of dislike. It was one of contempt.

Under the best of circumstances, therefore, a colony is in a false position. But if the colony is in a region where the colonizing race has to do its work by means of other inferior races the condition is much worse. From the standpoint of the race little or nothing has been gained by the English conquest and colonization of Jamaica. Jamaica has merely been turned into a negro island, with a future, seemingly, much like that of San Domingo. British Guiana, however well administered, is nothing but a colony where a few hundred or few thousand white men hold the superior positions, while the bulk of the population is composed of Indians, Negroes, and

Asiatics. Looked at through the vista of the centuries, such a colony contains less promise of true growth than does a State like Venezuela or Ecuador. The history of most of the South American republics has been both mean and bloody; but there is at least a chance that they may develop, after infinite tribulations and suffering, into a civilization quite as high and stable as that of such a European power as Portugal. But there is no such chance for any tropical American colony owned by a Northern European race. It is distinctly in the interest of civilization that the present States in the two Americas should develop along their own lines, and however desirable it is that many of them should receive European immigration, it is highly undesirable that any of them should be under European control.

So much for the general principles, and the justification, historically and morally, of the Monroe Doctrine. Now take the specific case at issue. Great Britain has a boundary dispute with Venezuela. She claims as her own a territory which Venezuela asserts to be hers, a territory which in point of size very nearly equals the Kingdom of Italy. Our government, of course, cannot, if it wishes to remain true to the traditions of the Monroe Doctrine submit to the acquisition by England of such an enormous tract of territory, and it must therefore find out whether the English claims are or are not well founded. It would, of course, be preposterous to lay down the rule that no European power should seize American territory which was not its own, and yet to permit the power itself to decide the question of the ownership of such territory. Great Britain refused to settle the question either by amicable agreement with Venezuela or by arbitration. All that remained for the United States, was to do what it actually did; that is, to try to find out the facts for itself, by its own commission. If the facts show England to be in the right, well and good. If they show England to be in the wrong, we most certainly ought not to permit her to profit, at Venezuela's expense, by her own wrong-doing.

We are doing exactly what England would very properly do in a like case. Recently, when the German Emperor started to interfere in the Transvaal, England promptly declared her own "Monroe Doctrine" for South Africa. We do not propose to see English filibusters try at the expense of Venezuela the same policy which recently came to such an ignominious end in the Transvaal, in a piece of weak, would-be buccaneering, which, it is perhaps not unfair to say was fittingly commemorated in the verse of the new poet-laureate.

It would be difficult to overestimate the good done in this country by the vigorous course already taken by the national executive and legislature in this matter. The lesson taught Lord Salisbury is one which will not soon be forgotten by English statesmen. His position is false, and is recognized as false by the best English statesmen and publicists. If he does not consent to arrange the matter with Venezuela, it will have to be arranged in some way by arbitration. In either case, the United States gains its point. The only possible danger of war comes from the action of the selfish and timid men on this side of the water, who clamorously strive to misrepresent American, and to mislead English, public opinion. If they succeed in persuading Lord Salisbury that the American people will back down if he presses them, they will do the greatest damage possible to both countries, for they will render war, at some time in the future, almost inevitable.

Such a war we would deplore; but it must be distinctly understood that we would deplore it very much more for England's sake than for our own; for whatever might be the initial fortunes of the struggle, or the temporary damage and loss to the United States, the mere fact that Canada would inevitably be rent from England in the end would make the outcome an English disaster.

We do not in any way seek to become the sponsor of the South American States. England has the same right to protect her own subjects, or even in exceptional cases to interfere to stop outrages in South America, that we have to interfere in Armenia—and it is to be regretted that our representatives do not see their way clear to interfere for Armenia. But England should not acquire territory at the expense of Venezuela any more than we should acquire it at the expense of Turkey.

The mention of Armenia brings up a peculiarly hypocritical plea which has been advanced against us in this controversy. It has been solemnly alleged that our action in Venezuela has hampered England in the East and has prevented her interfering on behalf of Armenia. We do not wish to indulge in recriminations, but when such a plea is advanced, the truth, however unpleasant, must be told. The great crime of this century against civilization has been the upholding of the Turk by certain Christian powers. To England's attitude in the Crimean War, and after the Russo—Turkish War of 1877, the present Armenian horror is primarily due. Moreover, for six months before the Venezuelan question arose England had looked on motionless while the Turks perpetrated on their wretched subjects wrongs that would blast the memory of Attila.

We do not wish to be misunderstood. We have no feeling against England. On the contrary, we regard her as being well in advance of the great powers of Continental Europe, and we have more sympathy with her. In general, her success tells for the success of civilization, and we wish her well. But where her interests enlist her against the progress of civilization and in favor of the oppression of other nationalities who are struggling upward, our sympathies are immediately forfeited.

It is a matter of serious concern to every college man, and, indeed, to every man who believes in the good effects of a liberal education, to see the false views which seem to obtain among so many of the leaders of educated thought, not only upon the Monroe Doctrine, but upon every question which involves the existence of a feeling of robust Americanism. Every educated man who puts himself out of touch with the current of American thought, and who on conspicuous occasions assumes an attitude hostile to the interest of America, is doing what he can to weaken the influence of educated men in American life. The crude, ill-conditioned jealousy of education, which is so often and so lamentably shown by large bodies of our people, is immensely stimulated by the action of those prominent educated men in whom education seems to have destroyed the strong, virile virtues and especially the spirit of Americanism.

No nation can achieve real greatness if its people are not both essentially moral and essentially manly; both sets of qualities are necessary. It is an admirable thing to possess refinement and cultivation, but the price is too dear if they must be paid for at the cost of the rugged fighting qualities which make a man able to do a man's work in the world, and which make his heart beat with that kind of love of country which is shown not only in readiness to try to make her civic life better, but also to stand up manfully for her when her honor and influence are at stake in a dispute with a foreign power. A heavy responsibility rests on the educated man. It is a double discredit to him to go wrong, whether his shortcomings take the form of shirking his everyday civic duties, or of abandonment of the nation's rights in a foreign quarrel. He must no more be misled by the sneers of those who always write "patriotism" between inverted commas than by the coarser, but equally dangerous, ridicule of the politicians who jeer at "reform." It is as unmanly to be taunted by one set of critics into cowardice as it is to be taunted by the other set into dishonesty.

There are many upright and honorable men who take the wrong side, that is, the anti-American side, of the Monroe Doctrine because they are too short-sighted or too unimaginative to realize the hurt to the nation that would be caused by the adoption of their views. There are other men who take the wrong view simply because they have not thought much of the matter, or are in unfortunate surroundings, by which they have been influenced to their own moral hurt. There are yet other men in whom the mainspring of the opposition to that branch of American policy known as the Monroe Doctrine is sheer timidity. This is sometimes the ordinary timidity of wealth. Sometimes, however, it is peculiarly developed among educated men whose education has tended to make them over-cultivated and over-sensitive to foreign opinion. They are generally men who undervalue the great fighting qualities, without which no nation can ever rise to the first rank.

The timidity of wealth is proverbial, and it was well illustrated by the attitude taken by too many people of means at the time of the Venezuela trouble. Many of them, including bankers, merchants, and railway magnates, criticised the action of the President and the Senate, on the ground that it had caused business disturbance. Such a position is essentially ignoble. When a question of national honor or of national right or wrong, is at stake, no question of financial interest should be considered for a moment. Those wealthy men who wish the abandonment of the Monroe Doctrine because its assertion may damage their business, bring discredit to themselves, and, so far as they are able, discredit to the nation of which they are a part.

It is an evil thing for any man of education to forget that education should intensify patriotism, and that patriotism must not only be shown by striving to do good to the country from within, but by readiness to uphold its interests and honor, at any cost, when menaced from without. Educated men owe to the community the serious performance of this duty. We need not concern ourselves with the emigré educated man, the American who deliberately takes up his permanent abode abroad, whether in London or Paris; he is usually a man of weak character, unfitted to do good work either abroad or at home, who does what he can for his country by relieving it of his presence. But the case is otherwise with the American who stays at home, and tries to teach the youth of his country to disbelieve in the country's rights, as against other countries, and to regard it as the sign of an enlightened spirit to decry the assertion of those rights by force of arms. This man may be inefficient for good; but he is capable at times of doing harm, because he tends to make other people inefficient likewise. In our municipal politics there has long been evident a tendency to gather in one group the people who have no scruples, but who are very efficient, and in another group the amiable people who are not efficient at all. This is but one manifestation of the general and very unwholesome tendency among certain educated people to lose the power of doing efficient work as they acquire refinement. Of course in the long run a really good education will give not only refinement, but also an increase of power, and of capacity for efficient work. But the man who forgets that a real education must include the cultivation of the fighting virtues is sure to manifest this tendency to inefficiency. It is exhibited on a national scale by the educated men who take the anti-American side of international questions. There are exceptions to the rule; but as a rule the healthy man, resolute to do the rough work of the world, and capable of feeling his veins tingle with pride over the great deeds of the men of his own nation, will naturally take the American side of such a question as the Monroe Doctrine. Similarly, the anæmic man of refinement and cultivation, whose intellect has been educated at the expense of his character, and who shrinks from all these struggles through which alone the world moves on to greatness, is inclined to consider any expression of the Monroe Doctrine as truculent and ill advised.

Of course, many strong men who are good citizens on ordinary occasions take the latter view simply because they have been misled. The colonial habit of thought dies hard. It is to be wished that those who are cursed with it would, in endeavoring to emulate the ways of the old world, endeavor to emulate one characteristic which has been shared by every old-world nation, and which is possessed to a marked degree by England. Every decent Englishman is devoted to his country, first, last, and all the time. An Englishman may or may not dislike America, but he is invariably for England and against America when any question arises between them; and I heartily respect him for so being. Let our own people of the partially colonial type copy this peculiarity and it will be much to their credit.

The finest speech that for many years has been delivered by a college man to other college men was that made last spring by Judge Holmes, himself a gallant soldier of the Civil War, in that hall which Harvard has erected to commemorate those of her sons who perished when the North strove with the South. It should be graven on the heart of every college man, for it has in it that lift of the soul toward things heroic that makes the eyes burn and the veins thrill. It must be read in its entirety, for no quotation could do justice to its fine scorn of the mere money-maker, its lofty fealty to a noble ideal, and, above all, its splendid love of country and splendid praise of the valor of those who strive on stricken fields that the honor of their nation may be upheld.

It is strange, indeed, that in a country where words like those of Judge Holmes can be spoken, there should exist men who actually oppose the building of a navy by the United States, nay, even more, actually oppose so much as the strengthening of the coast defences, on the ground that they prefer to have this country too feeble to resent any insult, in order that it may owe its safety to the contemptuous for-bearance which it is hoped this feebleness will inspire in foreign powers. No Tam-many alderman, no venal legislator, no demagogue or corrupt politician, ever strove more effectively than these men are striving to degrade the nation and to make one ashamed of the name of America. When we remember that among them there are college graduates, it is a relief to remember that the leaders on the side of manli-ness and of love of country are also college graduates. Every believer in scholarship and in a liberal education, every believer in the robust qualities of heart, mind, and body without which cultivation and refinement are of no avail, must rejoice to think that, in the present crisis, college men have been prominent among the lead-ers whose farsighted statesmanship and resolute love of country have made those of us who are really Americans proud of the nation. Secretary Olney is a graduate of Brown; Senator Lodge, who took the lead in the Senate on this matter, is a gradu-ate of Harvard; and no less than three members of the Boundary Commission are graduates of Yale.

XII
WASHINGTON'S FORGOTTEN MAXIM[19]

A CENTURY has passed since Washington wrote "To be prepared for war is the most effectual means to promote peace." We pay to this maxim the lip loyalty we so often pay to Washington's words; but it has never sunk deep into our hearts. Indeed of late years many persons have refused it even the poor tribute of lip loyalty, and prate about the iniquity of war as if somehow that was a justification for refusing to take the steps which can alone in the long run prevent war or avert the dreadful disasters it brings in its train. The truth of the maxim is so obvious to every man of really far-sighted patriotism that its mere statement seems trite and useless; and it is not over-creditable to either our intelligence or our love of country that there should be,

[19] Address as Assistant Secretary of the Navy, before the Naval War College, June, 1897.

as there is, need to dwell upon and amplify such a truism.

In this country there is not the slightest danger of an over-development of warlike spirit, and there never has been any such danger. In all our history there has never been a time when preparedness for war was any menace to peace. On the contrary, again and again we have owed peace to the fact that we were prepared for war; and in the only contest which we have had with a European power since the Revolution, the war of 1812, the struggle and all its attendant disasters, were due solely to the fact that we were not prepared to face, and were not ready instantly to resent, an attack upon our honor and interest; while the glorious triumphs at sea which redeemed that war were due to the few preparations which we had actually made. We are a great peaceful nation; a nation of merchants and manufacturers, of farmers and mechanics; a nation of workingmen, who labor incessantly with head or hand. It is idle to talk of such a nation ever being led into a course of wanton aggression or conflict with military powers by the possession of a sufficient navy.

The danger is of precisely the opposite character. If we forget that in the last resort we can only secure peace by being ready and willing to fight for it, we may some day have bitter cause to realize that a rich nation which is slothful, timid, or unwieldy is an easy prey for any people which still retains those most valuable of all qualities, the soldierly virtues. We but keep to the traditions of Washington, to the traditions of all the great Americans who struggled for the real greatness of America, when we strive to build up those fighting qualities for the lack of which in a nation, as in an individual, no refinement, no culture, no wealth, no material prosperity, can atone.

Preparation for war is the surest guaranty for peace. Arbitration is an excellent thing, but ultimately those who wish to see this country at peace with foreign nations will be wise if they place reliance upon a first-class fleet of first-class battleships rather than on any arbitration treaty which the wit of man can devise. Nelson said that the British fleet was the best negotiator in Europe, and there was much truth in the saying. Moreover, while we are sincere and earnest in our advocacy of peace, we must not forget that an ignoble peace is worse than any war. We should engrave in our legislative halls those splendid lines of Lowell:

"Come, Peace! not like a mourner bowed

For honor lost and dear ones wasted, But proud, to meet a people proud,

With eyes that tell of triumph tasted!"

Peace is a goddess only when she comes with sword girt on thigh. The ship of state can be steered safely only when it is always possible to bring her against any foe with "her leashed thunders gathering for the leap." A really great people, proud and high-spirited, would face all the disasters of war rather than purchase that base prosperity which is bought at the price of national honor. All the great masterful races have been fighting races, and the minute that a race loses the hard fighting virtues, then, no matter what else it may retain, no matter how skilled in commerce and finance, in science or art, it has lost its proud right to stand as the equal of the best. Cowardice in a race, as in an individual, is the unpardonable sin, and a wilful failure to prepare for danger may in its effects be as bad as cowardice. The timid man who cannot fight, and the selfish, shortsighted, or foolish man who will not take the steps that will enable him to fight, stand on almost the same plane.

It is not only true that a peace may be so ignoble and degrading as to be worse than any war; it is also true that it may be fraught with more bloodshed than most wars. Of this there has been melancholy proof during the last two years. Thanks largely to the very unhealthy influence of the men whose business it is to speculate in the money market, and who approach every subject from the financial standpoint, purely; and thanks quite as much to the cold-blooded brutality and calculating timidity of many European rulers and statesmen, the peace of Europe has been preserved, while the Turk has been allowed to butcher the Armenians with hideous and unmentionable barbarity, and has actually been helped to keep Crete in slavery. War has been averted at the cost of more bloodshed and infinitely more suffering and degradation to wretched women and children than have occurred in any European struggle since the days of Waterloo. No war of recent years, no matter how wanton, has been so productive of horrible misery as the peace which the powers have maintained during the continuance of the Armenian butcheries. The men who would preach this peace, and indeed the men who have preached universal peace in terms that have prepared the way for such a peace as this, have inflicted a wrong on humanity greater than could be inflicted by the most reckless and war-loving despot. Better a thousand times err on the side of over-readiness to fight, than to err on the side of tame submission to injury, or cold-blooded indifference to the misery of the oppressed.

Popular sentiment is just when it selects as popular heroes the men who have led in the struggle against malice domestic or foreign levy. No triumph of peace is quite so great as the supreme triumphs of war. The courage of the soldier, the courage of the statesman who has to meet storms which can be quelled only by soldierly qualities— this stands higher than any quality called out merely in time of peace. It is by no means necessary that we should have war to develop soldierly attributes and soldierly qualities; but if the peace we enjoy is of such a kind that it causes their loss, then it is far too dearly purchased, no matter what may be its attendant benefits. It may be that some time in the dim future of the race the need for war will vanish; but that time is yet ages distant. As yet no nation can hold its place in the world, or can do any work really worth doing, unless it stands ready to guard its rights with an armed hand. That orderly liberty which is both the foundation and the capstone of our civilization can be gained and kept only by men who are willing to fight for an ideal; who hold high the love of honor, love of faith, love of flag, and love of country. It is true that no nation can be really great unless it is great in peace; in industry, integrity, honesty. Skilled intelligence in civic affairs and industrial enterprises alike; the special ability of the artist, the man of letters, the man of science, and the man of business; the rigid determination to wrong no man, and to stand for righteousness—all these are necessary in a great nation. But it is also necessary that the nation should have physical no less than moral courage; the capacity to do and dare and die at need, and that grim and steadfast resolution which alone will carry a great people through a great peril. The occasion may come at any instant when

"'T is man's perdition to be safe When for the truth he ought to die."

All great nations have shown these qualities. The Dutch held but a little corner of Europe. Their industry, thrift, and enterprise in the pursuits of peace and their cultivation of the arts helped to render them great; but these qualities would have been barren had they not been backed by those sterner qualities which rendered them able to wrest their freedom from the cruel strength of Spain, and to guard it against the banded might of England and of France. The merchants and the artists of Holland did much for her; but even more was done by the famished burghers who fought to the death on the walls of Harlem and Leyden, and the great admirals who led their fleets to victory on the broad and narrow seas.

England's history is rich in splendid names and splendid deeds. Her literature is even greater than that of Greece. In commerce she has stood in the modern world as more than ever Carthage was when civilization clustered in a fringe around the Mediterranean. But she has risen far higher than ever Greece or Carthage rose, because she possesses also the great, masterful qualities which were possessed by the Romans who overthrew them both. England has been fertile in soldiers and administrators; in men who triumphed by sea and by land; in adventurers and explorers who won for her the world's waste spaces; and it is because of this that the English-speaking race now shares with the Slav the fate of the coming years.

We of the United States have passed most of our few years of national life in peace. We honor the architects of our wonderful material prosperity; we appreciate the necessity of thrift, energy, and business enterprise, and we know that even these are of no avail without the civic and social virtues. But we feel, after all, that the men who have dared greatly in war, or the work which is akin to war, are those who deserve best of the country. The men of Bunker Hill and Trenton, Saratoga and Yorktown, the men of New Orleans and Mobile Bay, Gettysburg and Appomattox are those to whom we owe most. None of our heroes of peace, save a few great constructive statesmen, can rank with our heroes of war. The Americans who stand highest on the list of the world's worthies are Washington, who fought to found the country which he afterward governed, and Lincoln, who saved it through the blood of the best and bravest in the land; Washington, the soldier and statesman, the man of cool head, dauntless heart, and iron will, the greatest of good men and the best of great men; and Lincoln, sad, patient, kindly Lincoln, who for four years toiled and suffered for the people, and when his work was done laid down his life that the flag which had been rent in sunder might once more be made whole and without a seam.

It is on men such as these, and not on the advocates of peace at any price, or upon those so shortsighted that they refuse to take into account the possibility of war, that we must rely in every crisis which deeply touches the true greatness and true honor of the Republic. The United States has never once in the course of its history suffered harm because of preparation for war, or because of entering into war. But we have suffered incalculable harm, again and again, from a foolish failure to prepare for war or from reluctance to fight when to fight was proper. The men who today protest against a navy, and protest also against every movement to carry out the traditional policy of the country in foreign affairs, and to uphold the honor of the flag, are themselves but following in the course of those who protested against the acquisition of the great West, and who failed to make proper preparations for the war of 1812, or refused to support it after it had been made. They are own brothers to the men whose short-sightedness and supine indifference prevented any reorganization of the *personnel* of the Navy during the middle of the century, so that we entered upon the Civil War with captains seventy years old. They are close kin to the men who, when the Southern States seceded, wished to let the Union be disrupted in peace rather than restored through the grim agony of armed conflict.

I do not believe that any considerable number of our citizens are stamped with this timid lack of patriotism. There are some *doctrinaires* whose eyes are so firmly fixed on the golden vision of universal peace that they cannot see the grim facts of real life until they stumble over them, to their own hurt, and, what is much worse, to the possible undoing of their fellows. There are some educated men in whom education merely serves to soften the fibre and to eliminate the higher, sterner qualities which tell for national greatness; and these men prate about love for mankind, or for another country, as being in some hidden way a substitute for love of their own country. What is of more weight, there are not a few men of means who have made the till their fatherland, and who are always ready to balance a temporary interruption of money-making, or a temporary financial and commercial disaster, against the self-sacrifice necessary in upholding the honor of the nation and the glory of the flag.

But after all these people, though often noisy, form but a small minority of the whole. They would be swept like chaff before the gust of popular fury which would surely come if ever the nation really saw and felt a danger or an insult. The real trouble is that in such a case this gust of popular fury would come too late. Unreadiness for war is merely rendered more disastrous by readiness to bluster; to talk defiance and advocate a vigorous policy in words, while refusing to back up these words by deeds, is cause for humiliation. It has always been true, and in this age it is more than ever true, that it is too late to prepare for war when the time for peace has passed. The shortsightedness of many people, the good-humored indifference to facts of others, the sheer ignorance of a vast number, and the selfish reluctance to insure against future danger by present sacrifice among yet others—these are the chief obstacles to building up a proper navy and carrying out a proper foreign policy.

The men who opposed the war of 1812, and preferred to have the nation humiliated by unre-ented insult from a foreign power rather than see her suffer the losses of an honorable conflict, occupied a position little short of contemptible; but it was not much worse than that of the men who brought on the war and yet deliberately refused to make the preparations necessary to carry it to a successful conclusion. The visionary schemes for defending the country by gunboats, instead of by a fleet of seagoing battle-ships; the refusal to increase the Navy to a proper size; the determination to place reliance upon militia instead of upon regularly trained troops; and the disasters which followed upon each and every one of these determinations should be studied in every school-book in the land so as to enforce in the minds of all our citizens the truth of Washington's adage, that in time of peace it is necessary to prepare for war.

All this applied in 1812; but it applies with tenfold greater force now. Then, as now, it was the Navy upon which the country had to depend in the event of war with a foreign power; and then, as now, one of the chief tasks of a wise and far-seeing statesmanship should have been the upbuilding of a formidable fighting navy. In 1812 untold evils followed from the failure to provide such a fighting navy; for the splendid feats of our few cruisers merely showed what could have been done if we had had a great fleet of battle—ships. But ships, guns, and men were much more easily provided in time of emergency at the beginning of this century than at the end. It takes months to build guns and ships now, where it then took days, or at the most, weeks; and it takes far longer now to train men to the management of the vast and complicated engines with which war is waged. Therefore preparation is much more difficult, and requires a much longer time; and yet wars are so much quicker, they last so comparatively short a period, and can be begun so instantaneously that there is very much less time than formerly in which to make preparations.

No battle-ship can be built inside of two years under no matter what stress of circumstances, for we have not in this country the plant to enable us to work faster. Cruisers would take almost as long. Even torpedo boats, the smallest of all, could not be put in first-class form under ninety days. Guns available for use against a hostile invader would require two or three months; and in the case of the larger guns, the only ones really available for the actual shock of battle, could not be made under eight months. Rifles and military munitions of every kind would require a corresponding length of time for preparation; in most cases we should have to build, not merely the weapons we need, but the plant with which to make them in any large quantity. Even if the enemy did not interfere with our efforts, which they undoubtedly would, it would, therefore, take from three to six months after the outbreak of a war, for which we were unprepared, before we could in the slightest degree remedy our unreadiness. During this six months it would be impossible to overestimate the damage that could be done by a resolute and powerful antagonist. Even at the end of that time we would only be beginning to prepare to parry his attack, for it would be two years before we could attempt to return it. Since the change in military conditions in modern times there has never been an instance in which a war between any two nations has lasted more than about two years. In most recent wars the operations of the first ninety days have decided the result of the conflict. All that followed has been a mere vain effort to strive against the stars in their courses by doing at the twelfth hour what it was useless to do after the eleventh.

We must therefore make up our minds once for all to the fact that it is too late to make ready for war when the fight has once begun. The preparation must come before that. In the case of the Civil War none of these conditions applied. In 1861 we had a good fleet, and the Southern Confederacy had not a ship. We were able to blockade the Southern ports at once, and we could improvise engines of war more than sufficient to put against those of an enemy who also had to improvise them, and who labored under even more serious disadvantages. The *Monitor* was got ready in the nick of time to meet the *Merrimac*, because the Confederates had to plan and build the latter while we were planning and building the former; but if ever we have to go to war with a modern military power we shall find its Merrimacs already built, and it will then be altogether too late to try to build Monitors to meet them.

If this point needs any emphasis surely the history of the war of 1812 applies to it. For twelve years before that war broke out even the blindest could see that we were almost certain to be drawn into hostilities with one or the other of the pair of combatants whose battle royal ended at Waterloo. Yet we made not the slightest preparation for war. The authorities at Washington contented themselves with trying to build a flotilla of gunboats which could defend our own harbors without making it necessary to take the offensive ourselves. We already possessed a dozen first-class cruisers, but not a battle-ship of any kind. With almost incredible folly the very Congress that declared war voted down the bill to increase the Navy by twenty battle-ships; though it was probably too late then, anyhow, for even under the simpler conditions of that day such a fleet could not have been built and put into first-class order in less than a couple of years. Bitterly did the nation pay for its want of foresight and forethought. Our cruisers won a number of striking victories, heartening and giving hope to the nation in the face of disaster; but they were powerless to do material harm to the gigantic naval strength of Great Britain. Efforts were made to increase our little Navy, but in the face of a hostile enemy already possessing command of the seas this was impossible. Two or three small cruisers were built; but practically almost all the fighting on the ocean was done by the handful of frigates and sloops which we possessed when the war broke out. Not a battleship was able to put to sea until after peace was restored. Meanwhile our coast was blockaded from one end to the other and was harried at will by the hostile squadrons. Our capital city was burned, and the ceaseless pressure of the block ade produced such suffering and irritation as nearly to bring about a civil war among ourselves. If in the first decade of the present century the American people and their rulers had possessed the wisdom to provide an efficient fleet of powerful battleships there would probably have been no war of 1812; and even if war had come, the immense loss to, and destruction of, trade and commerce by the blockade would have been prevented. Merely from the monetary standpoint the saving would have been incalculable; and yet this would have been the smallest part of the gain.

It can therefore be taken for granted that there must be adequate preparation for conflict, if conflict is not to mean disaster. Furthermore, this preparation must take the shape of an efficient fighting navy. We have no foe able to conquer or over-run our territory. Our small army should always be kept in first-class condition, and every attention should be paid to the National Guard; but neither on the North nor the South have we neighbors capable of menacing us with invasion or long resisting a serious effort on our part to invade them. The enemies we may have to face will come from over sea; they may come from Europe, or they may come from Asia. Events move fast in the West; but this generation has been forced to see that they move even faster in the oldest East. Our interests are as great in the Pacific as in the Atlantic, in the Hawaiian Islands as in the West Indies. Merely for the protection of our own shores we need a great navy; and what is more, we need it to protect our interests in the islands from which it is possible to command our shores and to protect our commerce on the high seas.

In building this navy, we must remember two things: First, that our ships and guns should be the very best of their kind; and second, that no matter how good they are, they will be useless unless the man in the conning tower and the man behind the guns are also the best of their kind. It is mere folly to send men to perish because they have arms with which they cannot win. With poor ships, were an Admiral Nelson and Farragut rolled in one, he might be beaten by any first-class fleet; and he surely would be beaten if his opponents were in any degree his equals in skill and courage; but without this skill and courage no perfection of material can avail, and with them very grave shortcomings in equipment may be overcome. The men who command our ships must have as perfect weapons ready to their hands as can be found in the civilized world, and they must be trained to the highest point in using them. They must have skill in handling the ships, skill in tactics, skill in strategy, for ignorant courage can not avail; but without courage neither will skill avail. They must have in them the dogged ability to bear punishment, the power and desire to inflict it, the daring, the resolution, the willingness to take risks and incur responsibility which have been possessed by the great captains of all ages, and without which no man can ever hope to stand in the front rank of fighting men.

Tame submission to foreign aggression of any kind is a mean and unworthy thing; but it is even meaner and more unworthy to bluster first, and then either submit or else refuse to make those preparations which can alone obviate the necessity for submission. I believe with all my heart in the Monroe Doctrine, and, I believe also that the great mass of the American people are loyal to it; but it is worse than idle to announce our adherence to this doctrine and yet to decline to take measures to show that ours is not mere lip loyalty. We had far better submit to interference by foreign powers with the affairs of this continent than to announce that we will not tolerate such interference, and yet refuse to make ready the means by which alone we can prevent it. In public as in private life, a bold front tends to insure peace and not strife. If we possess a formidable navy, small is the chance indeed that we shall ever be dragged into a war to uphold the Monroe Doctrine. If we do not possess such a navy, war may be forced on us at any time.

It is certain, then, that we need a first-class navy. It is equally certain that this should not be merely a navy for defense. Our chief harbors should, of course, be fortified and put in condition to resist the attack of an enemy's fleet; and one of our prime needs is an ample force of torpedo boats to use primarily for coast defense. But in war the mere defensive never pays, and can never result in anything but disaster. It is not enough to parry a blow. The surest way to prevent its repetition is to return it. No master of the prize ring ever fought his way to supremacy by mere dexterity in avoiding punishment. He had to win by inflicting punishment. If the enemy is given the choice of time and place to attack, sooner or later he will do irreparable damage, and if he is at any point beaten back, why, after all, it is merely a repulse, and there are no means of following it up and making it a rout. We cannot rely upon coast protection alone. Forts and heavy land guns and torpedo boats are indispensable, and the last, on occasion, may be used for offensive purposes also. But in the present state of naval and military knowledge we must rely mainly, as all great nations always have relied, on the battle-ship, the fighting ship of the line. Gunboats and light cruisers serve an excellent purpose, and we could not do without them. In time of peace they are the police of the seas; in time of war they would do some harrying of commerce, and a great deal of scouting and skirmishing; but our main reliance must be on the great armored battle-ships with their heavy guns and shot-proof vitals. In the last resort we most trust to the ships whose business it is to fight and not to run, and who can themselves go to sea and strike at the enemy when they choose, instead of waiting peacefully to receive his blow when and where he deems it best to deliver it. If in the event of war our fleet of battle-ships can destroy the hostile fleet, then our coasts are safe from the menace of serious attack; even a fight that ruined our fleet would probably so shatter the hostile fleet as to do away with all chance of invasion; but if we have no fleet wherewith to meet the enemy on the high seas, or to anticipate his stroke by our own, then every city within reach of the tides must spend men and money in preparation for an attack that may not come, but which would cause crushing and irredeemable disaster if it did come.

Still more is it necessary to have a fleet of great battle-ships if we intend to live up to the Monroe Doctrine, and to insist upon its observance in the two Americas and the islands on either side of them. If a foreign power, whether in Europe or Asia, should determine to assert its position in those lands wherein we feel that our influence should be supreme, there is but one way in which we can effectively interfere. Diplomacy is utterly useless where there is no force behind it; the diplomat is the servant, not the master, of the soldier. The prosperity of peace, commercial and material prosperity, gives no weight whatever when the clash of arms comes. Even great naked strength is useless if there is no immediate means through which that strength can manifest itself. If we mean to protect the people of the lands who look to us for protection from tyranny and aggression; if we mean to uphold our interests in the teeth of the formidable Old World powers, we can only do it by being ready at any time, if the provocation, is sufficient, to meet them on the seas, where the battle for supremacy must be fought. Unless we are prepared so to meet them, let us abandon all talk of devotion to the Monroe Doctrine or to the honor of the American name.

This nation cannot stand still if it is to retain its self-respect, and to keep undimmed the honorable traditions inherited from the men who with the sword founded it and by the sword preserved it. We ask that the work of upbuilding the Navy, and of putting the United States where it should be put among maritime powers, go forward without a break. We ask this not in the interest of war, but in the interest of peace. No nation should ever wage war wantonly, but no nation should ever avoid it at the cost of the loss of national honor. A nation should never fight unless forced to; but it should always be ready to fight. The mere fact that it is ready will generally spare it the necessity of fighting. If this country now had a fleet of twenty battle-ships their existence would make it all the more likely that we should not have war. It is very important that we should, as a race, keep the virile fighting qualities and should be ready to use them at need; but it is not at all important to use them unless there is need. One of the surest ways to attain these qualities is to keep our Navy in first-class trim. There never is, and never has been, on our part a desire to use a weapon because of it's being well-tempered. There is not the least danger that the possession of a good navy will render this country overbearing toward its neighbors. The direct contrary is the truth.

An unmanly desire to avoid a quarrel is often the surest way to precipitate one; and utter unreadiness to fight is even surer. If at the time of our trouble with Chili, six years ago, we had not already possessed the nucleus of the new navy we should almost certainly have been forced into fighting, and even as it was trouble was only averted because of the resolute stand then taken by the President and by the officers of the Navy who were on the spot. If at that time the Chilians had been able to get ready the battle-ship which was building for them, a war would almost certainly have followed, for we had no battle-ship to put against it.

If in the future we have war, it will almost certainly come because of some action, or lack of action, on our part in the way of refusing to accept responsibilities at the proper time, or failing to prepare for war when war does not threaten. An ignoble peace is even worse than an unsuccessful war; but an unsuccessful war would leave behind it a legacy of bitter memories which would hurt our national development for a generation to come. It is true that no nation could actually conquer us, owing to our isolated position; but we would be seriously harmed, even materially, by disasters that stopped far short of conquest; and in these matters, which are far more important than things material, we could readily be damaged beyond repair. No material loss can begin to compensate for the loss of national self-respect. The damage to our commercial interests by the destruction of one of our coast cities would be as nothing compared to the humiliation which would be felt by every American worthy of the name if we had to submit to such an injury without amply avenging it. It has been finely said that "a gentleman is one who is willing to lay down his life for little things "; that is for those things which seem little to the man who cares only whether shares rise or fall in value, and to the timid *doctrinaire* who preaches timid peace from his cloistered study.

Much of that which is best and highest in national character is made up of glorious memories and traditions. The fight well fought, the life honorably lived, the death bravely met—those count for more in building a high and fine type of temper in a nation than any possible success in the stock market, than any possible prosperity in commerce or manufactures. A rich banker may be a valuable and useful citizen, but not a thousand rich bankers can leave to the country such a heritage as Farragut left, when, lashed in the rigging of the *Hartford*, he forged past the forts and over the unseen death below, to try his wooden stem against the ironclad hull of the great Confederate ram. The people of some given section of our country may be better off because a shrewd and wealthy man has built up therein a great manufacturing business, or has extended a line of railroad past its doors; but the whole nation is better, the whole nation is braver, because Cushing pushed his little torpedo-boat through the darkness to sink beside the sinking *Albemarle* .

Every feat of heroism makes us forever indebted to the man who performed it. All daring and courage, all iron endurance of misfortune, all devotion to the ideal of honor and the glory of the flag, make for a finer and nobler type of manhood. It is not only those who do and dare and endure that are benefited; but also the countless thousands who are not themselves called upon to face the peril, to show the strength, or to win the reward. All of us lift our heads higher because those of our countrymen whose trade it is to meet danger have met it well and bravely. All of us are poorer for every base or ignoble deed done by an American, for every instance of sefishness or weakness or folly on the part of the people as a whole. We are all worse off when any of us fails at any point in his duty toward the State in time of peace, or his duty toward the State in time of war. It ever we had to meet defeat at the hands of a foreign foe, or had to submit tamely to wrong or insult, every man among us worthy of the name of American would feel dishonored and debased. On the other hand, the memory of every triumph won by Americans, by just so much helps to make each American nobler and better. Every man among us is more fit to meet the duties and responsibilities of citizenship because of the perils over which, in the past, the nation has triumphed; because of the blood and sweat and tears, the labor and the anguish, through which, in the days that have gone, our forefathers moved on to triumph. There are higher things in this life than the soft and easy enjoyment of material comfort. It is through strife, or the readiness for strife, that a nation must win greatness. We ask for a great navy, partly because we think that the possession of such a navy is the surest guaranty of peace, and partly because we feel that no national life is worth having if the nation is not willing, when the need shall arise, to stake everything on the supreme arbitrament of war, and to pour out its blood, its treasure, and its tears like water, rather than submit to the loss of honor and renown.

In closing, let me repeat that we ask for a great navy, we ask for an armament fit for the nation's needs, not primarily to fight, but to avert fighting. Preparedness deters the foe, and maintains right by the show of ready might without the use of violence. Peace, like freedom, is not a gift that tarries long in the hands of cowards, or of those too feeble or too short-sighted to deserve it; and we ask to be given the means to insure that honorable peace which alone is worth having.

XIII
NATIONAL LIFE AND CHARACTER[20]

IN *National Life and Character; a Forecast*, Mr. Charles H. Pearson, late fellow of Oriel College, Oxford, and sometime Minister of Education in Victoria, has produced one of the most notable books of the end of the century. Mr. Pearson is not always quite so careful as he might be about his facts; many of the conclusions he draws from them seem somewhat strained; and with much of his forecast most of us would radically disagree. Nevertheless, no one can read this book without feeling his thinking powers greatly stimulated; without being forced to ponder problems of which he was previously wholly ignorant, or which he but half understood; and without realizing that he is dealing with the work of a man of lofty thought and of deep and philosophic insight into the world-forces of the present.

Mr. Pearson belongs to the melancholy or pessimist school, which has become so prominent in

[20] *The Sewanee Review*, August, 1894.

England during the last two or three decades, and which has been represented there for half a century. In fact, the note of despondency seems to be the dominant note among Englishmen of high cultivation at the present time. It is as marked among their statesmen and publicists as among their men of letters, Mr. Balfour being particularly happy in his capacity to express in good English, and with much genuine elevation of thought, a profound disbelief in nineteenth century progress, and an equally profound distrust of the future toward which we are all traveling.

For much of this pessimism and for many of the prophecies which it evokes, there is no excuse whatsoever. There may possibly be good foundation for the pessimism as to the future shown by men like Mr. Pearson; but hitherto the writers of the stamp of the late "Cassandra" Greg who have been pessimistic about the present, have merely betrayed their own weakness or their own incapacity to judge contemporary persons and events. The weakling, the man who cannot struggle with his fellow-men and with the conditions that surround him, is very apt to think these men and these conditions bad; and if he has the gift of writing, he puts these thoughts down at some length on paper. Very strong men, moreover, if of morose and dyspeptic temper, are apt to rail at the present, and to praise the past simply because they do not live in it. To any man who will consider the subject from a scientific point of view, with a desire to get at the truth, it is needless to insist on the fact that at no period of the world's history has there been so much happiness generally diffused among mankind as now.

At no period of the world's history has life been so full of interest and of possibilities of excitement and enjoyment as for us who live in the latter half of the nineteenth century. This is not only true as far as the working classes are concerned, but it is especially true as regards the men of means, and above all of those men of means who also possess brains and ambition. Never before in the world's history have there been such opportunities thrown open to men, in the way of building new commonwealths, exploring new countries, conquering kingdoms, and trying to adapt the governmental policy of old nations to new and strange conditions. The half-century which is now closing, has held out to the people who have dwelt therein, some of the great prizes of history. Abraham Lincoln and Prince Bismarck have taken their places among the world's worthies. Mighty masters of war have arisen in America, in Germany, in Russia; Lee and Grant, Jackson and Farragut, Moltke, Skobeleff, and the Red Prince. The work of the chiefs of mechanical and electrical invention has never been equalled before, save perhaps by what was done in the first half of this same century. Never before have there been so many opportunities for commonwealth builders; new States have been pitched on the banks of the Saskatchewan, the Columbia, the Missouri, and the Colorado, on the seacoast of Australia, and in the interior of Central Africa. Vast regions have been won by the sword. Burmah and Turkestan, Egypt and Matabeleland, have rewarded the prowess of English and Russian conquerors, exactly as, when the glory of Rome was at its height, remote Mediterranean provinces furnished triumphs to the great military leaders of the Eternal City. English administrators govern subject empires larger than those conquered by Alexander. In letters no name has been produced that will stand with the first half-dozen of all literature, but there have been very many borne by men whose effect upon the literatures of their own countries has been profound, and whose works will last as long as the works of any men written in the same tongues. In science even more has been done; Darwin has fairly revolutionized thought; and many others stand but a step below him.

All this means only that the opportunities have been exceptionally great for the men of exceptionally great powers; but they have also been great for the men of ordinary powers. The workingman is, on the whole, better fed, better clothed, better housed, and provided with greater opportunities for pleasure and for mental and spiritual improvement than ever before. The man with ability enough to become a lawmaker has the fearful joy of grappling with problems as important as any the administrators and legislators of the past had to face. The ordinary man of adventurous tastes and a desire to get all out of life that can be gotten, is beyond measure better off than were his forefathers of one, two, or three centuries back. He can travel round the world; he can dwell in any country he wishes; he can explore strange regions; he can spend years by himself in the wilderness, hunting great game; he can take part in a campaign here and there. Withersoever his tastes lead him, he finds that he has far greater capacity conferred upon him by the conditions of nineteenth-century civilization to do something of note than ever a man of his kind had before. If he is observant, he notes all around him the play of vaster forces than have ever before been exerted, working, half blindly, half under control, to bring about immeasurable results. He sees going on before his eyes a great transfer of population and civilization, which is making America north of the Rio Grande, and Australia, English-speaking continents; which has filled Central and South America with States of uncertain possibilities; which is creating for the first time a huge Aryan nation across the entire north of Asia, and which is working changes in Africa infinitely surpassing in importance all those that have ever taken place there since the days when the Bantu peoples first built their beehive huts on the banks of the Congo and the Zambezi. Our century has teemed with life and interest.

Yet this is the very century at which Carlyle railed: and it is strange to think that he could speak of the men at that very moment engaged in doing such deeds, as belonging to a worn-out age. His vision was clear to see the importance and the true bearing of England's civil war of the seventeenth century, and yet he remained mole-blind to the vaster and more important civil war waged before his very eyes in nineteenth-century America. The heroism of Naseby and Worcester and Minden hid from him the heroism of Balaklava and Inker man, of Lucknow and Delhi. He could appreciate at their worth the campaigns of the Seven Year's War, and yet could hardly understand those waged between the armies of the Potomac and of Northern Virginia. He was fairly inspired by the fury and agony and terror of the struggle at Kunnersdorf; and yet could not appreciate the immensely greater importance of the death-wrestle that reeled round Gettysburg. His eyes were so dazzled by the great dramas of the past that he could not see the even greater drama of the present. It is but the bare truth to say that never have the rewards been greater, never has there been more chance for doing work of great and lasting value, than this last half of the nineteenth century has offered alike to statesman and soldier, to explorer and commonwealth-builder, to the captain of industry, to the man of letters, and to the man of science. Never has life been more interesting to each to take part in. Never has there been a greater output of good work done both by the few and by the many.

Nevertheless, signs do not fail that we are on the eve of great changes, and that in the next century we shall see the conditions of our lives, national and individual, modified after a sweeping and radical fashion. Many of the forces that make for national greatness and for individual happiness in the nineteenth century will be absent entirely, or will act with greatly diminished strength, in the twentieth. Many of the forces that now make for evil will by that time have gained greatly in volume and power. It is foolish to look at the future with blind and careless optimism; quite as foolish as to gaze at it only through the dun-colored mists that surround the preachers of pessimism. It is always best to look facts squarely in the face, without blinking them, and to remember that, as has been well said, in the long run even the most uncomfortable truth is a safer companion than the pleasantest falsehood.

Whether the future holds good or evil for us does not, it is true, alter our duty in the present. We must stand up valiantly in the fight for righteousness and wisdom as we see them, and must let the event turn out as it may. Nevertheless, even though there is little use in pondering over the future, most men of intelligence do ponder over it at times, and if we think of it at all, it is well to think clearly.

Mr. Pearson writes a forecast of what he believes probably will, or at least very possibly may, happen in the development of national life and character during the era upon which we are now entering. He is a man who has had exceptional advantages for his work; he has studied deeply and travelled widely; he has been a diligent reader of books and a keen observer of men. To a careful training in one of the oldest of the world' s universities he has added long experience as an executive officer in one of the world' s youngest commonwealths. He writes with power and charm. His book is interesting in manner, and is still more interesting in matter, for he has thought deeply and faithfully over subjects of immense importance to the future of all the human race. He possesses a mind of marked originality. Moreover, he always faithfully tries to see facts as they actually are. He is, it seems to me, unduly pessimistic; but he is not pessimistic of set purpose, nor does he adopt pessimism as a cult. He tries hard, and often successfully, to make himself see and to make himself state forces that are working for good. We may or may not differ from him, but it behooves us, if we do, to state our positions guardedly; for we are dealing with a man who has displayed much research in getting at his facts and much honesty in arriving at his rather melancholy conclusions.

The introduction to Mr. Pearson' s book is as readable as the chapters that follow, and may best be considered in connection with the first of these chapters, which is entitled "The Unchangeable Limits of the Higher Races." I am almost tempted to call this the most interesting of the six chapters of the book, and yet one can hardly do so when absorbed in reading any one of the other five. Mr. Pearson sees what ought to be evident to every one, but apparently is not, that what he calls the "higher races," that is, the races that for the last twenty-five hundred years (but, it must be remembered, only during the last twenty-five hundred years) have led the world, can prosper only under conditions of soil and climate analogous to those obtaining in their old European homes. Speaking roughly, this means that they can prosper only in the temperate zones, north and south.

Four hundred years ago the temperate zones, were very thinly peopled indeed, while the tropical and sub-tropical regions were already densely populated. The great feature in the world's history for the last four centuries has been the peopling of these vast, scantily inhabited regions by men of the European stocks; notably by men speaking English, but also by men speaking Russian and Spanish. During the same centuries these European peoples have for the first time acquired an enormous ascendency over all other races. Once before, during the days of the Greco-Macedonian and Roman supremacy, European peoples possessed a somewhat similar supremacy; but it was not nearly as great, for at that period America and Australia were unknown, Africa south of the Sahara was absolutely unaffected by either Roman or Greek, and all but an insignificant portion of Asia was not only without the pale of European influence, but held within itself immense powers of menace to Europe, and contained old and peculiar civilizations, still flourishing in their prime. All this has now been changed. Great English-speaking nations have sprung up in America north of the Rio Grande, and are springing up in Australia. The Russians, by a movement which has not yet fired the popular imagination, but which all thinking men recognize as of incalculable importance, are building a vast State in northern Asia, stretching from the Yellow Sea to the Ural Mountains. Tropical America is parcelled out among States partly of European blood, and mainly European in thought, speech and religion; while tropical Asia and Africa have been divided among European powers, and are held in more or less complete subjection by their military and civil agents. It is no wonder that men who are content to look at things superficially, and who think that the tendencies that have triumphed durthe last two centuries are as immutable in their workings as great natural laws, should speak as if it were a mere question of time when the civilized peoples should overrun and occupy the entire world, exactly as they now do Europe and North America.

Mr. Pearson points out with great clearness the groundlessness of this belief. He deserves especial praise for discriminating between the importance of ethnic, and of merely political, conquests. The conquest by one country of another populous country always attracts great attention at the time, and has wide momentary effects; but it is of insignificant importance when compared with the kind of armed settlement which causes new nations of an old stock to spring up in new countries. The campaigns carried on by the lieutenants of Justinian against Goth and Vandal, Bulgarian and Persian, seemed in the eyes of civilized Europe at that time of incalculably greater moment than the squalid warfare being waged in England between the descendants of Low Dutch sea-thieves and the aboriginal British. Yet, in reality, it was of hardly any consequence in history whether Belisarius did or did not succeed in overthrowing the Ostrogoth merely to make room for the Lombard, or whether the Vandal did or did not succumb to the Roman instead of succumbing to the Saracen a couple of centuries later; while it was of the most vital consequence to the whole future of the world that the English should supplant the Welsh as masters of Britain.

Again, in our own day, the histories written of Great Britain during the last century teem with her dealings with India, while Australia plays a very insignificant part indeed; yet, from the standpoint of the ages, the peopling of the great island-continent with men of the English stock is a thousand fold more important than the holding Hindoostan for a few centuries.

Mr. Pearson understands and brings out clearly that in the long run a conquest must fail when it means merely the erection of an insignificant governing caste. He shows clearly that the men of our stock do not prosper in tropical countries. In the New World they leave a thin strain of their blood among and impose their laws, language, and forms of government on the aboriginal races, which then develop on new and dimly drawn lines. In the Old World they fail to do even this. In Asia they may leave a few tens of thousands or possibly hundreds of thousands of Eurasians to form an additional caste in a caste-ridden community. In tropical Africa they may leave here and there a mulatto tribe like the Griquas. But it certainly has not yet been proved that the European can live and propagate permanently in the hot regions of India and Africa, and Mr. Pearson is right in anticipating for the whites who have conquered these tropical and sub-tropical regions of the Old World, the same fate which befell the Greek kingdoms in Bactria and the Chersonese. The Greek rulers of Bactria were untimately absorbed and vanished, as probably the English rulers of India will some day in the future—for the good of mankind, we sincerely hope and believe the very remote future—themselves be absorbed and vanish. In Africa south of the Zambezi (and possibly here and there on high plateaus north of it,) there may remain white States, although even these States will surely contain a large colored population, always threatening to swamp the whites; but in tropical Africa generally, it does not seem possible that any white State can ever be built up. Doubtless for many centuries European adventurers and Arab raiders will rule over huge territories in the country south of the Soudan and north of the Tropic of Capricorn, and the whole structure, not only social, but physical, of the negro and the negroid peoples will be profoundly changed by their influence and by the influence of the half-caste descendants of these European and Asiatic soldiers of fortune and industry. But it is hardly possible to conceive that the peoples of Africa, however ultimately changed, will be anything but negroid in type of body and mind. It is probable that the change will be in the direction of turning them into tribes like those of the Soudan, with a similar religion and morality. It is almost impossible that they will not in the end succeed in throwing off the yoke of the European outsiders, though this end may be, and we hope will be, many centuries distant. In America, most of the West Indies are becoming negro islands. The Spaniard, however, because of the ease with which he drops to a lower ethnic level, exerts a much more permanent influence than the Englishman upon tropic aboriginal races; and the tropical lands which the Spaniards and Portuguese once held, now contain, and always will contain, races which, though different from the Aryan of the temperate zone, yet bridge the gulf between him and the black, red, and yellow peoples who have dwelt from time immemorial on both sides of the equator.

Taking all this into consideration, therefore, it is most likely that a portion of Mr. Pearson's forecast, as regards the people of the tropic zones, will be justified by events. It is impossible for the dominant races of the temperate zones ever bodily to displace the peoples of the tropics. It is highly probable that these people will cast off the yoke of their European conquerors sooner or later, and will become independent nations once more; though it is also possible that the modern conditions of easy travel may permit the permanent rule in the tropics of a vigorous northern race, renewed by a complete change every generation.

Mr. Pearson's further proposition is that these black, red, and yellow nations, when thus freed, will threaten the dominance of the higher peoples, possibly by military, certainly by industrial, rivalry, and that the mere knowledge of the equality of these stocks will cow and dispirit the higher races.

This part of his argument is open to very serious objections. In the first place, Mr. Pearson entirely fails to take into account the difference in character among the nationalities produced in the tropics as the result of European conquest. In Asia, doubtless, the old races now submerged by European predominance will reappear, profoundly changed in themselves and in their relations to one another, but as un-European as ever, and not appreciably affected by any intermixture of European blood. In Africa, the native States will probably range somewhere between the Portuguese half-caste and quarter-caste communities now existing on certain of the tropic coasts, and pastoral or agricultural communities, with a Mohammedan religious cult and Asiatic type of government, produced by the infusion of a conquering Semitic or hamitic caste on a conquered negro people. There may be a dominant caste of European blood in some of these States, but that is all. In tropical America, the change has already taken place. The States that there exist will not materially alter their form. It is possible that here and there populations of Chinese, pure or half-caste, or even of coolies, may spring up; but taken as a whole, these States will be in the future what they are now, that is, they will be by blood partly white, but chiefly Indian or negro, with their language, law, religion, literature, and governmental system approaching those of Europe and North America.

Suppose that what Mr. Pearson foresees comes to pass, and that the black and yellow races of the world attain the same independence already achieved by the mongrel reddish race. Mr. Pearson thinks that this will expose us to two dangers. The first is that of actual physical distress caused by the competition of the teeming myriads of the tropics, or perhaps by their invasion of the Temperate zones. Mr. Pearson himself does not feel any very great anxiety about this invasion assuming a military type, and I think that even the fear he does express is unwarranted by the facts. He is immensely impressed by the teeming population of China. He thinks that the Chinese will some day constitute the dominant portion of the population, both politically and numerically, in the East Indies, New Guinea, and Farther India. In this he is probably quite right; but such a change would merely mean the destruction or submersion of Malay, Dyak, and Papuan and would be of hardly any real consequence to the white man. He further thinks that the Chinese may jeopardize Russia in Asia. Here I am inclined to think he is wrong. As far as it is possible to judge in the absence of statistics, the Chinaman at present is not increasing relatively as fast as the Slav and the Anglo-Saxon. Half a century or so more will put both of them within measurable distance of equality with him, even in point of numbers. The movement of population in China is toward the south, not the north; the menace is real for the English and French protectorates in the south; in the north the difficulty hitherto has been to keep Russian settlers from crossing the Chinese frontier. When the great Trans-Siberian railroad is built, and when a few millions more of Russian settlers stretch from the Volga to the valley of the Amoor, the danger of a military advance by the Chinese against Asiatic Russia will be entirely over, even granting that it now exists. The Chinaman never has been, and probably never will be, such a fighter as Turk or Tartar, and he would have to possess an absolutely overwhelming superiority of numbers to give him a chance in a war of aggression against a powerful military race. As yet, he has made no advance whatever towards developing an army capable of offensive work against European foes. In China there are no roads; the military profession is looked down on; Chinese troops would be formidable only under a European leader, and a European leader would be employed only from dire necessity; that is to repel, not to undertake an invasion. Moreover, China is merely an aggregate of provinces with a central knot at Pekin; and Pekin could be taken at any time by a small trained army. China will not menace Siberia until after undergoing some stupendous and undreamed-of internal revolution. It is scarcely within the bounds of possibility to conceive of the Chinaman expelling the European settler from lands in which that settler represents the bulk of a fairly thick population, not merely a small intrusive caste. It is, of course, always possible that in the far-distant future (though there is no sign of it now) China may travel on the path of Japan, may change her policy, may develop fleets and armies; but if she does do this, there is no reason why this fact should stunt and dwarf the people of the higher races. In Elizabeth's day the Turkish fleets and armies stood towards those of European powers in a far higher position than those of China, or of the tropics generally, can ever hope to stand in relation to the peoples of the Temperate zones; and yet this did not hinder the Elizabethan Age from being one of great note both in the field of thought and in the field of action.

The anticipation of what might happen if India became solidified seems even more ill-founded. Here Mr. Pearson's position is that the very continuance of European rule, doing away with war and famine, produces an increase of population and a solidity of the country, which will enable the people to overthrow that European rule. He assumes that the solidified and populous country will continue to remain such after the overthrow of the Europeans, and will be capable of deeds of aggression; but, of course, such an assumption is contrary to all probabilities. Once the European rule was removed, famine and internecine war would again become chronic, and India would sink back to her former place. Moreover, the long continuance of British rule undoubtedly weakens the war-like fibre of the natives, and makes the usurer rather than the soldier the dominant type.

The danger to which Mr. Pearson alludes, that even the negro peoples may in time become vast military powers, constituting a menace to Europe, really seems to belong to a period so remote that every condition will have changed to a degree rendering it impossible for us to make any estimate in reference thereto. By that time the descendant of the negro may be as intellectual as the Athenian. Even prophecy must not look too many thousand years ahead. It is perfectly possible that European settlements in Africa will be swamped some time by the rising of natives who outnumber them a hundred or a thousand to one, but it is not possible that the negroes will form a military menace to the people of the north, at least for a space of time longer than that which now separates us from the men of the River Drift. The negroid peoples, the so-called "hamatic," and bastard Semitic, races of eastern middle Africa are formidable fighters; but their strength is not fit for any such herculean tasks.

There is much more reason to fear the industrial competition of these races; but even this will be less formidable as the power of the State increases and especially as the democratic idea obtains more and more currency. The Russians are not democratic at all, but the State is very powerful with them; and therefore they keep the Chinese out of their Siberian provinces, which are being rapidly filled up with a population mainly Slav, the remainder of which is being Slavicized. From the United States and Australia the Chinaman is kept out because the democracy, with much clearness of vision, has seen that his presence is ruinous to the white race.

Nineteenth century democracy needs no more complete vindication for its existence than the fact that it has kept for the white race the best portions of the new worlds' surface, temperate America and Australia. Had these regions been under aristocratic governments, Chinese immigration would have been encouraged precisely as the slave trade is encouraged of necessity by any slave-holding oligarchy, and the result would in a few generations have been even more fatal to the white race; but the democracy, with the clear instinct of race selfishness, saw the race foe, and kept out the dangerous alien. The presence of the negro in our Southern States is a legacy from the time when we were ruled by a trans-oceanic aristocracy. The whole civilization of the future owes a debt of gratitude greater than can be expressed in words to that democratic policy which has kept the temperate zones of the new and the newest worlds a heritage for the white people.

As for the industrial competition, the Chinaman and the Hindoo may drive certain kinds of white traders from the tropics; but more than this they cannot do. They can never change the status of the white laborer in his own home, for the latter can always protect himself, and as soon as he is seriously menaced, always will protect himself, by protective tariffs and stringent immigration laws.

Mr. Pearson fears that when once the tropic races are independent, the white peoples will be humiliated and will lose heart: but this does not seem inevitable, and indeed seems very improbable. If the Englishman should lose his control over South Africa and India, it might indeed be a serious blow to the Englishman of Britain; though it may be well to remember that the generation of Englishmen which grew up immediately after. England had lost America, accomplished feats in arms, letters, and science such as, on the whole, no other English generation ever accomplished. Even granting that Britain were to suffer as Mr. Pearson thinks she would, the enormous majority of the English-speaking peoples, those whose homes are in America and Australia, would be absolutely unaffected; and Continental Europe would be little more affected than it was when the Portuguese and Dutch successively saw their African and Indian empires diminish. France has not been affected by the expulsion of the French from Hayti; nor have the freed negroes of Hayti been capable of the smallest aggressive movement. No American or Australian cares in the least that the tan-colored peoples of Brazil and Ecuador now live under governments of their own instead of being ruled by viceroys from Portugal and Spain;

and it is difficult to see why they should be materially affected by a similar change happening in regard to the people along the Ganges or the upper Nile. Even if China does become a military power on the European model, this fact will hardly affect the American and Australian at the end of the twentieth century more than Japan's effort to get admitted to the circle of civilized nations has affected us at the end of the nineteenth.

Finally, it must be borne in mind that if any one of the tropical races ever does reach a pitch of industrial and military prosperity which makes it a menace to European and American countries, it will almost necessarily mean that this nation has itself become civilized in the process; and we shall then simply be dealing with another civilized nation of non-aryan blood, precisely as we now deal with Magyar, Fin, and Basque, without any thought of their being ethnically distinct from Croat, Rouman, or Wend.

In Mr. Pearson's second chapter he deals with the stationary order of society, and strives to show that while we are all tending toward it, some nations, notably France, have practically come to it. He adds that when this stationary state is reached, it will produce general discouragement, and will probably affect the intellectual energy of the people concerned. He further points out that our races now tend to change from faith in private enterprises to faith in State organizations, and that this is likely to diminish the vigorous originality of any race. He even holds that we already see the beginning of a decadence, in the decline of speculative thought, and still more in the way of mechanical inventions @@@fectly true that the *laissez-faire* doctrine of the old school of political economists is receiving, less and less favor; but after all, if we look at events historically, we see that every race, as it has grown to civilized greatness, has used the power of the State more and more. A great State cannot rely on mere unrestricted individualism, any more than it can afford to crush out all individualism. Within limits, the mercilessness of private commercial warfare must be curbed as we have curbed the individual's right of private war proper. It was not until the power of the State had become great in England, and until the lawless individualism of feudal times had vanished, that the English people began that career of greatness which has put them on a level with the Greeks in point of intellectual achievement, and with the Romans in point of that material success which is measured by extension through settlement, by conquest, by triumphant warcraft and statecraft. As for Mr. Pearson's belief that we now see a decline in speculative thought and in mechanical invention, all that can be said is that the facts do not bear him out.

There is one side to this stationary state theory which Mr. Pearson scarcely seems to touch. He points out with emphasis the fact, which most people are prone to deny, that the higher orders of every society tend to die out; that there is a tendency, on the whole, for both lower classes and lower civilizations to increase faster than the higher. Taken in the rough, his position on this point is undoubtedly correct. Progressive societies, and the most progressive portions of society, fail to increase as fast as the others, and often positively decrease. The great commanders, great statesmen, great poets, great men of science of any period taken together do not average as many children who reach years of maturity as a similar number of mechanics, workmen, and farmers, taken at random. Nevertheless, society progresses, the improvement being due mainly to the transmission of acquired characters, a process which in every civilized State operates so strongly as to counterbalance the operation of that baleful law of natural selection which tells against the survival of some of the most desirable classes. Mr. Balfour, by the way, whose forecast for the race is in some respects not unlike Mr. Pearson's, seems inclined to adopt the view that acquired characteristics cannot be inherited; a position which, even though supported by a few eminent names, is hardly worthy serious refutation.

The point I wish to dwell upon here, however, is that it is precisely in those castes which have reached the stationary state, or which are positively diminishing in numbers, that the highest culture and best training, the keenest enjoyment of life, and the greatest power of doing good to the community, are to be found at present. Unquestionably, no community that is actually diminishing in numbers is in a healthy condition: and as the world is now, with huge waste places still to fill up, and with much of the competition between the races reducing itself to the warfare of the cradle, no race has any chance to win a great place unless it consists of good breeders as well as of good fighters. But it may well be that these conditions will change in the future, when the other changes to which Mr. Pearson looks forward with such melancholy, are themselves brought about. A nation sufficiently populous to be able to hold its own against aggression from without, a nation which, while developing the virtues of refinement, culture, and learning, has yet not lost those of courage, bold initiative, and military hardihood, might well play a great part in the world, even though it had come to that stationary state already reached by the dominant castes of thinkers and doers in most of the dominant races.

In Mr. Pearson's third chapter he dwells on some of the dangers of political development, and in especial upon the increase of the town at the expense of the country, and upon the growth of great standing armies. Excessive urban development undoubtedly does constitute a real and great danger. All that can be said about it is that it is quite impossible to prophesy how long this growth will continue. Moreover, some of the evils, as far as they really exist, will cure themselves. If townspeople do, generation by generation, tend to become stunted and weak, then they will die out, and the problem they cause will not be permanent; while on the other hand, if the cities can be made healthy, both physically and morally, the objections to them must largely disappear. As for standing armies, Mr. Pearson here seems to have too much thought of Europe only. In America and Australia there is no danger of the upgrowing of great standing armies: and, as he well shows, the fact that every citizen must undergo military training, is by no means altogether a curse to the nations of Continental Europe.

There is one point, by the way, although a small point, where it may be worth while to correct Mr. Pearson's statement of a fact. In dwelling on what is undoubtedly the truth, that raw militia are utterly incompetent to make head against trained regular forces, he finds it necessary to explain away the defeat at New Orleans. In doing this, he repeats the story as it has been told by British historians from Sir Archibald Alison to Goldwin Smith. I hasten to say that the misstatement is entirely natural on Mr. Pearson's part; he was simply copying, without sufficiently careful investigation, the legend adopted by one side to take the sting out of defeat. The way he puts it is that six thousand British under Pakenham, without artillery, were hurled against strong works defended by twice their numbers, and were beaten, as they would have been beaten had the works been defended by almost any troops in the world. In the first place. Pakenham did not have six thousand men; he had almost ten thousand. In the second place, the Americans, instead of being twice as numerous as the British, were but little more than half as numerous. In the third place, so far from being without artillery, the British were much superior to the Americans in this respect. Finally, they assailed a position very much less strong than that held by Soult when Wellington beat him at Toulouse with the same troops which were defeated by Jackson at New Orleans. The simple truth is that Jackson was a very good general, and that he had under him troops whom he had trained in successive campaigns against Indians and Spaniards, and that on the three occasions when he brought Pakenham to battle—that is, the night attack, the great artillery duel, and the open assault—the English soldiers, though they fought with the utmost gallantry, were fairly and decisively beaten.

This one badly-chosen premise does not, however, upset Mr. Pearson's conclusions. Plenty of instances can be taken from our war of 1812 to show how unable militia are to face trained regulars; and an equally striking example was that afforded at Castlebar, in Ireland, in1798, when a few hundred French regulars attacked with the bayonet and drove in headlong flight from a very strong position, defended by a powerful artillery, five times their number of English, Scotch, and Irish militia.

In Mr. Pearson's fourth chapter he deals, from a very noble standpoint, with some advantages of national feeling. With this chapter and with his praise of patriotism, and particularly of that patriotism which attaches itself to the whole country, and not to any section of it, we can only express our hearty agreement.

In his fifth chapter, on "The Decline of the Family" he sets forth, or seems to set forth, certain propositions with which I must as heartily disagree. He seems to lament the change which is making the irresponsible despot as much of an anomaly in the family as in the State. He seems to think that this will weaken the family. It may do so, in some instances, exactly as the abolition of a despotism may produce anarchy; but the movement is essentially as good in one case as in the other. To all who have known really happy family lives, that is to all who have known or have witnessed the greatest happiness which there can be on this earth, it is hardly necessary to say that the highest ideal of the family is attainable only where the father and mother stand to each other as lovers and friends, with equal rights. In these homes the children are bound to father and mother by ties of love, respect, and obedience, which are simply strengthened by the fact that they are treated as reasonable beings with rights of their own, and that the rule of the household is changed to suit the changing years, as childhood passes into manhood and womanhood. In such a home the family is not weakened; it is strengthened. This is no unattainable ideal. Every one knows hundreds of homes where it is more or less perfectly realized, and it is an ideal incomparably higher than the ideal of the beneficent autocrat which it has so largely supplanted.

The final chapter of Mr. Pearson's book is entitled "The Decay of Character." He believes that our world is becoming a world with less adventure and energy, less brightness and hope. He believes that all the great books have been written, all the great discoveries made, all the great deeds done. He thinks that the adoption of State socialism in some form will crush out individual merit and the higher kinds of individual happiness. Of course, as to this, all that can be said is that men differ as to what will be the effect of the forces whose working he portrays, and that most of us who live in the American democracy do not agree with him. It is to the last degree improbable that State socialism will ever be adopted in its extreme form, save in a few places. It exists, of course, to a certain extent wherever a police force and a fire department exist; and the sphere of the State's action may be vastly increased without in any way diminishing the happiness of either the many or the few. It is even conceivable that a combination of legislative enactments and natural forces may greatly reduce the inequalities of wealth without in any way diminishing the real power of enjoyment or power for good work of what are now the favored classes. In our own country the best work has always been produced by men who lived in castes or social circles where the standard of essential comfort was high; that is, where men were well clothed, well fed, well housed, and had plenty of books and the opportunity of using them; but where there was small room for extravagant luxury. We think that Mr. Pearson' s fundamental error here is his belief that the raising of the mass necessarily means the lowering of the standard of life for the fortunate few. Those of us who now live in communities where the native American element is largest and where there is least inequality of conditions, know well that there is no reason whatever in the nature of things why, in the future, communities should not spring up where there shall be no great extremes of poverty and wealth, and where, nevertheless, the power of civilization and the chances for happiness and for doing good work shall be greater than ever before.

As to what Mr. Pearson says about the work of the world which is best worth doing being now done, the facts do not bear him out. He thinks that the great poems have all been written, that the days of the drama and the epic are past. Yet one of the greatest plays that has ever been produced, always excepting the plays of

Shakespeare, was produced in this century; and if the world had to wait nearly two thousand years after the vanishing of the Athenian dramatists before Shakespeare appeared, and two hundred years more before Goethe wrote his one great play, we can well afford to suspend judgment for a few hundred years at least, before asserting that no country and no language will again produce another great drama. So it is with the epic. We are too near Milton, who came three thousand years after Homer, to assert that the centuries to come will never more see an epic. One race may grow feeble and decrepit and be unable to do any more work; but another may take its place. After a time the Greek and Latin writers found that they had no more to say; and a critic belonging to either nationality might have shaken his head and said that all the great themes had been used up and all the great ideas expressed; nevertheless, Dante, Cervantes, Moliere, Schiller, Chaucer, and Scott, then all lay in the future.

Again, Mr. Pearson speaks of statecraft at the present day as offering fewer prizes, and prizes of less worth than formerly, and as giving no chance for the development of men like Augustus Caesar, Richelieu, or Chatham. It is difficult to perceive how these men can be considered to belong to a different class from Bismarck, who is yet alive; nor do we see why any English-speaking people should regard a statesman like Chatham, or far greater that Chatham, as an impossibility nowadays or in the future. We Americans at least will with difficulty be persuaded that there has ever been a time when a nobler prize of achievement, suffering, and success was offered to any statesman than was offered both to Washington and to Lincoln. So, when Mr. Pearson speaks of the warfare of civilized countries offering less chance to the individual than the warfare of savage and barbarous times, and of its being far less possible now than in old days for a man to make his personal influence felt in warfare, we can only express our disagreement. No world-conqueror can arise save in or next to highly civilized States. There never has been a barbarian Alexander or Caesar, Hannibal or Napoleon. Sitting Bull and Rain-in-the-Face compare but ill with Von Moltke; and no Norse king of all the heroic viking age even so much as began to exercise the influence upon the warfare of his generation that Frederick the Great exercised on his.

It is not true that character of necessity decays with the growth of civilization. It may, of course, be true in some cases. Civilization may tend to develop upon the lines of Byzantine, Hindoo, and Inca; and there are sections of Europe and sections of the United States where we now tend to pay heed exclusively to the peaceful virtues and to develop only a race of merchants, lawyers, and professors, who will lack the virile qualities that have made our race great and splendid. This development may come, but it need not come necessarily, and, on the whole, the probabilities are against its coming at all.

Mr. Pearson is essentially a man of strength and courage. Looking into the future, the future seems to him gray and unattractive; but he does not preach any unmanly gospel of despair. He thinks that in time to come, though life will be freer than in the past from dangers and vicissitudes, yet it will contain fewer of the strong pleasures and of the opportunities for doing great deeds that are so dear to mighty souls. Nevertheless, he advises us all to front it bravely whether our hope be great or little; and he ends his book with these fine sentences: "Even so, there will still remain to us ourselves. Simply to do our work in life, and to abide the issue, if we stand erect before the eternal calm as cheerfully as our fathers faced the eternal unrest, may be nobler training for our souls than the faith in progress,"

We do not agree with him that there will be only this eternal calm to face; we do not agree with him that the future holds for us a time when we shall ask nothing from the day but to live, nor from the future but that we may not deteriorate. We do not agree with him that there is a day approaching when the lower races will predominate in the world and the higher races will have lost their noblest elements. But after all, it matters little what view we take of the future if, in our practice, we but do as he preaches, and face resolutely whatever fate may have in store. We, ourselves, are not certain that progress is assured; we only assert that it may be assured if we but live wise, brave, and upright lives. We do not know whether the future has in store for us calm or unrest. We cannot know beyond peradventure whether we can prevent the higher races from losing their nobler traits and from being overwhelmed by the lower races. On the whole, we think that the greatest victories are yet to be won, the greatest deeds yet to be done, and that there are yet in store for our peoples and for the causes that we uphold grander triumphs than have ever yet been scored. But be this as it may, we gladly agree that the one plain duty of every man is to face the future as he faces the present, regardless of what it may have in store for him, and, turning toward the light as he sees the light, to play his part manfully, as a man among men.

XIV
"SOCIAL EVOLUTION"[21]

MR. KIDD'S *Social Evolution* is a suggestive, but a very crude book; for the writer is burdened by a certain mixture of dogmatism and superficiality, which makes him content to accept half truths and insist that they are whole truths. Nevertheless, though the book appeals chiefly to minds of the kind which are uncharitably described as "half-baked," Mr. Kidd does suggest certain lines of thought which are worth following—though rarely to his conclusions.

He deserves credit for appreciating what he calls "the outlook." He sketches graphically, and with power, the problems which now loom up for settlement before all of us who dwell in Western lands; and he portrays the varying attitudes of interest, alarm, and hope with which the thinkers and workers of the day regard these problems. He points out that the problems which now face us are by no

[21] *North American Review*, July, 1895.

means parallel to those that were solved by our forefathers one, two, or three centuries ago. The great political revolutions seem to be about complete and the time of the great social revolutions has arrived. We are all peering eagerly into the future to try to forecast the action of the great dumb forces set in operation by the stupendous industrial revolution which has taken place during the present century. We do not know what to make of the vast displacements of population, the expansion of the towns, the unrest and discontent of the masses, and the uneasiness of those who are devoted to the present order of things.

Mr. Kidd sees these problems, but he gropes blindly when he tries to forecast their solution. He sees that the progress of mankind in past ages can only have been made under and in accordance with certain biological laws, and that these laws continue to work in human society at the present day. He realizes the all-importance of the laws which govern the reproduction of mankind from generation to generation, precisely as they govern the reproduction of the lower animals, and which, therefore, largely govern his progress. But he makes a cardinal mistake in treating of this kind of progress. He states with the utmost positive-ness that, left to himself, man has not the slightest innate tendency to make any onward progress whatever, and that if the conditions of life allowed each man to follow his own inclinations the average of one generation would always tend to sink below the average of the preceding. This is one of the sweeping generalizations of which Mr. Kidd is fond, and which mar so much of his work. He evidently finds great difficulty in stating a general law with the proper reservations and with the proper moderation of phrase; and so he enunciates as truths statements which contain a truth, but which also contain a falsehood. What he here says is undoubtedly true of the world, taken as a whole. It is in all probability entirely false of the highest sections of society. At any rate, there are numerous instances where the law he states does not work; and of course a single instance oversets a sweeping declaration of such a kind.

There can be but little quarrel with what Mr. Kidd says as to the record of the world being a record of ceaseless progress on the one hand, and ceaseless stress and competition on the other; although even here his statement is too broad, and his terms are used carelessly. When he speaks of progress being ceaseless, he evidently means by progress simply change, so that as he uses the word it must be understood to mean progress backward as well as forward. As a matter of fact, in many forms of life and for long ages there is absolutely no progress whatever and no change, the forms remaining practically stationary.

Mr. Kidd further points out that the first necessity for every successful form engaged in this struggle is the capacity for reproduction beyond the limits for which the conditions of life comfortably provide, so that competition and selection must not only always accompany progress, but must prevail in every form of life which is not actually retrograding. As already said, he accepts without reservation the proposition that if all the individuals of every generation in any species were allowed to propagate their kind equally, the average of each generation would tend to fall below the preceding.

From this position he draws as a corollary, that the wider the limits of selection, the keener the rivalry and the more rigid the selection, just so much greater will be the progress; while for any progress at all there must be some rivalry in selection, so that every progressive form must lead a life of continual strain and stress as it travels its upward path. This again is true in a measure, but is not true as broadly as Mr. Kidd has stated it. The rivalry of natural selection is but one of the features in progress. Other things being equal, the species where this rivalry is keenest will make most progress; but then "other things" never are equal. In actual life those species make most progress which are farthest removed from the point where the limits of selection are very wide, the selection itself very rigid, and the rivalry very keen. Of course the selection is most rigid where the fecundity of the animal is greatest; but it is precisely the forms which have most fecundity that have made least progress. Some time in the remote past the guinea pig and the dog had a common ancestor. The fecundity of the guinea pig is much greater than that of the dog. Of a given number of guinea pigs born, a much smaller pro-portion are able to survive in the keen rivalry, so that the limits of selection are wider, and the selection itself more rigid; nevertheless the progress made by the progenitors of the dog since eocene days has been much more marked and rapid than the progress made by the progenitors of the guinea pig in the same time.

Moreover, in speaking of the rise that has come through the stress of competition in our modern societies, and of the keenness of this stress in the societies that have gone fastest, Mr. Kidd overlooks certain very curious features in human society. In the first place he speaks as though the stress under which nations make progress was primarily the stress produced by multiplication beyond the limits of subsistence. This, of course, would mean that in progressive societies the number of births and the number of deaths would both be at a maximum, for it is where the births and deaths are largest that the struggle for life is keenest. If, as Mr. Kidd' s hypothesis assumes, progress was most marked where the struggle for life was keenest, the European peoples standing highest in the scale would be the South Italians, the Polish Jews, and the people who live in the congested districts of Ireland. As a matter of fact, however, these are precisely the peoples who have made least progress when compared with the dominant strains among, for instance, the English or Germans. So far is Mr. Kidd' s proposition from being true that, when studied in the light of the facts, it is difficult to refrain from calling it the reverse of the truth. The race existing under conditions which make the competition for bare existence keenest, never progresses as fast as the race which exists under less stringent conditions. There must undoubtedly be a certain amount of competition, a certain amount of stress and strain, but it is equally undoubted that if this competition becomes too severe the race goes down and not up; and it is further true that the race existing under the severest stress as regards this competition often fails to go ahead as fast even in population as does the race where the competition is less severe. No matter how large the number of births may be, a race cannot increase if the number of deaths also grows at an accelerating rate.

To increase greatly a race must be prolific, and there is no curse so great as the curse of barrenness, whether for a nation or an individual. When a people gets to the position even now occupied by the mass of the French and by sections of the New Englanders, where the death rate surpasses the birth rate, then that race is not only fated to extinction but it deserves extinction. When the capacity and desire for fatherhood and motherhood is lost the race goes down, and should go down; and we need to have the plainest kind of plain speaking addressed to those individuals who fear to bring children into the world. But while this is all true, it remains equally true that immoderate increase in no way furthers the development of a race, and does not always help its increase even in numbers. The English-speaking peoples during the past two centuries and a half have increased faster than any others, yet there have been many other peoples whose birth rate during the same period has stood higher.

Yet, again, Mr. Kidd, in speaking of the stress of the conditions of progress in our modern societies fails to see that most of the stress to which he refers does not have anything to do with increased difficulty in obtaining a living, or with the propagation of the race. The great prizes are battled for among the men who wage no war whatever for mere subsistence, while the fight for mere subsistence is keenest among precisely the classes which contribute very little indeed to the progress of the race. The generals and admirals, the poets, philosophers, historians and musicians, the statesmen and judges, the law-makers and law-givers, the men of arts and of letters, the great captains of war and of industry—all these come from the classes where the struggle for the bare means of subsistence is least severe, and where the rate of increase is relatively smaller than in the classes below. In civilized societies the rivalry of natural selection works against progress. Progress is made in spite of it, for progress results not from the crowding out of the lower classes by the upper, but on the contrary from the steady rise of the lower classes to the level of the upper, as the latter tend to vanish, or at most barely hold their own. In progressive societies it is often the least fit who survive; but, on the other hand, they and their children often tend to grow more fit. The mere statement of these facts is sufficient to show not only how incorrect are many of Mr. Kidd' s premises and conclusions, but also how unwarranted are some of the fears which he expresses for the future. It is plain that the societies and sections of societies where the individual's happiness is on the whole highest, and where progress is most real and valuable, are precisely these where the grinding competition and the struggle for mere existence is least severe. Undoubtedly in every progressive society there must be a certain sacrifice of individuals, so that there must be a certain proportion of failures in every generation; but the actual facts of life prove beyond shadow of doubt that the extent of this sacrifice has nothing to do with the rapidity or worth of the progress. The nations that make most progress may do so at the expense of ten or fifteen individuals out of a hundred, whereas the nations that make least progress, or even go backwards, may sacrifice almost every man out of the hundred.

This last statement is in itself partly an answer to the position taken by Mr. Kidd, that there is for the individual no "rational sanction" for the conditions of progress. In a progressive community, where the conditions provide for the happiness of four-fifths or ninetenths of the people, there is undoubtedly a rational sanction for progress both for the community at large and for the great bulk of its members; and if these members are on the whole vigorous and intelligent, the attitude of the smaller fraction who have failed will be a matter of little consequence. In such a community the conflict between the interests of the individual and the organism of which he is a part, upon which Mr. Kidd lays so much emphasis, is at a minimum. The stress is severest, the misery and suffering greatest, among precisely the communities which have made least progress—among the Bushmen, Australian black fellows, and root-digger Indians, for instance.

Moreover, Mr. Kidd does not define what he means by "rational sanction." Indeed one of his great troubles throughout is his failure to make proper definitions, and the extreme looseness with which he often uses the definitions he does make. Apparently by "rational" he means merely selfish, and proceeds upon the assumption that "reason" must always dictate to every man to do that which will give him the greatest amount of individual gratification at the moment, no matter what the cost may be to others or to the community at large. This is not so. Side by side with the selfish development in life there has been almost from the beginning a certain amount of unselfish development too; and in the evolution of humanity the unselfish side has, on the whole, tended steadily to increase at the expense of the selfish, notably in the progressive communities about whose future development Mr. Kidd is so ill at ease. A more supreme instance of unselfishness than is afforded by motherhood cannot be imagined; and when Mr. Kidd implies, as he does very clearly, that there is no rational sanction for the unselfihnsess of motherhood, for the unselfishness of duty, or loyalty, he merely misuses the word rational. When a creature has reached a certain stage of development it will cause the female more pain to see her offspring starve than to work for it, and she then has a very rational reason for so working. When humanity has reached a certain stage it will cause the individual more pain, a greater sense of degradation and shame and misery, to steal, to murder, or to lie, than to work hard and suffer discomfort. When man has reached this stage he has a very rational sanction for being truthful and honest. It might also parenthetically be stated that when he has reached this stage he has a tendency to relieve the sufferings of others, and he has for this course the excellent rational sanction that it makes him more uncomfortable to see misery unrelieved than it does to deny himself a little in order to relieve it.

However, we can cordially agree with Mr. Kidd's proposition that many of the social plans advanced by would-be reformers in the interest of oppressed individuals are entirely destructive of all growth and of all progress in society. Certain cults, not only Christian, but also Buddhistic and Brahminic, tend to develop an altruism which is as "supra-natural" as Mr. Kidd seemingly desires religion to be; for it really is without foundation in reason, and therefore to be condemned.

Mr. Kidd repeats again and again that the scientific development of the nineteenth century confronts us with the fact that the interests of the social organism and of the individual are, and must remain, antagonistic, and the latter predominant, and that there can never be found any sanction in individual reason for individual good conduct in societies where the conditions of progress prevail. From what has been said above it is evident that this statement is entirely without basis, and therefore that the whole scheme of mystic and highly irrational philosophy which he founds upon it at once falls to the ground. There is no such necessary antagonism as that which he alleges. On the contrary, in the most truly progressive societies, even now, for the great mass of the individuals composing them the interests of the social organism and of the individual are largely identical instead of antagonistic; and even where this is not true, there is a sanction of individual reason, if we use the word *reason* properly, for conduct on the part of the individual which is subordinate to the welfare of the general society.

We can measure the truth of his statements by applying them, not to great societies in the abstract, but to small social organisms in the concrete. Take for instance the life of a regiment or the organization of a police department or fire department. The first duty of a regiment is to fight, and fighting means the death and disabling of a large proportion of the men in the regiment. The case against the identity of interests between the individual and the organism, as put by Mr. Kidd, would be far stronger in a regiment than in any ordinary civilized society of the day. Yet as a matter of fact we know that in the great multitude of regiments there is much more subordination of the individual to the organism than is the case in any civilized state taken as a whole. Moreover, this subordination is greatest in precisely those regiments where the average individual is best off, because it is greatest in those regiments where the individual feels that high, stern pride in his own endurance and suffering, and in the great name of the organism of which he forms a part, that in itself yields one of the loftiest of all human pleasures. If Mr. Kidd means anything when he says that there is no rational sanction for progress he must also mean that there is no rational sanction for a soldier not flinching from the enemy when he can do so unobserved, for a sentinel not leaving his post, for an officer not deserting to the enemy. Yet when he says this he utters what is a mere jugglery on words. In the process of evolution men and societies have often reached such a stage that the best type of soldier or citizen feels infinitely more shame and misery from neglect of duty, from cowardice or dishonesty, from selfish abandonment of the interests of the organism of which he is part, than can be offset by the gratification of any of his desires. This, be it also observed, often takes place, entirely independent of any religious considerations. The habit of useful self-sacrifice may be developed by civilization in a great society as well as by military training in a regiment. The habit of useless self-sacrifice may also, unfortunately, be developed; and those who practice it are but one degree less noxious than the individuals who sacrifice good people to bad.

The religious element in our development is that on which Mr. Kidd most strongly dwells, entitling it "the central feature of human history." A very startling feature of his treatment is that in religious matters he seemingly sets no value on the difference between truth and falsehood, for he groups all religions together. In a would-be teacher of ethics such an attitude warrants severe rebuke; for it is essentially dishonest and immoral. Throughout his book he treats all religious beliefs from the same standpoint, as if they were all substantially similar and substantially of the same value; whereas it is, of course, a mere truism to say that most of them are mutually destructive. Not only has he no idea of differentiating the true from the false, but he seems not to understand that the truth of a particular belief is of any moment. Thus he says, in speaking of the future survival of religious beliefs in general, that the most notable result of the scientific revolution begun by Darwin must be "to establish them on a foundation as broad, deep, and lasting as any the theologians ever dreamed of." If this sentence means anything it means that all these religious beliefs will be established on the same foundation. It hardly seems necessary to point out that this cannot be the fact. If the God of the Christians be in very truth the one God, and if the belief in Him be established, as Christians believe it will, then the foundation for the religious belief in Mumbo Jumbo can be neither broad, deep, nor lasting. In the same way the beliefs in Mohammed and Buddha are mutually exclusive, and the various forms of ancestor worship and fetichism cannot all be established on a permanent basis, as they would be according to Mr. Kidd's theory.

Again, when Mr. Kidd rebukes science for its failure to approach religion in a scientific spirit he shows that he fails to grasp the full bearing of the subject which he is considering. This failure comes in part from the very large, not to say loose, way in which he uses the words "science" and "religion." There are many sciences and many religions, and there are many different kinds of men who profess the one or advocate the other. Where the intolerant professors of a given religious belief endeavor by any form of persecution to prevent scientific men of any kind from seeking to find out and establish the truth, then it is quite idle to blame these scientific men for attacking with heat and acerbity the religious belief which prompts such persecution. The exigencies of a life and death struggle unfit a man for the coldness of a mere scientific inquiry. Even the most enthusiastic naturalist, if attacked by a man-eating shark, would be much more interested in evading or repelling the attack than in determining the precise specific relations of the shark. A less important but amusing feature of his argument is that he speaks as if he himself had made an entirely new discovery when he learned of the important part played in man' s history by his religious beliefs. But Mr. Kidd surely cannot mean this. He must be aware that all the great historians have given their full importance to such religious movements as the birth and growth of Christianity, the Reformation, the growth of Islamism, and the like. Mr. Kidd is quite right in insisting upon the importance of the part played by religious beliefs, but he has fallen into a vast error if he fails to understand that the great majority of the historical and sociological writers have given proper weight to this importance.

Mr. Kidd's greatest failing is his tendency to use words in false senses. He uses "reason" in the false sense "selfish." He then, in a spirit of mental tautology, assumes that reason must be necessarily purely selfish and brutal. He assumes that the man who risks his life to save a friend, the woman who watches over a sick child, and the soldier who dies at his post, are unreasonable, and that the more their reason is developed the less likely they will be to act in these ways. The mere statement of the assertion in such a form is sufficient to show its nonsense to any one who will take the pains to think whether the people who ordinarily perform such feats of self-sacrifice and self-denial are people of brutish minds or of fair intelligence.

If none of the ethical qualities are developed at the same time with a man's reason, then he may become a peculiarly noxious kind of wild beast; but this is not in the least a necessity of the development of his reason. It would be just as wise to say that it was a necessity of the development of his bodily strength. Undoubtedly the man with reason who is selfish and unscrupulous will, because of his added power, behave even worse than the man without reason who is selfish and unscrupulous; but the same is true of the man of vast bodily strength. He has power to do greater harm to himself and to others; but, because of this, to speak of bodily strength or of reason as in itself "profoundly anti-social and anti-evolutionary" is foolishness. Mr. Kidd, as so often, is misled by a confusion of names for which he is himself responsible. The growth of rationalism, unaccompanied by any growth in ethics or morality, works badly. The society in which such a growth takes place will die out, and ought to die out. But this does not imply that other communities quite as intelligent may not also be deeply moral and be able to take firm root in the world.

Mr. Kidd's definitions of "supranatural" and "ultrarational" sanctions, the definitions upon which he insists so strongly and at such length, would apply quite as well to every crazy superstition of the most brutal savage as to the teachings of the New Testament. The trouble with his argument is that, when he insists upon the importance of this ultra-rational sanction, defining it as loosely as he does, he insists upon too much. He apparently denies that men can come to a certain state at which it will be rational for them to do right even to their own hurt. It is perfectly possible to build up a civilization which, by its surroundings and by its inheritances, working through long ages, shall make the bulk of the men and women develop such characteristics of unselfishness, as well as of wisdom, that it will be the rational thing for them as individuals to act in accordance with the highest dictates of honor and courage and morality. If the intellectual development of such a civilized community goes on at an equal pace with the ethical, it will persistently war against the individuals in whom the spirit of selfishness, which apparently Mr. Kidd considers the only rational spirit, shows itself strongly. It will weed out these individuals and forbid them propagating, and therefore will steadily tend to produce a society in which the rational sanction for progress shall be identical in the individual and the State. This ideal has never yet been reached, but long steps have been taken towards reaching it; and in most progressive civilizations it is reached to the extent that the sanction for progress is the same not only for the State but for each one of the bulk of the individuals composing it. When this ceases to be the case progress itself will generally cease and the community ultimately disappear.

Mr. Kidd, having treated of religion in a preliminary way, and with much mystic vagueness, then attempts to describe the functions of religious belief in the evolution of society. He has already given definitions of religion quoted from different authors, and he now proceeds to give his own definition. But first he again insists upon his favorite theory, that there can be no rational basis for individual good conduct in society; using the word rational, according to his usual habit, as a synonym of selfish; and then asserts that there can be no such thing as a rational religion. Apparently all that Mr. Kidd demands on this point is that it shall be what he calls ultra-rational, a word which he prefers to irrational. In other words he casts aside as irrelevant all discussion as to a creed's truth.

Mr. Kidd then defines religion as being "a form of belief providing an ultra-rational sanction for that large class of conduct in the individual where his interests and the interests of the social organism are antagonistic, and by which the former are rendered subordinate to the latter in the general interest of the evolution which the race is undergoing," and says that we have here the principle at the base of all religions. Of course this is simply not true. All those religions which busy themselves exclusively with the future life, and which even Mr. Kidd could hardly deny to be religious, do not have this principle at their base at all. They have nothing to do with the general interests of the evolution which the race is undergoing on this earth. They have to do only with the soul of the individual in the future life. They are not concerned with this world, they are concerned with the world to come. All religions, and all forms of religions, in which the principle of asceticism receives any marked development are positively antagonistic to the development of the social organism. They are against its interests. They do not tend in the least to subordinate the interests of the individual to the interests of the organism "in the general interest of the evolution which the race is undergoing." A religion like that of the Shakers means the almost immediate extinction of the organism in which it develops. Such a religion distinctly subordinates the interests of the organism to the interests of the individual. The same is equally true of many of the more ascetic developments of Christianity and Islam. There is strong probability that there was a Celtic population in Iceland before the arrival of the Norsemen, but these Celts belonged to the Culdee sect of Christians. They were anchorites, and professed a creed which completely subordinated the development of the race on this earth to the well-being of the individual in the next. In consequence they died out and left no successors. There are creeds, such as most of the present day creeds of Christianity, both Protestant and Catholic, which do very noble work for the race because they teach its individuals to subordinate their own interests to the interests of mankind; but it is idle to say this of every form of religious belief.

It is equally idle to pretend that this principle, which Mr. Kidd says lies at the base of all religions, does not also lie at the base of many forms of ethical belief which could hardly be called religious. His definition of religion could just as appropriately be used to define some forms of altruism or humanitarianism, while it does not define religion at all, if we use the word religion in the way in which it generally is used. If Mr. Kidd should write a book about horses, and should define a horse as a striped equine animal found wild in South Africa, his definition would apply to certain members of the horse family, but would not apply to that animal which we ordinarily mean when we talk of a horse; and, moreover, it would still be sufficiently loose to include two or three entirely distinct species. This is precisely the trouble with Mr. Kidd's definition of religion. It does not define religion at all as the word is ordinarily used, and while it does apply to certain religious beliefs, it also applies quite as well to certain nonreligious beliefs. We must, therefore, recollect that throughout Mr. Kidd's argument on behalf of the part that religion plays he does not mean what is generally understood by religion, but the special form or forms which he here defines.

Undoubtedly, in the race for life, that group of beings will tend ultimately to survive in which the general feeling of the members, whether due to humanitarianism, to altruism, or to some form of religious belief proper, is such that the average individual has an unselfish—what Mr. Kidd would call an ultra-rational—tendency to work for the ultimate benefit of the community as a whole. Mr. Kidd's argument is so loose that it may be construed as meaning that, in the evolution of society, irrational superstitions grow up from time to time, affect large bodies of the human race in their course of development, and then die away; and that this succession of evanescent religious beliefs will continue for a very long time to come, perhaps as long as the human race exists. He may further mean that, except for this belief in a long succession of lies, humanity could not go forward. His words, I repeat, are sufficiently involved to make it possible that he means this, but, if so, his book can hardly be taken as a satisfactory defence of religion.

If there is justification for any given religion, and justification for the acceptance of supernatural authority as regards this religion, then there can be no justification for the acceptance of all religions, good and bad alike. There can, at the outside, be a justification for but one or two. Mr. Kidd's grouping of all religions together is offensive to every earnest believer. Moreover, in his anxiety to insist only on the irrational side of religion, he naturally tends to exalt precisely those forms of superstition which are most repugnant to reasoning beings with moral instincts, and which are most heartily condemned by believers in the loftiest religions. He apparently condemns Lecky for what Lecky says of that species of unpleasant and noxious anchorite best typified by St. Simeon Stylites and the other pillar hermits. He corrects Lecky for his estimate of this ideal of the fourth century, and says that instead of being condemned it should be praised, as affording striking evidence and example of the vigor of the immature social forces at work. This is not true. The type of anchorite of which Mr. Lecky speaks with such just condemnation flourished most rankly in Christian Africa and Asia Minor, the very countries where Christianity was so speedily overthrown by Islam. It was not an example of the vigor of the immature social forces at work; on the contrary, it was a proof that those social forces were rotten and had lost their vigor. Where an anchorite of the type Lecky describes, and Mr. Kidd impliedly commends, was accepted as the true type of the church, and set the tone for religious thought, the church was corrupt, and was unable to make any effective defence against the scarcely baser form of superstition which received its development in Islamism. As a matter of fact, asceticism of this kind had very little in common with the really vigorous and growing part of European Christianity, even at that time. Such asceticism is far more closely related to the practices of some loathsome Mohammedan dervish than to any creed which has properly developed from the pure and lofty teachings of the Four Gospels. St. Simeon Stylites is more nearly kin to a Hindoo fakir than to Phillips Brooks or Archbishop Ireland.

Mr. Kidd deserves praise for insisting as he does upon the great importance of the development of humanitarian feelings and of the ethical element in humanity during the past few centuries, when compared with the mere material development. He is, of course, entirely right in laying the utmost stress upon the enormous part taken by Christianity in the growth of Western civilization. He would do well to remember, however, that there are other elements than that of merely ceremonial Christianity at work, and that such ceremonial Christianity in other races produces quite different results, as he will see at a glance, if he will recall that Abyssinia and Hayti are Christian countries.

In short, whatever Mr. Kidd says in reference to religion must be understood as being strictly limited by his own improper terminology. If we should accept the words religion and religious belief in their ordinary meaning, and should then accept as true what he states, we should apparently have to conclude that progress depended largely upon the fervor of the religious spirit, without regard to whether the religion itself was false or true. If such were the fact, progress would be most rapid in a country like Morocco, where the religious spirit is very strong indeed, far stronger than in any enlightened Christian country, but where, in reality, the religious development has largely crushed out the ethical and moral development, so that the country has gone steadily backward. A little philosophic study would convince Mr. Kidd that while the ethical and moral development of a nation may, in the case of certain religions, be based on those religions and develop with them and on the lines laid down by them, yet that in other countries where they develop at all they have to develop right in the teeth of the dominant religious beliefs, while in yet others they may develop entirely independent of them. If he doubts this let him examine the condition of the Soudan under the Mahdi, where what he calls the ultrarational and supra-natural sanctions were accepted without question, and governed the lives of the people to the exclusion alike of reason and morality. He will hardly assert that the Soudan is more progressive than say Scotland or Minnesota, where there is less of the spirit which he calls religious and which old-fashioned folk would call superstitious.

Mr. Kidd's position in reference to the central feature of his argument is radically false; but he handles some of his other themes very well. He shows clearly in his excellent chapter on modern socialism that a state of retrogression must ensue if all incentives to strife and competition are withdrawn. He does not show quite as clearly as he should that over-competition and too severe stress make the race deteriorate instead of improving; but he does show that there must be some competition, that there must be some strife. He makes it clear also that the true function of the State, as it interferes in social life, should be to make the chances of competition more even, not to abolish them. We wish the best men; and though we pity the man that falls or lags behind in the race, we do not on that account crown him with the victor's wreath. We insist that the race shall be run on fairer terms than before because we remove all handicaps. We thus tend to make it more than ever a test of the real merits of the victor, and this means that the victor must strive heart and soul for success. Mr. Kidd's attitude in describing socialism is excellent. He sympathizes with the wrongs which the socialistic reformer seeks to redress, but he insists that these wrongs must not be redressed, as the socialists would have them, at the cost of the welfare of mankind.

Mr. Kidd also sees that the movement for political equality has nearly come to an end, for its purpose has been nearly achieved. To it must now succeed a movement to bring all people into the rivalry of life on equal conditions of social opportunity. This is a very important point, and he deserves the utmost credit for bringing it out. It is the great central feature in the development of our time, and Mr. Kidd has seen it so clearly and presented it so forcibly that we cannot but regret that he should be so befogged in other portions of his argument.

Mr. Kidd has our cordial sympathy when he lays stress on the fact that our evolution cannot be called primarily intellectual. Of course there must be an intellectual evolution, too, and Mr. Kidd perhaps fails in not making this sufficiently plain. A perfectly stupid race can never rise to a very high plane; the negro, for instance, has been kept down as much by lack of intellectual development as by anything else; but the prime factor in the preservation of a race is its power to attain a high degree of social efficiency. Love of order, ability to fight well and breed well, capacity to subordinate the interests of the individual to the interests of the community, these and similar rather humdrum qualities go to make up the sum of social efficiency. The race that has them is sure to overturn the race whose members have brilliant intellects, but who are cold and selfish and timid, who do not breed well or fight well, and who are not capable of disinterested love of the community. In other words, character is far more important than intellect to the race as to the individual. We need intellect, and there is no reason why we should not have it together with character; but if we must choose between the two we choose character without a moment's hesitation.

XV
THE LAW OF CIVILIZATION AND DECAY[22]

FEW more melancholy books have been written than Mr. Brooks Adams's *Law of Civilization and Decay* . It is a marvel of compressed statement. In a volume of less than four hundred pages Mr. Adams singles out some of the vital factors in the growth and evolution of civilized life during the last two thousand years; and so brilliant is his discussion of these factors as to give, though but a glimpse, yet one of the most vivid glimpses ever given, of some of the most important features in the world-life of Christendom. Of some of the features only; for a fundamentally defective point in Mr. Adams's brilliant book is his failure to present certain phases of the life of the nations,—phases which are just as important as those which he discusses with such vigorous ability. Furthermore, he disregards not a few facts

[22] The *Forum,* January, 1897.

which would throw light on others, the weight of which he fully recognizes. Both these shortcomings are very natural in a writer who possesses an entirely original point of view, who is the first man to see clearly certain things that to his predecessors have been nebulous, and who writes with a fervent intensity of conviction, even in his bitterest cynicism, such as we are apt to associate rather with the prophet and reformer than with a historian to whom prophet and reformer alike appeal no more than do their antitypes. It is a rare thing for a historian to make a distinct contribution to the philosophy of history; and this Mr. Adams has done. Naturally enough, he, like other men who break new ground, tends here and there to draw a devious furrow.

The book is replete with vivid writing, and with sentences and paragraphs which stand out in the memory as marvels in the art of presenting the vital features of a subject with a few master-strokes. The story of the Crusades, the outline of the English conquest of India, and the short tale of the rise of the house of Rothschild, are masterpieces. Nowhere else is it possible to find in the same compass any description of the Crusades so profound in its appreciation of the motives behind them, so startling in the vigor with which the chief actors, and the chief events, are portrayed. Indeed, one is almost tempted to say that it is in the description of the Crusades that Mr. Adams is at his best. He is dealing with a giant movement of humanity; and he grasps not only the colossal outward manifestations, but also the spirit itself, and, above all, the strange and sinister changes which that spirit underwent. His mere description of the Baronies set up by the Crusaders in the conquered Holy Land, with their loose feudal government, brings them before the reader's eyes as few volumes specially devoted to the subject could. It is difficult to write of a fortress and make a pen-picture which will always stay in the mind; yet this is what Mr. Adams has done in dealing with the grim religious castles, terrible in size and power, which were built by the Knights of the Temple and the Hospital as bulwarks against Saracen might. He is not only a scholar of much research, but a student of art, who is so much more than a mere student as to be thrilled and possessed by what he studies. He shows, with a beauty and vigor of style not unbecoming his subject, how profoundly the art of Europe was affected by the Crusades. It is not every one who can write with equal interest of sacred architecture and military engineering, who can appreciate alike the marvels of Gothic cathedrals and the frowning strength of feudal fortresses, and who furthermore can trace their interrelation.

The story of the taking of Constantinople by the Crusaders who followed the lead of the blind Doge Dandolo is told with an almost brutal ruthlessness quite befitting the deed itself. Nowhere else in the book is Mr. Adams happier in his insistence upon the conflict between what he calls the economic and the imaginative spirits. The incident sets well with his favorite theory of the inevitable triumph of the economic over the imaginative man, as societies grow centralized, and the no less inevitable fossilization and ruin of the body politic which this very triumph itself ultimately entails. The history of the English conquest of India is only less vividly told. Incidentally, it may be mentioned that one of Mr. Adams's many merits is his contemptuous refusal to be misled by modern criticism of Macaulay. He sees Macaulay's greatness as a historian, and his essential truthfulness on many of the very points where he has been most sharply criticised.

Mr. Adams's book, however, is far more than a mere succession of brilliant episodes. He fully sees that the value of facts lies in their relation to one another; and from the facts as he sees them he deduces certain laws with more than a Thucydidean indifference as to his own individual approval or disapproval of the development. The life of nations, like any other form of life, is but one manifestation of energy; and Mr. Adams's decidedly gloomy philosophy of life may be gathered from the fact that he places fear and greed as the two forms of energy which stand conspicuously predominant; fear in the earlier, and greed in the later, stages of evolution from barbarism to civilization. Civilization itself he regards merely as the history of the movement from a condition of physical distribution to one of physical concentration. During the earlier stages of this movement the imaginative man—the man who stands in fear of a priesthood—is, in his opinion, the representative type, while with him, and almost equally typical, stand the soldier and the artist. As consolidation advances, the economic man—the man of industry, trade, and capital—tends to supplant the emotional and artistic types of manhood, and finally himself develops along two lines,— "the usurer in his most formidable aspect, and the peasant whose nervous system is best adapted to thrive on scanty nutriment." These two very unattractive types are, in his belief, the inevitable final products of all civilization, as civilization has hitherto developed; and when they have once been produced there follows either a stationary period, during which the whole body politic gradually ossifies and atrophies, or else a period of utter disintegration.

This is not a pleasant theory; it is in many respects an entirely false theory; but nevertheless there is in it a very ugly element of truth. One does not have to accept either all Mr. Adams's theories or all his facts in order to recognize more than one disagreeable resemblance between the world as it is to-day, and the Roman world under the Empire, or the Greek world under the successors of Alexander. Where he errs is in his failure to appreciate the fundamental differences which utterly destroy any real parallelism between the two sets of cases. Indeed, his zeal in championing his theories leads him at times into positions which are seen at a glance to be untenable.

Probably Mr. Adams's account of the English Reformation, and of Henry VIII. and his instruments, is far nearer the truth than Froude's. But his view of the evils upon which the reformers as a whole waged war, and of the spirit which lay behind the real leaders and spurred them on, is certainly less accurate than the view given by Froude in his *Erasmus and Council of Trent* . It can be partly corrected by the study of a much less readable book—Mr. Henry C. Lea's work on *The Inquisition* . Yet Mr. Adams's description of the English Reformation is very powerful, and has in it a vein of bitter truth; though on the whole it is perhaps not so well done as his account of the suppression of the Templars in France. If he can be said to have any heroes, the Templars must certainly be numbered among them.

He is at his best in describing the imaginative man, and especially the imaginative man whose energy manifests itself in the profession of arms. His description of the tremendous change which passed over Europe during the centuries which saw, what is commonly called, the decay of faith is especially noteworthy. In no other history are there to be found two sentences which portray more vividly the reasons for the triumph of the great Pope Hildebrand over the Emperor Henry, than these:

"To Henry's soldiers the world was a vast space peopled by those fantastic beings which are still seen on Gothic towers. These demons obeyed the monk of Rome, and his army, melling from the Emperor under a nameless horror, left him helpless."

His account of the contrast between the relations of Philip Augustus and of Philip the Fair with the Church is dramatic in its intensity. To Mr. Adams, Philip the Fair, even more than Henry VIII., is the incarnation of the economic spirit in its conflict with the Church; and he makes him an even more repulsive, though perhaps an abler, man than Henry. In this he is probably quite right. His account of the hounding down of Boniface, and the cruel destruction of the Templars, is as stirring as it is truthful; but he certainly pushes his theory to an altogether impossible extreme when he states that the moneyed class, the *bourgeoisie*, was already the dominant force in France. The heroes of Froissart still lay in the future; and for centuries to come the burgher was to be outweighed by king, priest, and noble. The economic man, the man of trade and money, was, at that time, in no sense dominant.

That there is grave reason for some of Mr. Adams's melancholy forebodings, no serious student of the times, no sociologist or reformer, and no practical politician who is interested in more than momentary success, will deny. A foolish optimist is only less noxious than an utter pessimist; and the pre-requisite for any effort, whether hopeful or hopeless, to better our conditions is an accurate knowledge of what these conditions are. There is no use in blinding ourselves to certain of the tendencies and results of our high-pressure civilization. Some very ominous facts have become more and more apparent during the present century, in which the social movement of the white race has gone on with such unexampled and ever-accelerating rapidity. The rich have undoubtedly grown richer; and, while the most careful students are inclined to answer with an emphatic negative the proposition that the poor have grown poorer, it is nevertheless certain that there has been a large absolute, though not relative, increase of poverty, and that the very poor tend to huddle in immense masses in the cities. Even though these masses are, relatively to the rest of the population, smaller than they formerly were, they constitute a standing menace, not merely to our prosperity, but to our existence. The improvement in the means of communication, moreover, has so far immensely increased the tendency of the urban population to grow at the expense of the rural; and philosophers have usually been inclined to regard the ultimate safety of a nation as resting upon its peasantry. The improvement in machinery, the very perfection of scientific processes, cause great, even though temporary, suffering to unskilled laborers. Moreover, there is a certain softness of fibre in civilized nations which, if it were to prove progressive, might mean the development of a cultured and refined people quite unable to hold its own in those conflicts through which alone any great race can ultimately march to victory. There is also a tendency to become fixed, and to lose flexibility. Most ominous of all, there has become evident, during the last two generations, a very pronounced tendency among the most highly civilized races, and among the most highly civilized portions of all races, to lose the power of multiplying, and even to decrease; so much so as to make the fears of the disciples of Malthus a century ago seem rather absurd to the dweller in France or New England to-day.

Mr. Adams does not believe that any individual or group of individuals can influence the destiny of a race for good or for evil. All of us admit that it is very hard by individual effort thus to make any alteration in destiny; but we do not think it impossible; and Mr. Adams will have performed a great service if he succeeds in fixing the eyes of the men who ought to know thoroughly the problems set us to solve, upon the essential features of these problems. I do not think his diagnosis of the disease is in all respects accurate. I believe there is an immense amount of healthy tissue as to the existence of which he is blind; but there is disease, and it is serious enough to warrant very careful examination.

However, Mr. Adams is certainly in error in putting the immense importance he does upon the question of the expansion or contraction of the currency. There is no doubt whatever that a nation is profoundly affected by the character of its currency; but there seems to be equally little doubt that the currency is only one, and by no means the most important, among a hundred causes which profoundly affect it. The United States has been on a gold basis, and on a silver basis; it has been on a paper basis, and on a basis of what might be called the scraps and odds and ends of the currencies of a dozen other nations; but it has kept on developing along the same lines no matter what its currency has been. If a change of currency were so enacted as to amount to dishonesty, that is, to the repudiation of debts, it would be a very bad thing morally; or, if a change took place in a manner that would temporarily reduce the purchasing power of the wage-earner, it would be a very bad thing materially; but the current of the national life would not be wholly diverted or arrested, it would merely be checked, even by such a radical change. The forces that most profoundly shape the course of a nation's life lie far deeper than the mere use of gold or of silver, the mere question of the appreciation or depreciation of one metal when compared with the other, or when compared with commodities generally.

Mr. Adams unconsciously shows this in his first and extremely interesting chapter on the Romans. In one part of this chapter he seems to ascribe the ruin of the Roman Empire to the contraction of the currency, saying, "with contraction came that fall of prices which first ruined, then enslaved, and finally exterminated the native rural population of Italy." This he attributes to the growth of the economic or capitalistic spirit. As he puts it, "the stronger type exterminated the weaker, the money-lender killed out the husbandman, the soldiers vanished, and the farms on which they once flourished were left desolate."

But, curiously enough, Mr. Adams himself shows that all this really occurred during the two centuries, or thereabouts, extending from the end of the second Punic war through the reign of the first of the Roman emperors; and this was a period of currency expansion, not of currency contraction. Moreover, it was emphatically a period when the military and not the economic type was supreme. The great Romans of the first and second centuries before Christ were soldiers, not merchants or usurers, and they could only be said to possess the economic instinct incidentally, in so far as it is possessed by every man of the military type who seizes the goods accumulated by the man of the economic type. It was during these centuries, when the military type was supreme, and when prices were rising, that the ruin, the enslavement and the extermination of the old rural population of Italy began. It was during these centuries that the husbandmen left the soil and became the mob of Rome, clamoring for free bread and the games of the amphitheatre. It was toward the close of this period that the Roman army became an army no longer of Roman citizens, but of barbarians trained in the Roman manner; it was toward the close of this period that celibacy became so crying an evil as to invoke the vain action of the legislature, and that the Roman race lost the power of self-perpetuation. What happened in the succeeding centuries,—the period of the contraction of the currency and the rise of prices,—was merely the completion of the ruin which had already been practically accomplished.

These facts seem to show clearly that the question of the currency had really little or nothing to do with the decay of the Roman fibre. This decay began under one set of currency conditions, and continued unchanged when these conditions became precisely reversed. An infinitely more important cause, as Mr. Adams himself shows, was the immense damage done to the Italian husbandman by the importation of Asiatic and African slaves; which was in all probability the chief of the causes that conspired to ruin him. He was forced into competition with races of lower vitality; races tenacious of life, who possessed a very low standard of living, and who furnished to the great slave-owner his cheap labor. Mr. Adams shows that the husbandman was affected, not only by the importation of vast droves of slaves to compete with him in Italy, but by the competition with low-class labor in Egypt and elsewhere. These very points, if developed with Mr. Adams's skill, would have enabled him to show in a very striking manner the radical contrast between the present political and social life of civilized states, and the political and social life of Rome during what he calls the capitalistic or closing period. At present, the minute that the democracy becomes convinced that the workman and the peasant are suffering from competition with cheap labor, whether this cheap labor take the form of alien immigration, or of the importation of goods manufactured abroad by low-class workingmen, or of commodities produced by convicts, it at once puts a stop to the competition. We keep out the Chinese, very wisely; we have put an end to the rivalry of convict contract labor with free labor; we are able to protect ourselves, whenever necessary, by heavy import duties, against the effect of too cheap labor in any foreign country; and, finally, in the civil war, we utterly destroyed the system of slavery, which really was threatening the life of the free working-man in a way in which it cannot possibly be threatened by any conceivable development of the "capitalistic" spirit. Mr. Adams possesses a very intimate knowledge of finance, and there are many of his discussions on this subject into which only an expert would be competent to enter. Nevertheless, on certain financial and economic questions, touching matters open to discussion by the man of merely ordinary knowledge, his terminology is decidedly vague. This is especially true when he speaks of "the producer." Now the producer, as portrayed by the Populist stump orator or writer of political and economic pamphlets, is a being with whom we became quite intimate during the recent campaign; but we have found it difficult to understand at all definitely who this "producer" actually is. According to one school of Populistic thinkers the farmer is the producer; but according to another and more radical school this is not so, unless the farmer works with his hands and not his head, this school limiting the application of the term "producer" to the working-man who does the immediate manual work of production. On the other hand those who speak with scientific precision must necessarily class as producers all men whose work results directly or indirectly in production. Under this definition, inventors and men who improve the methods of transportation, like railway presidents, and men who enable other producers to work, such as bankers who loan money wisely, are all themselves to be classed as producers, and often indeed as producers of the most effective kind.

The great mass of the population consists of producers; and in consequence the majority of the sales by producers are sales to other producers. It requires one set of producers to make a market for any other set of producers; and in consequence the rise or fall of prices is a good or a bad thing for different bodies of producers according to the different circumstances of each case. Mr. Adams says that the period from the middle of the twelfth to the middle of the thirteenth centuries was an interval of "almost unparalleled prosperity," which he apparently ascribes to the expansion of the currency, with which, he says, "went a rise in prices, all producers grew rich, and for more than two generations the strain of competition was so relaxed that the different classes of the population preyed upon each other less savagely than they are wont to do in less happy times." It is not exactly clear how a rise in the prices both of what one producer sells another, and of what he in return buys from that other, can somehow make both of them rich, and relax the strain of competition. Certainly in the present century, competition has been just as severe in times of high prices; and some of the periods of greatest prosperity have coincided with the periods of very low prices. There is reason to believe that low prices are ultimately of great benefit to the wage-earners. A rise in prices generally injures them. Moreover, in the century of which Mr. Adams speaks, the real non-producers were the great territorial feudal lords and the kings and clergymen; and these were then supreme. It was the period of the ferocious Albigensian crusades. It is true that it ushered in a rather worse period,—that of the struggle between England and France, with its attendant peasant wars and Jacqueries, and huge bands of marauding free-companies. But the alteration for the worse was due to a fresh outbreak of "imaginative" spirit; and the first period was full of recurring plagues and famines, besides the ordinary unrest, murder, oppression, pillage, and general corruption. Mr. Adams says that the different classes of the population during that happy time "preyed upon each other less savagely" than at other times. All that need be said in answer is that there is not now a civilized community, under no matter what stress of capitalistic competition, in which the different classes prey upon one another with one-tenth the savagery they then showed; or in which famine and disease, even leaving war out of account, come anywhere near causing so much misery to poor people, and above all to the wage-earners, or working-men, the under strata and base of the producing classes.

From many of the statements in Mr. Adams's very interesting concluding chapter I should equally differ; and yet this chapter is one which is not merely interesting but soul-stirring, and it contains much with which most of us would heartily agree. Through the cold impartiality with which he strives to work merely as a recorder of facts, there break now and then flashes of pent-up wrath and vehement scorn for all that is mean and petty in a purely materialistic, purely capitalistic, civilization. With his scorn of what is ignoble and base in our development, his impatient contempt of the deification of the stockmarket, the trading-counter, and the factory, all generous souls must agree. When we see prominent men deprecating the assertion of national honor because it "has a bad effect upon business," or because it "impairs the value of securities"; when we see men seriously accepting Mr. Edward Atkinson's pleasant theory that patriotism is of no consequence when compared with the price of cotton sheeting or the capacity to undersell our competitors in foreign markets, it is no wonder that a man who has in him the stuff of ancestors who helped to found our Government, and helped to bring it safely through the Civil War should think blackly of the future. But Mr. Adams should re-member that there always have been men of this merely huckstering type, or of other types not much higher.

It is not a nice thing that Mr. Eliot, the president of one of the greatest education-al institutions of the land, should reflect discredit upon the educated men of the country by his attitude on the Venezuela affair, carrying his desertion of American principles so far as to find himself left in the lurch by the very English statesman whose cause he was championing; but Mr. Adams by turning to the "History" of the administration of Madison, by his brother, Henry Adams, would find that Mr. Eliot had plenty of intellectual ancestors among the "blue lights" federalists of that day. Timothy Pickering showed the same eager desire to stand by another country to the hurt of his own country's honor, and Timothy Pickering was a United States Sena-tor whose conduct was far more reprehensible than that of any private individual could be. We have advanced, not retrograded, since 1812.

This applies also to what Mr. Adams says of the fall of the soldier and the rise of the usurer. He quite overstates his case in asserting that in Europe the soldier has lost his importance since 1871, and that the administration of society since then has fallen into the hands of the "economic man," thereby making a change "more radical than any that happened at Rome or even at Byzantium." In the first place, a period of a quarter of a century is altogether too short to admit of such a gener-alization. In the next place, the facts do not support this particular generalization. The Germans are quite as military in type as ever they were, and very much more so than they were at any period during the two centuries preceding Bismarck and Moltke. Nor is it true to say that "the ruler of the French people has passed for the first time from the martial to the moneyed type." Louis XV. and Louis Philippe can hardly be held to belong to any recognized martial type; and the reason of the comparative sinking of the military man in France is due not in the least to the rise of his economic fellow-countryman, but to the rise of the other military man in Germany. Mr. Adams says that since the capitulation of Paris the soldier has tended to sink more and more, until he merely receives his orders from financiers (which term when used by Mr. Adams includes all business and working-men) with his salary, without being allowed a voice, even in the questions which involve peace and war. Now this is precisely the position which the soldier has occupied for two centuries among English speaking races; and it is during these very centuries that the English-speaking race has produced its greatest soldiers. Marlborough and Wel-lington, Nelson and Farragut, Grant and Lee, exactly fill Mr. Adams's definition of the position into which soldiers have "sunk"; and the United States has just elected as President, as it so frequently has done before, a man who owes his place in politics in large part to his having done gallant service as a soldier, and who is in no sense a representative of the moneyed type.

Again, Mr. Adams gloomily remarks that "producers have become the subjects of the possessors of hoarded wealth," and that among capitalists the money-lenders form an aristocracy, while debtors are helpless and the servants of the creditors. All this is really quite unworthy of Mr. Adams, or of anyone above the intellectual level of Mr. Bryan, Mr. Henry George, or Mr. Bellamy. Any man who has had the slightest practical knowledge of legislation, whether as Congressman or as State legislator, knows that nowadays laws are passed much more often with a view to benefiting the debtors than the creditors; always excepting that very large portion of the creditor class which includes the wage-earners. "Producers"—whoever they may be—are not the subjects of "hoarded wealth," nor of anyone nor anything else. Capital is not absolute; and it is idle to compare the position of the capitalist nowadays with his position when his workmen were slaves and the law-makers were his creatures. The money-lender, by whom I suppose Mr. Adams means the banker, is not an aristocrat as compared to other capitalists,—at any rate in the United States. The merchant, the manufacturer, the railroad man, stand just as the banker does; and bankers vary among themselves just as any other business men do. They do not form a "class" at all; anyone who wishes to can go into the business; men fail and succeed in it just as in other businesses. As for the debtors being powerless, if Mr. Adams knows any persons who have lent money in Kansas or similar States they will speedily en-lighten him on this subject, and will give him an exact idea of the extent to which the debtor is the servant of the creditor. In those States the creditor—and especially the Eastern money-lender or "gold-bug"—is the man who has lost all his money. Mr. Adams can readily find this out by the simple endeavor to persuade some "moneylender," or other "Wall Street shark" to go into the business of lending money on Far-Western farm property. The money-lender in the most civilized portions of the United States always loses if the debtor is loser, or if the debtor is dishonest. Of course there are "sharpers" among bankers, as there are among producers. Moreover, the private, as distinguished from the corporate, debtor borrows for comparatively short periods, so that he is practically not at all affected by an appreciating currency; the rise is much too small to count in the case of the individual, though it may count in the long-term bonds of a nation or corporation. The wage of the working-man rises, while interest, which is the wage of the capitalist, sinks.

Mr. Adams's study of the rise of the usurer in India and the ruin of the martial races is very interesting; but it has not the slightest bearing upon anything which is now happening in Western civilization. The debtor, in America at least, is amply able to take care of his own interests. Our experience shows conclusively that the creditors only prosper when the debtors prosper, and the danger lies less in the accumulation of debts, than in their repudiation. Among us the communities which repudiate their debts, which inveigh loudest against their creditors, and which offer the poorest field for the operations of the honest banker (whom they likewise always call" money-lender, ") are precisely those which are least prosperous and least self-respecting. There are, of course, individuals here and there who are unable to cope with the moneylender, and even sections of the country where this is true; but this only means that a weak or thriftless man can be robbed by a sharp money-lender just as he can be robbed by the sharp producer from whom he buys or to whom he sells. There is, in certain points, a very evident incompatibility of interest between the farmer who wishes to sell his product at a high rate, and the working-man who wishes to buy that product at a low rate; but the success of the capitalist, and especially of the banker, is conditioned upon the prosperity of both workingman and farmer.

When Mr. Adams speaks of the change in the relations of women and men he touches on the vital weakness of our present civilization. If we are, in truth, tending toward a point where the race will cease to be able to perpetuate itself, our civilization is of course a failure. No quality in a race atones for the failure to produce an abundance of healthy children. The problem upon which Mr. Adams here touches is the most serious of all problems, for it lies at the root of, and indeed itself is, national life. But it is hard to accept seriously Mr. Adams's plea that "martial" men loved their wives more than "economic" men do, and showed their love by buying them. Of course the only reason why a woman was bought in early times was because she was looked upon like any other chattel; she was "loved" more than she is now only as a negro was "loved" more by the negrotrader in 1860 than at present.

The worship of women during the Middle Ages was, in its practical effects, worship of a very queer kind. The "economic man" of the present day is beyond comparison gentler and more tender and more loving to women than the "emotional man" of the Middle Ages.

Mr. Adams closes with some really fine paragraphs, of which the general purport is, that the advent of the capitalist and the economic man, and especially the advent of the usurer, mark a condition of consolidation which means the beginning of utter decay, so that our society, as a result of this accelerated movement away from emotionalism and towards capitalism, is now in a condition like that of the society of the later Roman Empire. He forgets, however, that there are plenty of modern states which have entirely escaped the general accelerated movement of our time. Spain on the one hand, and Russia on the other, though alike in nothing else, are alike in being entirely outside the current of modern capitalistic development. Spain never suffered from capitalists. She exterminated the economic man in the interest of the emotional and martial man. As a result she has sunk to a condition just above that of Morocco—another state, by the way, which still clings to the martial and emotional type, and is entirely free from the vices of capitalistic development, and from the presence of the usurer, save as the usurer existed in the days of Isaac of York. Soldiers and artists have sunk lower in Spain than elsewhere, although they have had no competition from the economic man. Russia is in an entirely different position. Russia is eminently emotional, and her capitalists are of the most archaic type; but it is difficult to say exactly what Russia has done for art, or in what respect her soldiers are superior to other soldiers; and certainly the life of the lower classes in Russia is on the average far less happy than the life of the workingman and farmer in any English-speaking country. Evidently, as Spain and Russia show, national decay, or non-development may have little to do with economic progress.

Mr. Adams has shown well that the progress of civilization and centralization has depended largely upon the growing mastery of the attack over the defence; but when he says that the martial type necessarily decays as civilization progresses, he goes beyond what he can prove. The economic man in England, Holland, and the United States has for several centuries proved a much better fighter than the martial emotionalist of the Spanish countries. It is Spain which is now decaying; not the nations with capitalists. The causes which make Russia formidable are connected with the extent of her territory and her population, for she has certainly failed so far to produce fighting men at all superior to the fighting men of the economic civilizations. In a pent-up territory she would rise less rapidly, and fall more rapidly, than they would; and her freedom from centralization and capitalization would not help her. Spain, which is wholly untouched by modern economic growth, suffers far more than any English-speaking country from maladies like those of Rome in its decadence; and Rome did not decay from the same causes which affect modern America or Europe; while Russia owes her immunity from a few of the evils that affect the rest of us, to causes unconnected with her backwardness in civilization, and moreover has worse evils of her own to contend with. The English-speaking man has so far out-built, outfought, and out-administered the Russian; and he is as far as the poles away from the Roman of the later Empire.

Moreover, instead of the mercenary or paid police growing in relative strength, as Mr. Adams says, it has everywhere shrunk during the last fifty years, when compared with the mass of armed farmers and wage-earners who make up a modern army. The capitalist can no longer, as in ages past, count upon the soldiers as being of his party; he can only count upon them when they are convinced that in fighting his battle they are fighting their own; although under modern industrial conditions this is generally the case. Again, Mr. Adams is in error in his facts, when he thinks that producers have prospered in the silver-using, as compared with the gold-using, countries. The wage-earner and small farmer of the United States, or even of Europe, stand waist high above their brothers in Mexico and the other communities that use only silver. The prosperity of the wage-earning class is more important to the state than the prosperity of any other class in the community, for it numbers within its ranks two-thirds of the people of the community. The fact that modern society rests upon the wage-earner, whereas ancient society rested upon the slave, is of such transcendent importance as to forbid any exact comparison between the two, save by way of contrast.

While there is in modern times a decrease in emotional religion, there is an immense increase in practical morality. There is a decrease of the martial type found among savages and the people of the Middle Ages, except as it still survives in the slums of great cities; but there remains a martial type infinitely more efficient than any that preceded it. There are great branches of industry which call forth in those that follow them more hardihood, manliness, and courage than any industry of ancient times. The immense masses of men connected with the railroads are continually called upon to exercise qualities of mind and body such as in antiquity no trade and no handicraft demanded. There are, it is true, influences at work to shake the vitality, courage, and manliness of the race; but there are other influences which tell in exactly the opposite direction; and, whatever may come in the future, hitherto the last set of influences have been strongest. As yet, while men are more gentle and more honest than before, it cannot be said that they are less brave; and they are certainly more efficient as fighters. If our population decreases; if we lose the virile, manly qualities, and sink into a nation of mere hucksters, putting gain above national honor, and subordinating everything to mere ease of life; then we shall indeed reach a condition worse than that of the ancient civilizations in the years of their decay. But at present no comparison could be less apt than that of Byzantium, or Rome in its later years, with a great modern state where the thronging millions who make up the bulk of the population are wage-earners, who themselves decide their own destinies; a state which is able in time of need to put into the field armies, composed exclusively of its own citizens, more numerous than any which the world has ever before seen, and with a record of fighting in the immediate past with which there is nothing in the annals of antiquity to compare.

THE END.

The Codes Of Hammurabi And Moses
W. W. Davies

QTY

The discovery of the Hammurabi Code is one of the greatest achievements of archaeology, and is of paramount interest, not only to the student of the Bible, but also to all those interested in ancient history...

Religion   **ISBN:** *1-59462-338-4*   Pages:132

MSRP $12.95

The Theory of Moral Sentiments
Adam Smith

QTY

This work from 1749. contains original theories of conscience amd moral judgment and it is the foundation for systemof morals.

Philosophy   ISBN: *1-59462-777-0*   Pages:536

MSRP $19.95

Jessica's First Prayer
Hesba Stretton

QTY

In a screened and secluded corner of one of the many railway-bridges which span the streets of London there could be seen a few years ago, from five o'clock every morning until half past eight, a tidily set-out coffee-stall, consisting of a trestle and board, upon which stood two large tin cans, with a small fire of charcoal burning under each so as to keep the coffee boiling during the early hours of the morning when the work-people were thronging into the city on their way to their daily toil...

Pages:84

Childrens   ISBN: *1-59462-373-2*   *MSRP $9.95*

My Life and Work
Henry Ford

QTY

Henry Ford revolutionized the world with his implementation of mass production for the Model T automobile. Gain valuable business insight into his life and work with his own auto-biography... "We have only started on our development of our country we have not as yet, with all our talk of wonderful progress, done more than scratch the surface. The progress has been wonderful enough but..."

Pages:300

Biographies/   ISBN: *1-59462-198-5*   *MSRP $21.95*

The Art of Cross-Examination
Francis Wellman

QTY

I presume it is the experience of every author, after his first book is published upon an important subject, to be almost overwhelmed with a wealth of ideas and illustrations which could readily have been included in his book, and which to his own mind, at least, seem to make a second edition inevitable. Such certainly was the case with me; and when the first edition had reached its sixth impression in five months, I rejoiced to learn that it seemed to my publishers that the book had met with a sufficiently favorable reception to justify a second and considerably enlarged edition. ..

Reference   **ISBN:** *1-59462-647-2*

Pages:412
MSRP $19.95

On the Duty of Civil Disobedience
Henry David Thoreau

QTY

Thoreau wrote his famous essay, On the Duty of Civil Disobedience, as a protest against an unjust but popular war and the immoral but popular institution of slave-owning. He did more than write—he declined to pay his taxes, and was hauled off to gaol in consequence. Who can say how much this refusal of his hastened the end of the war and of slavery ?

Law   **ISBN:** *1-59462-747-9*

Pages:48
MSRP $7.45

Dream Psychology Psychoanalysis for Beginners
Sigmund Freud

QTY

Sigmund Freud, born Sigismund Schlomo Freud (May 6, 1856 - September 23, 1939), was a Jewish-Austrian neurologist and psychiatrist who co-founded the psychoanalytic school of psychology. Freud is best known for his theories of the unconscious mind, especially involving the mechanism of repression; his redefinition of sexual desire as mobile and directed towards a wide variety of objects; and his therapeutic techniques, especially his understanding of transference in the therapeutic relationship and the presumed value of dreams as sources of insight into unconscious desires.

Psychology   **ISBN:** *1-59462-905-6*

Pages:196
MSRP $15.45

The Miracle of Right Thought
Orison Swett Marden

QTY

Believe with all of your heart that you will do what you were made to do. When the mind has once formed the habit of holding cheerful, happy, prosperous pictures, it will not be easy to form the opposite habit. It does not matter how improbable or how far away this realization may see, or how dark the prospects may be, if we visualize them as best we can, as vividly as possible, hold tenaciously to them and vigorously struggle to attain them, they will gradually become actualized, realized in the life. But a desire, a longing without endeavor, a yearning abandoned or held indifferently will vanish without realization.

Self Help   **ISBN:** *1-59462-644-8*

Pages:360
MSRP $25.45

QTY

☐ **The Rosicrucian Cosmo-Conception Mystic Christianity** by *Max Heindel*   ISBN: *1-59462-188-8*   **$38.95**
The Rosicrucian Cosmo-conception is not dogmatic, neither does it appeal to any other authority than the reason of the student. It is: not controversial, but is: sent forth in the, hope that it may help to clear...   New Age/Religion Pages 646

☐ **Abandonment To Divine Providence** by *Jean-Pierre de Caussade*   ISBN: *1-59462-228-0*   **$25.95**
"The Rev. Jean Pierre de Caussade was one of the most remarkable spiritual writers of the Society of Jesus in France in the 18th Century. His death took place at Toulouse in 1751. His works have gone through many editions and have been republished...   Inspirational/Religion Pages 400

☐ **Mental Chemistry** by *Charles Haanel*   ISBN: *1-59462-192-6*   **$23.95**
Mental Chemistry allows the change of material conditions by combining and appropriately utilizing the power of the mind. Much like applied chemistry creates something new and unique out of careful combinations of chemicals the mastery of mental chemistry...   New Age Pages 354

☐ **The Letters of Robert Browning and Elizabeth Barret Barrett 1845-1846 vol II**   ISBN: *1-59462-193-4*   **$35.95**
by *Robert Browning* and *Elizabeth Barrett*   Biographies Pages 596

☐ **Gleanings In Genesis (volume I)** by *Arthur W. Pink*   ISBN: *1-59462-130-6*   **$27.45**
Appropriately has Genesis been termed "the seed plot of the Bible" for in it we have, in germ form, almost all of the great doctrines which are afterwards fully developed in the books of Scripture which follow...   Religion/Inspirational Pages 420

☐ **The Master Key** by *L. W. de Laurence*   ISBN: *1-59462-001-6*   **$30.95**
In no branch of human knowledge has there been a more lively increase of the spirit of research during the past few years than in the study of Psychology, Concentration and Mental Discipline. The requests for authentic lessons in Thought Control, Mental Discipline and...   New Age/Business Pages 422

☐ **The Lesser Key Of Solomon Goetia** by *L. W. de Laurence*   ISBN: *1-59462-092-X*   **$9.95**
This translation of the first book of the "Lernegton" which is now for the first time made accessible to students of Talismanic Magic was done, after careful collation and edition, from numerous Ancient Manuscripts in Hebrew, Latin, and French...   New Age/Occult Pages 92

☐ **Rubaiyat Of Omar Khayyam** by *Edward Fitzgerald*   ISBN: *1-59462-332-5*   **$13.95**
Edward Fitzgerald, whom the world has already learned, in spite of his own efforts to remain within the shadow of anonymity, to look upon as one of the rarest poets of the century, was born at Bredfield, in Suffolk, on the 31st of March, 1809. He was the third son of John Purcell...   Music Pages 172

☐ **Ancient Law** by *Henry Maine*   ISBN: *1-59462-128-4*   **$29.95**
The chief object of the following pages is to indicate some of the earliest ideas of mankind, as they are reflected in Ancient Law, and to point out the relation of those ideas to modern thought.   Religion/History Pages 452

☐ **Far-Away Stories** by *William J. Locke*   ISBN: *1-59462-129-2*   **$19.45**
"Good wine needs no bush, but a collection of mixed vintages does. And this book is just such a collection. Some of the stories I do not want to remain buried for ever in the museum files of dead magazine-numbers an author's not unpardonable vanity..."   Fiction Pages 272

☐ **Life of David Crockett** by *David Crockett*   ISBN: *1-59462-250-7*   **$27.45**
"Colonel David Crockett was one of the most remarkable men of the times in which he lived. Born in humble life, but gifted with a strong will, an indomitable courage, and unremitting perseverance...   Biographies/New Age Pages 424

☐ **Lip-Reading** by *Edward Nitchie*   ISBN: *1-59462-206-X*   **$25.95**
Edward B. Nitchie, founder of the New York School for the Hard of Hearing, now the Nitchie School of Lip-Reading, Inc, wrote "LIP-READING Principles and Practice". The development and perfecting of this meritorious work on lip-reading was an undertaking...   How-to Pages 400

☐ **A Handbook of Suggestive Therapeutics, Applied Hypnotism, Psychic Science**   ISBN: *1-59462-214-0*   **$24.95**
by *Henry Munro*   Health/New Age/Health/Self-help Pages 376

☐ **A Doll's House: and Two Other Plays** by *Henrik Ibsen*   ISBN: *1-59462-112-8*   **$19.95**
Henrik Ibsen created this classic when in revolutionary 1848 Rome. Introducing some striking concepts in playwriting for the realist genre, this play has been studied the world over.   Fiction/Classics/Plays 308

☐ **The Light of Asia** by *sir Edwin Arnold*   ISBN: *1-59462-204-3*   **$13.95**
In this poetic masterpiece, Edwin Arnold describes the life and teachings of Buddha. The man who was to become known as Buddha to the world was born as Prince Gautama of India but he rejected the worldly riches and abandoned the reigns of power when...   Religion/History/Biographies Pages 170

☐ **The Complete Works of Guy de Maupassant** by *Guy de Maupassant*   ISBN: *1-59462-157-8*   **$16.95**
"For days and days, nights and nights, I had dreamed of that first kiss which was to consecrate our engagement, and I knew not on what spot I should put my lips..."   Fiction/Classics Pages 240

☐ **The Art of Cross-Examination** by *Francis L. Wellman*   ISBN: *1-59462-309-0*   **$26.95**
Written by a renowned trial lawyer, Wellman imparts his experience and uses case studies to explain how to use psychology to extract desired information through questioning.   How-to/Science/Reference Pages 408

☐ **Answered or Unanswered?** by *Louisa Vaughan*   ISBN: *1-59462-248-5*   **$10.95**
Miracles of Faith in China   Religion Pages 112

☐ **The Edinburgh Lectures on Mental Science (1909)** by *Thomas*   ISBN: *1-59462-008-3*   **$11.95**
This book contains the substance of a course of lectures recently given by the writer in the Queen Street Hall, Edinburgh. Its purpose is to indicate the Natural Principles governing the relation between Mental Action and Material Conditions...   New Age/Psychology Pages 148

☐ **Ayesha** by *H. Rider Haggard*   ISBN: *1-59462-301-5*   **$24.95**
Verily and indeed it is the unexpected that happens! Probably if there was one person upon the earth from whom the Editor of this, and of a certain previous history, did not expect to hear again...   Classics Pages 380

☐ **Ayala's Angel** by *Anthony Trollope*   ISBN: *1-59462-352-X*   **$29.95**
The two girls were both pretty, but Lucy who was twenty-one who supposed to be simple and comparatively unattractive, whereas Ayala was credited, as her Bombwhat romantic name might show, with poetic charm and a taste for romance. Ayala when her father died was nineteen...   Fiction Pages 484

☐ **The American Commonwealth** by *James Bryce*   ISBN: *1-59462-286-8*   **$34.45**
An interpretation of American democratic political theory. It examines political mechanics and society from the perspective of Scotsman James Bryce   Politics Pages 572

☐ **Stories of the Pilgrims** by *Margaret P. Pumphrey*   ISBN: *1-59462-116-0*   **$17.95**
This book explores pilgrims religious oppression in England as well as their escape to Holland and eventual crossing to America on the Mayflower, and their early days in New England...   History Pages 268

www.bookjungle.com *email: sales@bookjungle.com fax: 630-214-0564 mail: Book Jungle PO Box 2226 Champaign, IL 61825*

QTY

The Fasting Cure *by Sinclair Upton*   ISBN: *1-59462-222-1*   **$13.95**
In the Cosmopolitan Magazine for May, 1910, and in the Contemporary Review (London) for April, 1910, I published an article dealing with my experiences in fasting. I have written a great many magazine articles, but never one which attracted so much attention... New Age/Self Help/Health Pages 164

Hebrew Astrology *by Sepharial*   ISBN: *1-59462-308-2*   **$13.45**
In these days of advanced thinking it is a matter of common observation that we have left many of the old landmarks behind and that we are now pressing forward to greater heights and to a wider horizon than that which represented the mind-content of our progenitors... Astrology Pages 144

Thought Vibration or The Law of Attraction in the Thought World   ISBN: *1-59462-127-6*   **$12.95**
by William Walker Atkinson   Psychology/Religion Pages 144

Optimism *by Helen Keller*   ISBN: *1-59462-108-X*   **$15.95**
Helen Keller was blind, deaf, and mute since 19 months old, yet famously learned how to overcome these handicaps, communicate with the world, and spread her lectures promoting optimism. An inspiring read for everyone... Biographies/Inspirational Pages 84

Sara Crewe *by Frances Burnett*   ISBN: *1-59462-360-0*   **$9.45**
In the first place, Miss Minchin lived in London. Her home was a large, dull, tall one, in a large, dull square, where all the houses were alike, and all the sparrows were alike, and where all the door-knockers made the same heavy sound... Childrens/Classic Pages 88

The Autobiography of Benjamin Franklin *by Benjamin Franklin*   ISBN: *1-59462-135-7*   **$24.95**
The Autobiography of Benjamin Franklin has probably been more extensively read than any other American historical work, and no other book of its kind has had such ups and downs of fortune. Franklin lived for many years in England, where he was agent... Biographies/History Pages 332

Name	
Email	
Telephone	
Address	
City, State ZIP	

☐ **Credit Card**   ☐ **Check / Money Order**

Credit Card Number	
Expiration Date	
Signature	

Please Mail to: Book Jungle
PO Box 2226
Champaign, IL 61825
or Fax to: 630-214-0564

ORDERING INFORMATION

web*: www.bookjungle.com*
email*: sales@bookjungle.com*
fax*: 630-214-0564*
mail*: Book Jungle PO Box 2226 Champaign, IL 61825*
or PayPal *to sales@bookjungle.com*

Please contact us for bulk discounts

DIRECT-ORDER TERMS

**20% Discount if You Order
Two or More Books**
Free Domestic Shipping!
Accepted: Master Card, Visa,
Discover, American Express

www.ingramcontent.com/pod-product-compliance
Lightning Source LLC
Chambersburg PA
CBHW080903020726
47502CB00008B/2329